THE DARK PRAIRIE

Liminal Books

Liminal Books is an imprint of Between the Lines Publishing. The Liminal Books name and logo are trademarks of Between the Lines Publishing.

Copyright © 2023 by John W. Jarrett

Cover design by Cherie Fox

Between the Lines Publishing
1769 Lexington Ave N., Ste 286
Roseville, MN 55113
btwnthelines.com

Published: February 2023

Original ISBN (Paperback) 978-1-958901-23-6

Original ISBN (eBook) 978-1-958901-24-3

THE DARK PRAIRIE

John W. Jarrett

To the "incandescents" — both living and deceased. Within the abyss, your light and warmth bring comfort.

A special dedication to my wife, Belinda, and daughters, Sophia and Sayde.

ONE

"And who's this?" a rough voice broke like dark lightning through the eventide. I stepped out of the shade of the pecan grove and looked over at a patchy-haired vagrant stooped to his knees before my younger sister Bethany. Atop this hard-packed ridge that bordered the northern side of our Kansas homestead, she stood frozen, eyes wide, unable to move.

The man turned to look at me, then raised his hand and brushed her porcelain cheek with long fingernails packed with crescents of dirt. His drunken gaze was both hostile and meek. I followed the tips of his nails, scratching ever so lightly, and was shocked by his odor—a mixture of alcohol, grease, vomit, and shit. My eyes watered as I studied the small encampment behind him, just past the hill crest—a firepit with empty tin cans and liquor bottles littering the ground.

"You know this boy?" the man asked Bethany in tobacco-pitted texture.

With my eyes locked on the man, I walked slowly to her side and reached behind her, feeling for the whittling knife she'd stolen from me and run off with. She knew better—we both knew better—than to come up here to the Santa Fe Trail by ourselves. But our game of chase had sent us meandering. I pried the knife from her sweaty hand, hoping he wouldn't notice. "Janet," I said, looking back at the grove of trees. The setting sun threw contorted shadows of those leafless limbs long across the golden February earth, their skinny branches like panicked strangers warning away incomers. "Best be coming now. Pa's right behind me, and you know how vicious his temper gets when he finds us here."

The man looked at me. "I'm a pa, too," he said slowly and with purpose. His bloodshot eyes were shrouded in loose skin, and wild black whiskers shot up from arbitrary folds and blotches on his weathered face. He wore old beige suit pants and an oversized, oily brown jacket. He returned his gaze to Bethany, one eye catching up with the other. "Three little girls of my own. All grown now, moved on—no decency to even speak to their father anymore. That isn't nice, is it?"

He glanced down at Bethany's dress, rubbing the hem between his pudgy yellow fingers before moving his hand beneath her underskirt. "I'm guessing you're eight or nine, is that right?" His words were listless and took an eternity to bubble out of his mouth. "You remind me of them—my daughters," he continued, half-smiling.

"Like I said," I interrupted, my hands shaking as I maneuvered the knife to my other side, squeezing it tight. I could barely talk. "Pa's on his way, Bethany." My stomach twisted. She stood there, petrified, tears streaming down her face. I envisioned driving the blade deep into the man's face, waiting for the moment.

Behind us there was rustling in a bush by the edge of the pecan grove. I turned, surprised my bluff might be true after all. Terrified and hoping, I watched while Spooks, our large and muscular black cat, popped out into the clearing, prowling next to Bethany. His back was arched while he hissed at the creep, pawing the ground with claws extended.

"I thought you said your name was Janet?" the man asked, feigning puzzlement. He looked down at her feet and her leather shoes stitched in purple thread with her initials. "*BT*," he said, reading the embroidery. Slowly, he lowered his hand to where I could see it, cupping the bottom of her calf, then the back of her shoe. "Bethany ... *Tempting? Tantalizing?*" The other corner of his mouth raised, a broad smile revealing his rotten teeth.

I squeezed that knife as hard as I could, trembling in place, just waiting, yet paralyzed.

"Guess your pa's running late," the man said, raising his hand to Bethany's side, grazing her dress with his fingertips up to her shoulder, then down the front of her collar. He fingered the top button. "More time to get acquainted with you two children."

Just then, Spooks sprang upon the man's face and buried his fangs into his eyebrow. The man bolted upright and

3

yanked hard on the cat, tearing off his eyelid and half his brow, which dangled over a now-protruding eyeball. Blood streamed down his face as he tried to patch the fleshy bit back in place. Furious, his attention refocused on his prey.

"*Run,*" I yelled at Bethany. She sprinted into the pecan grove with me, now veiled in shadow. The vagrant was quick for a man with a limp and galloped like a three-legged dog. We disappeared into the darkness, leaning hard as we splashed through the rushing stream that braided through those trees. Skirting rocks barely visible in the last rays of daylight, I jumped and darted left and right, twisting between the trunks until I tripped, flying face-first into the freezing water, panicking that the man would catch me. I could hear his heavy feet, his labored breath. He was close. I looked back, but it was hard to see in the shadows. Gasping, I forced myself up, grasping over my outstretched feet, sprinting as fast as I could.

Near the border of the pecan grove, on the veranda of our house, I saw a kerosene lamp glowing brightly over the surrounding flat trodden ground. White smoke was visible in the moonlight, flowing from the chimney, and for an instant I recalled the bliss I'd felt moments ago before witnessing Bethany's molestation. Standing beside a tree at the top of the hill, I gazed on the purple sunset, swallowed in a dream. Surrounding me were God's creations, gleaming, sparkling. A thousand species of spellbinding nymphs, startled by my sudden arrival, transformed into the harmless shapes of land and flora: the distant rolling hills that ended at the horizon, capped in beacons of light—whitewater on waves of provincial grit shining back at the sky and carpeted in gilded yellow bluestem and beaked panic grass. All the tiny elements coalesced into a meticulous stained-glass panorama, freezing the sprites in a moment of eternity. I inhaled deeply, unable to contain the glory that engulfed me. *I see you*, I thought to myself, mesmerized. The nymphs, however, had frozen for something altogether different.

I made it into the wide clearing at the bottom of the hill and caught up to Bethany, standing at the edge of the yard, her body shaking uncontrollably. "You're okay, Bethany," I said, gathering her to my side and looking back for the man. I hurried her as fast as possible, seeing Ma standing under the large oak tree between the barn and our house. She was a tall woman and wore a tattered toile dress and polka dot apron. Her hands were on her hips; she squinted her face as we approached, a curious expression turning blank once she recognized it was us.

"You two up to no good?" Ma yelled. "Get over here, Bethany, and knock off that boo-hooing. It's unbecoming a starlet's daughter." Still shaking with fear, Bethany hurried to her side. Ma caressed her shoulder and tried ushering her toward the house, postponing Bethany's tears and apprehension.

"There was a ..." I started to say, shivering wet and holding myself at the knees to catch my breath.

Without a word, Ma abruptly turned and walked away, as I'd seen her do many times to foreign pilgrims passing through our town of Leavenworth. "One of *those* people," I'd overheard her say in private conversation with other women in town. She had little respect, and less patience, for any of the great unwashed who lacked a sufficient New England bourgeois sensibility.

"Don't just stand there, Bethany. Move yourself. And James, be a gentleman and open the door for us," she called over her shoulder. "I shouldn't have to tell you."

"Where's Pa?" I asked between breaths.

Ma looked back at me and huffed, then leaned towards Bethany. "Is everything okay, dear? Why are you crying? I made your favorite cookies. Chocolate chip," she said, loud enough for me to hear. We all knew that was Pa's favorite, not Bethany's. "No matter why you're crying, I guarantee a cookie will sooth your feelings."

"*Where's Pa!*" I demanded.

"What's the matter with you?" Ma asked. "Why aren't you tending your sister the way I am? Seriously James, you need to learn some empathy."

Ma wasn't ever bad or wicked toward me, but distant. Disconnected. Now and again, I'd see her act that way toward Bethany, too. Wasn't she curious to know what happened to her? Didn't she care? But the perimeter of Ma's world only sometimes reached far enough to include Pa or Bethany. Rarely me.

Ma smiled at Bethany, who was still crying with a look of pain. She went toward the house, moving gingerly, her knees slightly bent, and her feet spread far apart with each step. "Don't walk like that, Bethany," she said, tugging on her arm. "You remind me of that cabbage head at the lumber mill. Now let's get you a cookie. They're warm, and the

6

chocolate is all melty still." She glanced back at me. "No cookies for you, James, until you apologize for your tone."

"*Pa!*" I yelled. "Where are you?"

He walked around from the side of the house and into the light of the porch lamp. Seeing Bethany's state, he ran over.

"What is it?" he asked, kneeling on the ground next to her and taking her hand in his. As he did, Bethany lost it. She pulled her hand away and sobbed, covering her face, trembling. "What is it, sweetheart? Why are you walking like that? Did something happen?" But she couldn't get a word out. "Calm down, for God's sake, and speak. Tell me what happened!"

Pa had a switch I envied—something that triggered in times of stress which sharpened his senses and intellect. He looked up at me and asked the same question, now impatient for an answer. There was anger in his voice, and an obvious intolerance for those who didn't share his fortitude.

"Take her to the house," he said to Ma, then turned to me. "*Talk.*" He gripped my shoulders as if answers would squeeze out like juice. I glanced slantwise toward the trees, not wanting to look away from him, having been slapped for such disrespect in the past. By now the sky above was black, and the full moon shined white on us, casting angular shadows down our faces like broken shards of Acoma Pueblo pottery. The night fell quiet as Ma closed the door behind her and Bethany, and Pa awaited my response. I stood there shivering, sensing the world all around me and the universe around all of that—like a cocoon swaddling too tight. In the distance, the trees hid their details in impervious obscurity. I wondered if that man was in there, watching us. "Look at me when I'm speaking to you."

"A man," I said, dropping the knife from my hand. "A drifter. He was chasing us. He was touching Bethany—under her dress. At the road."

"Get my rifle off the wall and protect the girls." Without another word, he snatched up my knife and nimbly darted into the void, slipping into the tangle of pecan arms. I waited a moment, watching, listening, hoping I'd hear battle cries of the pa I grew up in awe of; the pa whose hints of Mexican American war memories from the dinner table built him into a mysterious and terrifying bulwark against menace and uncertainty; the pa who I couldn't help but turn into a hero.

I could guess what Ma thought about me—a mild revulsion, like milk that had soured but didn't quite force you to spit it from your mouth—though it plagued me that I never knew how Pa felt about me. I didn't want to care as much as I did for his approval. I tried uprooting this concern, believing a real man shouldn't mind such childish things, but the feeling always grew back. A curse to consider, but maybe I wasn't a real man yet. I often wondered if he was waiting for me to do something or say something, before our relationship would change and he'd open up to me. I never asked him, and felt stupid anytime I was about to. I wasn't a sissy—real men weren't sissies—and asking sounded sissyish.

The cold fell quick as the last simmering glow of navy flickered away in the west, and after going inside the house with Bethany, Ma didn't come back out, perhaps assuming I was with Pa ... or perhaps not giving my whereabouts any thought whatsoever. Night sounds grabbed my attention, amplified in the cavern of this pristine expanse—crickets and katydids, a creaking stack of firewood beside the house, our chickens nestling on their roosts, and what I thought were jackrabbits scurrying to their dens. Normally I'd pay no attention, but the climate had turned eerie. After ten or fifteen minutes of standing soggy-clothed in the icy air—my skin tingly—smoke began piping from the stove chimney and I knew Ma was making Bethany cinnamon tea. It was something she did every night before sitting down in her rocker to read a book and insisting that Bethany rub her neck. The thought of asking Ma for a hot cup myself didn't outweigh my aversion for her company, so I decided to wait a little longer for Pa. Until the cold was too much and I had to get my blood flowing.

Our horses, Clyde and Fred, hadn't yet been barned but sauntered around the paddock, stopping by the fence and watching me. Clyde was always talking to me, blowing air through his closed lips, or yanking them back to show those horse teeth and gums in all their splotchy ugliness. He'd creep up behind me and bring that grill of his next to my head. Whenever I turned to see what was there, it was him— his hot alfalfa breath in my face, scaring the crap out of me. I'd swear his smile reached ear to ear.

"What are you boys doing?" I asked them both, petting their noses one at a time. I was glad to be in their company and not alone, feeling like I was being watched. There was no telling if Pa ever found the creep. Maybe he got away. Or maybe the creep hurt Pa in some way. I tried to force the thoughts from my mind.

Clyde nudged Fred's nose out of the way and got under my hand before Fred had time to push back. If I could read animals' minds, Fred was surely asking if I would let Clyde get away with that. "Actually, yes, Fred. I am," I told him. "Your lonely dog eyes don't make up for your laziness."

I pushed on the heavy sliding barn door. The handle was freezing. The wheels creaked loudly, bouncing along the roller track, and it took more effort than I expected to get it open. Just inside, I lit a lantern which cast wide, errant shadows that glided over the canvas of this uncanny interior. I couldn't shake the image of that creep touching Bethany and looked back at my empty hand where the knife had been, hating myself for not using it.

"Let's go, boys," I said, walking both horses into their shared stall. They looked at me, expectant in some way, and I only realized what they wanted when Clyde tossed his head in the direction of the hay bales. Scooping up an armful, sweat prickled from my skin. Something felt so wrong about that night. It was indescribable. I felt trapped in the barn, and the hair on my arms stood on end, so I threw the hay over the rail for the horses and went back outside. The air was even colder than before, but I could catch my breath. *Pa's all right*, I thought to myself, faking confidence. I scoured the land for any sign of that creep. *He's all right.*

Standing under the oak tree, moonlight shined through the leaves and made fuzzy, elaborate patterns of shadows on the ground. There was something about how the dark and light lay down over the dirt and dead prairie grass, the margins between them a gray mixture shrouding something both there and not there. Where was that creep? All I could do was hope Pa caught him, and whatever business he tended, he tended it quietly.

"Get out of the way, Buster!" I said, nearly tripping over our fat yellow-and-white-haired spaniel dog as I walked in the house. He slept day and night just past the swing of the front door—cozy, as if he hadn't been kicked a hundred times already. He stirred and looked at me with a dopey, wide-open side-eye, not raising his head, then closing his eye again as I stepped past.

"You want a cup of tea, James?" Ma asked.

A mug sat on the table next to her, and in the stone fireplace silent flames stormed atop oak branches. The tongues of fire lapped the air, wavering and darting into the space above, filling the otherwise dark room with flickering orange light. My eyes rose over the mantle and fixed on Pa's Henry repeating rifle, and his .42 caliber LeMat pistol. I looked at Ma relaxing in her chair, certain that Bethany hadn't told her what happened. "Help yourself," she said. "I'm just settling in."

"Did she tell you?" I asked.

"Bethany?" she asked, looking over her shoulder where Bethany stood behind her chair, massaging her neck. "No—she didn't say anything." Ma smiled, glancing at the plate of cookies on the table. "I think I know why. Are you all better now, dear?" she asked.

Bethany didn't answer. Her eyes welled with tears.

"It's okay," Ma went on. "Have another cookie if you need to. A little harder, now, right there," Ma said, pointing to the side of her neck. She moaned while Bethany worked her fingers into the muscle. "I've had a rough day."

"You should tell her," I said, hoping I wouldn't have to.

Bethany looked stricken and again she didn't say anything. She raised the corner of her mouth, trying to smile at me, probably wanting to pretend like nothing had happened out there.

"Is there something I should know about?" Ma asked. "You two *were* up to no good ... I thought so." Though no longer dripping, I was still cold, so I stood beside the stove and kept my mouth shut, letting Bethany decide to say something if she wanted to. Ma turned and faced her. "Well?"

"I'm ..." Bethany said, clearing her throat. "I ... I mean ..." She cleared her throat again.

"Do you need something to drink?" Ma asked. "Crumbs in your throat?"

"Enough with the damned cookies, Ma. *Geez*. She doesn't even like chocolate chip!"

Ma sat up in her rocker, glaring at me. "I thought we left that nasty tone of yours outside," she said. "I guess I was wrong."

Bethany ran upstairs to her room, leaving me alone with Ma. Once she was gone, I couldn't help but blurt out, "You're so oblivious. Your daughter was molested tonight!" I wasn't sure how she'd react to hearing that, her expression so dull most of the time. This time I was amazed as life did enter her face. She flushed red, mad or embarrassed I couldn't tell, and squinted her eyes at me in uncertainty or disbelief. "I found her at the top of the hill," I said. "Some creep got his hands on her."

Tears wet her eyes, and without a word, she got out of her chair, walked to the staircase and looked up, holding the banister. I knew it had to be a heavy fact to shoulder. I was moved to compassion for her, in spite of how she treated me. "There's nothing any of us could have done, Ma," I said.

"Is that so?" she asked. She turned to me, her face twisting in anger. "So you're telling me that not only did you leave her alone while you were playing, you went up to the trail where your pa has told you countless times to stay away!? You certainly *could* have done something to prevent this—but you didn't. This is your fault, James!" I couldn't believe Ma was blaming me for what happened to Bethany. She straightened her dress about the waist, brushed off the creases, then wiped her eyes. "That must be where your pa is," she said softly, then went upstairs. I waited a few minutes, picking through the plate of cookies but not feeling like eating, until Ma returned.

"Is Bethany okay?" I asked. "Does she need anything? Can I get her anything?"

Ma sat in her chair, rolling her eyes at me. "Don't be dramatic," she said. "Your sister's going to be fine."

"Easy for you to say," I blurted out before thinking how rude my comment was. Not knowing what to expect from her, I stopped and watched, ready to dash upstairs for a quick getaway if need be. Instead, she looked at me, then laid her head back.

"You know about easy," she said, getting comfortable, "don't you. Must be proud of yourself. You've sure got the good life here." She closed her eyes. "All good things…"

Her words cut so deep sometimes, like all I cared about was myself. Sometimes I just wanted to lash out and make her feel the way she made me feel. "Pa's out there still," I said, "unless you don't care."

"There you go again," she said. "Please, I've had enough for one day." She leaned her head forward and looked at me. "I'm not a heartless witch, you know. You've got no clue about the things girls have to deal with. What they have to put up with. The world's not a pretty place, and it might be shocking to learn, but your sister's not alone." She grabbed a knitted blanket from a sewing basket next to her chair and flung it open, draping it over her body, then laid her head back down and closed her eyes again. "And your father's fine. He can take care of himself. You've heard his stories. God help that man if your pa gets his hands on him."

I tried pouring tea into my favorite mug—a squash-colored mochaware cup with the image of a seaweed plant on it—discovering none left in the pot but a couple drops. There was still hot water on the stove, though, so I filled my cup and loaded the strainer with loose leaf black tea and a teaspoon of cinnamon powder, then dropped it into my mug. The smell was amazing. I stirred in a few tablespoons of sugar and took a sip, the steam cutting through my sinuses as I lifted it to my mouth. Sucking a narrow stream over my tightening lips, the tea was sweet and spicy, burning the back of my throat, causing the chill under my skin to fall off my body like dry sand.

Ma watched me the whole time. I often wondered what ran through her mind. "Will you read to me?" she asked.

"Are you serious?"

"Of course I am," she said. "My eyes are tired."

Unbelievable. I threw on my wool coat from the rack beside the fireplace and opened the door to leave just as Pa walked up, standing in the dark with flickers of firelight shining on him. He loosened his shoestrings and left his boots on the veranda, took off his blood-speckled clothes and wiped himself with them. Then he entered the house naked except for his socks and underwear, eyeballing the rifle on the mantle.

"Did I not give you an instruction? Was it not clear enough?" he asked.

"It was," I said. "Did you find him?"

Pa was a big man—six foot two inches and shoulders twice as wide as any fellow in Leavenworth, Kansas—but he wasn't the biggest. That distinction belonged to his wealthy friend William Elton whose slightly bigger frame carried quite a bit more muscle, always draped with an emerald green mantle cape fastened with an ornate frog closure at the chest. The two of them became close friends on September 6, 1847. Each were infantrymen leading the Battle of El Molino invasion of Mexico City in the 8th Infantry, and each helped the other fight their way to survival while their unit took heavy casualties. According to Pa, Mr. Elton had been a fierce warrior who hated Mexicans and used that animosity to fuel his hostility in the war.

I caught myself as Pa brushed past, nearly knocking me down with his anvil shoulders as he went to the kitchen basin to wash his arms and face. "I gave you a simple instruction," he said, his broad back toward me.

Bethany came downstairs holding her blue kitty stuffed animal toy, stopping halfway when she saw him. His glance sent her back up without a word.

"So did you find the creep?" I asked again.

Pa looked over at Ma, seeing her quiet in her chair, eyes closed. "You didn't defend your sister at the top of the hill," he said, drying his body with a dishtowel. The house was silent except for the quiet whoosh and pop from the fireplace. Orange light and shadows danced over everything like the breezy shimmers on the bottom of a translucent pond. He laid down the towel and faced me. "You did not defend her or your Ma. How many times have I instructed you about duty?"

Ma's rocker creaked, and she pulled the blanket higher under her chin. She rustled and turned her head toward us. "I've learned not to count on this boy, Daryl," she said softly. Her voice carried a tone of satisfaction, savoring the words as they came off her tongue. "What happened tonight is his fault. He makes excuses and doesn't follow instruction. He's a disappointment. A coward even, yet to grow up."

"Cess, he is my son. And yours. Do not speak about him in that way."

Ma often jumped to conclusions and was frank in

16

discussion, a feistiness Pa told me he admired. But he was a different sort. A deductive man of facts, always working from principles to particulars, and in him there was no room for inference. Ma, on the other hand, lived in exaggeration, in fantastic embellishments of reality—evidence that reality was nowhere close to satisfactory for her. I thought of this as I repeated her words in my mind, that I was a coward, yet to grow up. She always exaggerated, and even Pa corrected her. But he didn't, I realized, replaying his words next. I filled with sadness and looked at Ma, torn between repudiating her ugly comments, and agreeing with them.

"It's time for bed," Pa said to me. "That man won't bother your sister any longer."

TWO

I woke up late the following morning, Sunday, still
groggy from a lousy sleep, and once again, as for the past two
weeks, a black crow perched on my windowsill looking in at
me. Behind him the sky was a gray slate tombstone, the
pecan grove ascending from one corner of the window to the
other. Imagining the cold caused my body to shiver, and I
second-guessed getting out of bed. I sat up anyway and
pulled on my boots, stomping to get my heels all the way in.
The bird sat calmly, just watching, a fresh snow having fallen
during the night. Wondering how effective those feathers
really were against winter, I figured he wanted to come
inside. But that wasn't going to happen.

A few years back, Minnie Finny found her husband
Joseph dead in their house and a hunchbacked scaly-faced
wood stork gracefully moving along the body, tearing chunks
of bloody flesh from his corpse with its long bent-tipped

beak. After that, the town simmered with murmurs that wild birds in the house were a grave and binding omen. I double-checked the window latch was locked, tapping on the glass as if to say hi. The bird tilted and snapped his head left and right. He looked friendly enough, and despite leaving pine nuts outside on the sill for him, I vowed to keep that window shut.

Perhaps the crow was curious, maybe hopeful even, not knowing the sinister folklore attached to his delicate down figure. Staring at him, I saw myself outside as well, closed off from a connection with my parents and left in the cold to wonder what I needed to do to get in. Was there something sinister attached to me that caused my predicament? Ma called me a coward—was that it? Is that what Pa thought too? The crow never turned about, seeing the vast potential available to him if only he'd the will to fly into that unbounded expanse. Maybe there was something I couldn't see either, but the walls of this house, not to mention my duty as a member of this family, confined my options.

I wondered how a man becomes such, other than being forced by the hands of time which would move any creature into maturity with or without cooperation. I wasn't interested in adulthood, though, as much as wisdom. Pa was a man of few words, and like so many other things about him, his actions last night were a mystery. All that was left for me was to emulate his character in hopes it might become my own one day. Perhaps that would unfasten the latch that kept me out.

"You awake up there, James?" Ma called from

downstairs. "Got some food if you're hungry."

I stood and walked to the railing by the head of the stairs, looking down over the kitchen and great room, decorated with unupholstered lathe-spun furniture. The drapes were pulled open and a gray aura caused the windows to glow, imparting that strange light which cast no shadows throughout the room. There was Ma sitting in her rocker, and I wondered if she'd been there all night. Wouldn't be a first. The chairs were all pushed in around our New Hampshire birchwood dining table, and it seemed that both Pa and Bethany weren't home.

"Where's Bethany?" I asked as I walked downstairs. Images of the creep popped into my mind—memories of last night's nightmares where the man had become a giant, his hands grabbing me alongside Bethany, throwing us under his arms as he walked into a dense forest home, an old cave shrouded in kudzu and spider webs. I could only assume how hard Bethany's night would have been for her. "She's not in her room."

"She's not here," Ma said, buried in her reading.

I unfolded a towel by the sink, finding a small pile of cold flapjacks inside. "No meat?" I asked, but Ma just glanced at me. After a moment she lowered her book.

"The truth can be a cruel thing, James, if you're not ready for it," she said. I guess that was my warning for what she said next. "You're sixteen years old," she went on. "Old enough to be married and starting a family of your own, yet there you stand in your mama's kitchen asking her if she made you breakfast. How do you think that makes you look?

20

I won't say another word about what you did yesterday, and what you failed to do, but I will tell you—this is enough. You acting like a child. It's enough."

I was so embarrassed; I could feel my face warming up. Her words stung more than I wanted to admit. I turned my back toward her and ate the tepid pancakes. "Where'd Bethany go then?" I asked, mid-chew.

"She's with your Pa. They went off somewhere. Tell me, do you know any business your pa has with the sheriff?"

"I don't know," I answered.

All I knew was that Pa hated Sheriff Lock. Henry—Hank, or *Hanky* as Pa liked to call him—Lock. He was some years younger than Ma, actually just ten years older than me, and a veteran of the War of the Rebellion. "Not an honorable soldier," Pa had said, telling me that weeks after his unit deployed, he made haste to throw up his arms and surrender to the Confederacy without even firing his rifle. He spent the remainder of his service in a Georgia prisoner-of-war camp, growing skinnier and skinnier. There was more, Pa said, but he'd spare me the details.

In spite of these things, I knew Ma liked the sheriff. We'd lived in Leavenworth since 1857, when I was three, moving from Dover, New Hampshire, where Pa and Ma first bet before the Mexican War. For as long as I could remember, Sheriff Lock—son of Leavenworth's ambitious, yet feebleminded mayor, Robin Lock—was around.

"The sheriff came by this morning," Ma said. "He didn't even say hi, just knocked on the door and off with your pa."

A cold chill ran through my body, and I feared Henry

wanted to talk to Pa about the vagrant. He didn't say what he did to the man last night, though it was obvious that the blood he washed off wasn't his own. I walked to the window and looked out, only seeing footsteps in the snow leading over to the pecan grove. Maybe Ma and Henry being friends would help Pa in some way, if it was trouble they were talking about.

"Throw another log in the fire, will you?" Ma asked me.

She was unlike any of the other women in Leavenworth. I'd really only known Midwestern geniality and grew uncomfortable whenever the gears of her New England temperament didn't line up with the townsfolks'. But she rarely went out anymore, preferring a book, that chair, and her favorite toile dress—a sentimental remnant from before her *Great Regret*—that she'd wear day after day. Whenever she did go out, pretty much only to the library since Pa did the day-to-day shopping, she wore sunhats that grew bigger each year, her skin turning whiter and whiter. What were once light blue veins under her skin had become algae-colored strands of kelp. She wasn't always a hermit, though. With her history of acting, she tried it years ago locally at the Wanderlust Drama Stage, but finally exchanged that distraction for an account at the library. She mentioned how reliable good novels were at getting her out of Kansas.

"Drama just doesn't cut it," she'd said on a picnic one spring afternoon. Her long brown hair was pulled into a ponytail, low on the back of her head, and she wore a wide-brimmed sunhat that drooped past her narrow shoulders. We sat on a blanket by the shore of a pond, watching Pa and

Bethany splash in the water. "We're not in New Hampshire anymore," she said, "that's for sure."

"What do you mean?" I asked.

"Oh, nothing," she answered, gazing far off. "Your pa's made sacrifices—I know that. But this place ... I'm just not suited for it. I thought I'd be and gave it a shot for a while." She leaned back on her bony hands, elbows straightened. "Mr. Elton swore this was the Promised Land, and he's always been generous, putting up travelers at his home who were passing through. But there's no city here. No excitement. No *glory*." She looked at me, biting her upper lip while I tried to understand what she was really saying. "Oh, I don't mean to persuade you against your home. It's a fine place for a child to grow up." She rifled through the picnic basket and pulled out a small bottle of liquor, then held it up for me to see. "This here's your pa's. I'm not one for whiskey. So instead, I read. That's my escape."

After putting more wood in the fireplace, I walked over to Ma's room, noticing the end table by her bed, littered with crinkled papers. "Mind your business, boy, and get away from my room," she said.

She'd warned me and Bethany from her "private space" before, which was ridiculous—our house wasn't that big. If anything, I thought she'd worry I'd find her secret stash of money stuffed in an iron pipe under the sink. "I'm just saying," she went on, "you don't go in there. Or your sister. If I catch you, by God you'll pay. I'll whip you myself, and that'll be a lesson you never forget."

"I'm not going in your room," I said. "I'm just looking."

"Well don't look. There's nothing in there that concerns you."

I went to the coatrack and put on my jacket, staring down at Buster. Sometimes I really envied that dumb dog. "Mind my words, boy," Ma whispered while I opened the front door. She was intimidating and ironic like a soft-spoken bully. "Get the horses fed and warmed up. We're going to town when your pa and Bethany get back."

"Why do you hassle me, Ma?" I asked, genuinely wanting to know, but thinking she'd never be straight with me.

"I told you last night," she bristled. She was straight, and had been straight all along apparently, regardless of my unwillingness to hear her. "Don't be so dense. Now close the door. You're letting the cold air in."

I grabbed my hat, Pa's old Stetson from when he was my age, and went to the barn. What else hadn't I been hearing? As I walked through the snow, insecurity and a mild self-loathing kindled inside me. I felt lost with nowhere to go. *Was this life?* I wondered. *Do people feel this way, then just get used to it?*

Fred looked at me with a wary expression as I pushed open the sliding door. Weird, until I saw the hay from last night kicked onto his side of the stall, soaked with steaming, bubbly piss. The searing stench of it hit me at the same time I saw it. "Really, Fred?" I asked. Again, Clyde tossed his head in the direction of the hay bales. I'm sure he was hungry.

"Here you go, Clyde," I said, tossing food onto his side. He raised his head and blew through his lips, heavy strings of spit shooting like yarn through the air. "Damn it," I said, ducking. "That's nasty!" I managed to wipe my sleeve on Clyde's nose. "Fred was always my favorite, you know," I lied.

Fred looked at me with pathetic eyes, glancing back and forth at the wet hay on his side. "That's your share, Fred. Don't get moody with me—you did it."

I hopped onto the pyramid of hay bales and leaned my back against the wall, making sure Fred didn't try anything with Clyde's food. *Maybe they should have their own stalls*, I thought. Then Fred's outbursts couldn't affect Clyde. But they'd always shared a stall, and in spite of his brother's personality, I knew Clyde enjoyed Fred's company. Pa had been doing carpentry for Mr. Elton and planned on bringing home a third horse as payment for his work whenever he finished. Should be any day, he'd said—a tall, strong chestnut stallion named Buck. Perhaps we'd build him a separate pen.

When Clyde finished eating, I opened their stall. "Let's go, you two," I said, pulling their bridles to get them outside. Of course Clyde was excited to stretch his legs, but Fred gave me a tantrum, planting his feet and shaking his head side to side in a figure eight. I dropped my knee into the back of his front leg, caving in his joint and forcing him to take a step. He reared up and gave me a look I can only describe as a cranky old man's, and with his head down, he squinted up at me, baring his teeth.

"What do you want, Fred? Just tell me." He watched Clyde jog outside into the skift, looked at me again, then tossed his glance back toward the east door on the other side of the barn. The most dramatic animal I've ever known. "If that's what it takes, okay," I said, walking to the door. He kept his eyes on me until I disappeared behind the staircase leading up to the loft, then he raised his head high with triumph and pranced out.

Unlike some folks I knew who could barely talk when it got below freezing, the cold never bothered me that much. After closing the sliding door, I stood outside in the frigid winter air watching the boys play. They ran into each other, muzzled a layer of ice on their water trough, and jogged side by side out of the sunshine and into a square of shade at the corner of the paddock. They did this over and over, into the light, then into the shade. It felt so innocent, so harmless. The way life was supposed to be.

I imagined it was me and Bethany playing, the way we'd done a thousand times, not knowing if things would be different now. A sense of doom infused every breath I took. I looked around, anxious the vagrant was nearby—and if not last night's vagrant, then another one. Was there a way back to innocence after what happened? A way forward into a harmless world? For the moment, at least, watching these horses play with such joy lifted the sandbags from my chest. It lifted the genuine, soul-shattering guilt I felt for not protecting Bethany.

Tears poured down my face as I watched Clyde and Fred play, their steamy white breath rolling and tumbling out of their noses the way I envisioned lava flowing into the ocean. Their shiny hair glimmered in the daylight. Forgetting myself, I breathed in the smell of dry grass and honeysuckle and noticed dry primrose bowing in the whispering breeze. I knew it wasn't real, but I weaved my way through to a different place. A place I wanted to stay so badly, but a place I didn't deserve. I remembered the oak leaf shadows from the night before, finding something there, yet not there. Here I was in this moment. Innocence, yet not innocent. Serenity, yet not serene. A speck of joy in an ocean of misery. If death would guarantee my presence in this sentiment, I'd gladly take it. But dying, I knew from my memories of the War of the Rebellion, was easy. When sins demanded retribution, death was often an insufficient wage. I looked around for Bethany, wiping my face clean. I owed her a part of my spirit, for the spirit I allowed to be stolen from her.

Mr. Grumpy rooted himself next to the sliding barn door, waiting to go back inside. "Clyde—get over here and join your daisy brother," I said, yanking the barn door open along the steel roller guides. The door banged as I pulled on it, ringing out over the vast prairie that fanned open south, past our reverend magnolia tree, and shuttering the peace that had come to me like a thief in the night. I wondered how to get it back, but it was gone without a trace. I inhaled deeply, as through gelatin, a tremor in my hands.

The boys walked into their stall, and Fred eyeballed a fifty-pound bag of oats next to the stack of hay. "You want a treat now?" I asked him. "After that performance? Forget it. And besides, you've got a warm breakfast already." They both rested their heads on the rail of their closed stall door, looking at me as I brought over a handful of oats. "Clyde, on the other hand," I said, just as Fred lowered his shoulder and shoved Clyde out of his way.

Fred was licking his lips, staring at me and my hand with gigantic wide eyes. "You got mettle, Fred. When you want to." So I fed him from the palm of my hand. "Don't worry Clyde. You're next."

I heard footsteps across the paddock and glanced over as Pa walked up, then leaned on the sliding door. "You get these horses warm?" he asked.

I pushed the rest of the oats into Fred's mouth and wiped my hand on my pants. "I'd say so, Pa. We've been out for a while. We going to town?"

"Soon," he answered, walking to the stall. He studied it then smiled. "Think we've got room for one more?"

"You finished your work at Mr. Elton's?" I tried to play it cool, excited for another horse, but Pa could probably tell.

"It's all right, son," he said. "I'm glad you're happy. I'm finished there. William will bring the animal by later today, giving us time to make some changes here." He opened the stall door and shooed the horses back into the paddock. "Get these two hitched to the wagon. Your ma will be staying here after all and not joining us."

"And Bethany? Is she going?" I asked.

"That will be her decision," he said. I could see sadness in his eyes. "She's welcome if she wants to, but if she'd rather not, that's fine." He squinted at me, seemingly suspicious that I even asked. "I don't see how it matters to you, however."

I hesitated before answering him, unsure if he too

28

blamed me for what happened. "I just haven't seen her today. That's all." I drifted into the paddock and watched the horses, yearning that this was all a dream. Pa walked out beside me and put his hand on my shoulder.

"All right, then," he said. It felt like he had more to say, but he looked at me, nodded, then walked off.

Town was southeast of our home a couple miles down a narrow dirt lane that wound through low hills, crossing frozen streams through sparsely set trees. The sky cleared as we rode in our bumpy buckboard wagon, the leaf springs under our seat too cold to flex so that every rock and divot we hit shot straight up through our bodies. Infinitely far off over this mostly level terrain, the horizon touched the baby blue sky. The immensity of space under which we conducted our lives was intimidating. It felt like a magnifying glass was aimed at every meaningless detail so that nothing went unseen. Almost as if some giant with his water globe toy stood above us all, peering in with one eyeball, hidden by that celestial light-blue bedsheet. A part of me yearned for the calm of night, when the cloak of daytime was drawn back.

We rode to the lumber mill. It was a splintered, weather-beaten eyesore—ironic as a premier supplier of quality wood in this part of the country. Pa parked our wagon in the back by the loading dock and we went inside. Balding Buddy Burton, the owner's adult son—who we kids called *Lobster Boy* because both his hands lost the last three fingers in separate ripsaw accidents—shuffled out to greet us. Not exactly the way Bethany walked last night, but there was a resemblance. His potbelly pushed on his coffee-stained smock, elbows bent and arms parallel with the ground while each hand's remaining fingers were tapping like pincers, never once lifting his heels from the ground.

"Good day, Buddy," Pa said to him.

Buddy was a high-pitched speed talker and responded with an incoherent mumble, staring at the ground. He finished his address and raised his head. "Oh, it Daryl … that's Daryl … hi Daryl. Oh," he said, seeing me, "and *him*." Disdain dripped from his tongue. That pissed me off. *Fresh Catch* had an uncanny ability to be rude in random moments, the way lunatics can. This wasn't the first time I was tempted, but I never did call him names to his face.

After asking Buddy to load six twelve-foot lengths of standard board onto the wagon, we headed inside to wait till he finished. I stopped by the door a moment, watching him pile the stack and square each one perfectly on top of the next, then fuss and bustle about on all corners, correcting the imperceptible misalignments. His life couldn't be easy, I recognized, feeling bad for getting angry earlier.

"Took weeks to save this up," Pa said, waving three dollars at me as I walked in. "It's worth it, James. A horse this special needs proper quarters." He looked out through the front window and down the road at the horse supply store. "Suppose we'll need more food, as well." His head dropped, looking at his cash.

"We have enough?" I asked, but he didn't answer.

Buddy burst in from the loading dock, intent on his trajectory. As if navigating obstacles, he shuffled over the wood plank floor. I'd never noticed before, but his prickly pear shoes were worn out, ripped, and covered in splinters. "All loaded up, Mr. Tuck. All loaded up. Yes sir. That'll be two dollars, sir, if you don't mind. Two dollars. One, two. Dollars, if you didn't hear me the first time."

Pa hesitated, clearly calculating in his mind, looking at his cash. "Two?"

"That's what I said, I said two, one two. That'll be two dollars, sir. It's what I said." Staring at Pa a second, his eyes momentarily unmoored and rolled in his head like corks on a lake shore. "TWO DOLLARS!" he shouted, eyes clenched shut, his breath smelling like copper and butt crack.

"How many boards was that again?" Pa asked.

"Two. Two by two. Four. Four boards, Mr. Tuck. Four perfectly squared boards. Two dollars, sir," he said, now extending one lobster claw to take the money. "You should be happy I don't charge for my meticulous attention to detail. Perfectly squared. A deal. Only two dollars." And again he went to tapping those two fingers together.

We watched Buddy load six boards, but here he was charging us for four. *Pa*, I thought, staring intently at him as if he could read my mind, *give him two dollars and let's buy that hay we need*. Perhaps he could read minds. His expression hardened.

"Buddy," he said, placing three dollars into the pincers, "you loaded six boards onto my wagon. I want six boards, and I owe you for them."

I don't think Buddy was accustomed to being wrong, or at least called out for being wrong. "Seeing is believing, Mr. Tuck. Seeing is believing. If you'll excuse me." He dashed for the loading dock, his gut in full swing, forcing each hip to jump back with every step. A moment later he returned, his face red. "Watch out for those nasty, I mean nasty, cockroaches on the trail. Dirty migrants. Raising hell, they are, I hear. Raising hell, little devils." He sat down on a stool behind the counter and retrieved an exceptionally long whittling knife and a diminutive block of Paulownia wood, which he labored to balance on his lap, then went to carving with aggression. "Have a good day, sir," he said to Pa. "A good day." Buddy glanced up at me as I walked away. "But not you," he whispered.

"You tell him about Bethany?" Pa asked as we rode down the bumpy street. The planks of wood jostled out of Buddy's precious alignment.

"No, Pa, I didn't say anything," I said.

"I suppose there's been some rumoring about crime and such, on the rise," he said. We both looked at the horse supply store as we passed it for home, then Pa turned to me. "I saw it in your eyes, son."

"What, Pa?"

"You know what I'm talking about. We're Tucks." I could tell this was going to be one of those rare moments when thoughts jammed up in his mind and he had to let them out. He went on, "We're an honorable family. If you are to be a member of this family, you'll be likewise. That means we don't thieve from anyone, no matter how much you might think you need something. You hungry? You work for your fill. Our horses hungry? They work for their fill, same as we do. And while you're healthy, you work extra for those who aren't. Have I made myself clear?"

It was always about clarity with him. "Yes, sir," I said, hoping we could leave it in the past.

Ahead of us was the General Store and Cordelia's Confectionary. The candy shop name was written in rainbow-script above a window at the corner of the building. Inside the window sat shelf upon shelf of large Victorian glass jars, each filled to the brim with rainbow gumdrops, hard tack, candy sticks, Gibraltars, orange circus peanuts, Pixy Stix, candy buttons, licorice lace, yellow-wrapped molasses pulls, Turkish delights, and pastel sugar plums. "Suppose we could make a quick stop, Pa?" I asked, staring at utopia as we passed by. I imagined their grainy sugar sticking between my teeth, then scraping it out and sucking on my fingernails till my fingers were soft and wrinkled. "Pa?" I asked again. "Ned Brown'll put it on credit, you know..." I was saying what he already knew. Without looking at me, Pa just shook his head, and I couldn't help believing what Ma told me was true: I was a disappointment, yet to grow up.

We rode on, approaching the sheriff's station at the end of the town's main road. Contrasted to the lumber mill, this small-town building was beautiful and new, and something Sherriff Lock himself built—no coincidence his dad was mayor, I'm sure. It replaced the old sheriff's station that sat a few hundred feet back, decaying and decrepit in overgrown weeds, windows missing and gunshot holes blasted through the walls. It had its own outhouse whose burial was overdue by decades—a suffocating chamber of horror even the roughest kids in town avoided, with flies the size of hawk moths.

Outside, Sheriff Lock and a few others, including a couple deputies and the mayor himself, gathered around the back of a wagon. The mayor was dressed in an Abraham Lincoln suit and top hat that added a foot to his petite stature. At first, the sheriff glanced at us, then back at the wagon, but then he turned to face us full-on, staring as we passed. His associates did likewise, including Deputy Charlie Elton, Pa's friend William's son. Charlie hated his boyhood name and reminded folks it was Charles now, but that was too much pretention for me. He'd always be Charlie.

Pa nodded at the silent group, their expressions seeming to be a mixture of awe and terror. None of them nodded back, but just watched us as we passed. Pa snapped the reins, and Clyde and Fred's pace synchronized. The cobble of hoofs on icy ground became a single throbbing rhythm, the grinding wagon wheels spitting muddy razors through the snow like a muted downpour of sleet.

"When I ask a question, I expect an answer."

"I did, Pa. I answered you. I said yes, you've made yourself clear."

"You're young. In youth, it's fundamentals. Nuance comes later," he finished as we left town. Gray clouds were again filling the heavens as we reentered the infinite expanse of prairie.

"Why'd they look at us like that?" I asked, turning back to see them shrink as we rode further away. I pushed my hat lower on my head, believing it was the vagrant they gathered around in that wagon—dead. A surge of excitement filled my body as I considered the possibility, and that the reason those men wore expressions of fear was that they recognized who my pa was. Who he could be, if he needed to. And I believed that was somebody none of those men back there could ever become. They feared my pa because they were in awe of him. A true man among so-called men and everything I could ever hope to become.

"Never mind them. Bunch of stodgy cowards. Not one of them is man enough to run a town, keep its residents safe."

"You mean that guy on the trail last night."

"Precisely, son." He looked at me with steel eyes—an expression seldom donned—then back at the road. I never heard any battle cries, never heard anything as a matter of fact, when he chased after the man. He was like fire without smoke, burning hot and all surprise.

"That was him, wasn't it?" I asked. "In the wagon back there."

"Don't ask questions you already know the answer to," he said.

Seeing him speckled with blood, anyone could have guessed what he did. But all I'd known were stories, never evidence. I'd never seen him act violently toward anyone in person—and technically, I still hadn't. But now I knew for certain. Pa was a man of words *and* actions. Mr. Elton shared the most with us, on long summer evenings when he and Pa sat drinking on the veranda. Not just about Pa's abilities, but his willingness to exercise them.

Pa's reputation had always been enviable in my eyes,

and I imagined it was me the Sheriff and the others looked on with such esteem. Hanky and his boys would see a real man who took care of business when they didn't. I would have murdered that molester, and they'd be jealous I did, knowing in their bones they wouldn't have my courage. I turned again to look at them before we rounded a hillside, and saw them so small in the distance. Literally small, and figuratively. I sat there beside my hero, smug in my satisfaction of an achievement I'd only fantasized.

Remembering last night and the man gazing up at Bethany, him smiling like a kid reaching into a cookie jar, I had the opportunity. It was right there. I was still feeling that knife in my hand. I had it. But instead, I stood there. All of a sudden, I didn't feel so smug anymore. Pa stared ahead at the road, unaffected by his actions. Would I be the same if that was me? Was it right to kill that man? Wasn't that exactly why we had law enforcement? *In a perfect world,* I told myself. Where towns didn't have to suffer incompetent law men like Hanky and associates. Pa had his opportunity, and he didn't hesitate. He took it, and I swore right then, as eldest son and inheritor of the fabled Daryl Tuck, I'd never let an opportunity like that pass me by again.

"Hey, Pa?" I asked. "What's it like in war?"

"You mean what is it like in battle? In a fight?" he asked in return.

"Yeah, I guess so."

"Have I not told you enough stories? And William?"

"You've said a lot about what happens, but not what it's like." I paused. "Do you get scared?"

36

He sat there gently flicking the reins. The leaf springs were at last moving, creaking a discordant but welcome incursion into the hypnotic harmony of our travel home, relieving our backsides as we bumped along. Large flakes of snow floated slowly around us as if they materialized out of the pewter sky just as they were spotted. We were alone on the road. "These clouds look ominous," he said. "Better get home."

"Where else would we go, Pa?" I asked.

His face was long, with deep furrows from cheek to chin. A scar on his mouth twisted his lower lip and aided his perception of resolve, or for those who knew him well, revealed his pensive spirit in moments of concentrated thought. "We'll be indoors hanging these rails. Snow be damned."

Through the crisp winter air, I heard a horseman riding fast in our direction from a distance behind us.

"I'm not avoiding your question, son," he said. "Just thinking on how best to answer it. I'll start by saying there are all kinds of battles, big ones and little ones. I can only speak for myself, but there's little fear when surrendering to instinct. The more thought you give it, the more time for fear to wriggle in. And big battles with many men gives lots of time for pondering. Some people thought I was brave, volunteering for reconnaissance, which put me hand to hand with the enemy." He looked at me. "But I was not brave. It was easier. Less time for thought. And I happened to be handy with a blade."

Stunned by his honesty, absorbed in his words, I sat

there envisioning the war, lost in my imagination.

"I have taken on many a man who was much larger, stronger, even faster than me. But none of those strengths mattered when their first knowledge of my presence was the chill of cold steel pushing through their ribcage."

We were within a quarter mile of home when I noticed Mr. Elton approaching on a road north of us, donning his green cape and riding horseback on his prized black Arabian, a large chestnut horse in tow. The snow flurry quickened, and a cold wind reddened my pa's nose. At the intersection of our two roads, beside a colossal dome-shaped walnut tree, we waited for him and were quickly met by Sheriff Lock, who rode up behind us.

"Whoa," he said, bringing his horse to a stop, then walking him in front of Clyde and Fred to block our way.

"Hanky," Pa said straight-faced, addressing the sheriff.

Henry's eyes squinted, watching Pa wipe his finger under his nose—a taunt Pa couldn't help do, and one he'd done so often I was surprised it upset Henry anymore. He puffed out his chest and turned his horse in a circle.

"What are you doing?" Pa asked.

"You need to come with me this time," the sheriff answered.

"Tuck," Mr. Elton called out, yanking his horse to a stop beside us all. "A piece of fortune to meet you on the road." He was an imposing man—low voice, thick jaw muscles, and deep-sunk eyes. His gray threadbare charro hat—a souvenir from his time in the Mexican War—drooped at the brim under the weight of the snow. "Sheriff," he said, addressing

Henry and tipping his hat.

"Good day, William," Henry said. He always extended a cordiality to families of his deputies, a charity he offered nobody else. "I've got business with Daryl here. If you'd be kind enough, we need to finish that business."

"I've got business with him as well," Mr. Elton replied. He didn't like Henry—a skinny, petty man who mistook authority for esteem—and neither did Mr. Elton's son, Charlie, but Henry was too self-absorbed to notice.

"Daryl," Mr. Elton said. "The barn is incredible—warm, sturdy, it'll stand for decades against the worst of winter."

"Excuse me," the sheriff interrupted. I think I was the only one who actually paid him any attention.

"I can't thank you enough," Mr. Elton continued. "Buck here is one of my best. You've earned him." He handed Buck's reins to Pa.

"Thank you, William," Pa said. "I'm always happy to help a friend. And you be sure to let Charles know if he needs help with any repairs at his place of employment to tell me. I've seen its condition. Shiny and new, but not well built. Damn thing must be drafty. Not enviable."

"Okay, that's enough," the sheriff said in a loud voice. "William, if you wouldn't mind, I need to take this culprit into custody."

"Culprit?" Mr. Elton asked.

Pa gave Henry a look of disbelief. "We had an understanding this morning," he said.

"Situation's changed," Henry said, the corners of his mouth rising.

"Nothing's changed. You asked me about that man you found, and I told you. End of story."

"What's this about a man?" Mr. Elton asked.

"We found a man, dead, in a gully by the trail early this morning. And the honorable mayor has reason to believe Daryl here is the culprit." My heart stopped, worried Pa might get arrested. "Look at the boy," the sheriff continued, pointing at me. "Clearly there's more to the story Daryl isn't telling us."

"No there ain't," I insisted, glancing at Pa.

"Needless to say, you're coming with me, Daryl."

"There's no reason to be hasty, sheriff," Mr. Elton said. "I need Daryl here to shelter his new horse before this weather gets any worse. You can spare a day or two for that."

The sheriff looked back and forth between Mr. Elton and Pa until I noticed the corners of my pa's lips rising and Henry's eyes settling on his countenance. "That won't do, William. Boy," he said, addressing me, "you ride this team back home and get them buttoned up. Daryl, you're lucky Mr. Elton brought you transportation. Wouldn't want you to walk all the way to town in this snow."

"And where do you propose Buck keeps warm in that shit-shack you call a sheriff's station?" Pa asked.

"None of your concern, Daryl," the sheriff said, his body twitchy, and his hand brushing over the grip of his six-shooter. "Now mount up and let's ride. William, with all due respect, you need to go." He turned to me, visibly frustrated. "Boy, take this rig home and get yourself a warm milky."

"You will not speak to my son that way," Pa replied.

"And if you think you're man enough to take me on, let's have a go."

Mr. Elton knew my father long enough to know his words were matter of fact, and not bravado. "Buck's welfare is my concern, Henry," William said. "Mind who you're speaking to and the consequence of your requests."

"These are no requests, William," Henry replied. "You will leave at once or be arrested for obstruction of justice."

Mr. Elton hopped off his horse, handed the rein to me, then proceeded to Henry's side and yanked him from his horse. The sheriff fell into the icy dirt face-first. In a moment he was scrambling to his feet, scraped up and covered with mud. I watched tensely as he pulled his sidearm, took a couple unsteady steps backward, and waved it at all of us with a quaking hand. By the time he focused on the scene before him, Pa had his revolver directed tranquilly at him, and Mr. Elton was taking the sheriff's horse into possession.

"Give me my horse back," Henry said. "Don't mess with the sheriff of this town. You respect the sheriff. Now do as I say or face my wrath."

Pa and Mr. Elton couldn't help but laugh out loud when Henry said that. "Son," Mr. Elton said, "you got no idea what wrath is. Are we going to end this peacefully, or will your deputies find *you* in a gully by the trail?" Pa just watched as William continued. "I suggest you make haste, Henry, before the storm gets any worse."

"Make haste?"

"Get on back to your precious little castle. Whatever dispute you've got with Daryl here won't be resolved today.

He'll be in to visit a day or two hence, and in the meantime, I know he's got some work to do building his fine new horse's quarters."

"Give me my horse," the sheriff said, his voice cracking.

"I've got a better idea," Mr. Elton said. "Give me that jacket of yours. That's right, take it off and toss it to me."

Henry looked at him with puzzlement.

"You're testing my patience, boy," he said, pulling his own revolver and aiming at the sheriff.

"You wouldn't," Henry said. "I'll tell everyone in town. They'll hate you once I'm done."

"I'm sure you'll tell everyone," Mr. Elton said. Henry's reputation as a ribald gossip was well known. "This town won't hate us though, and you know it," Mr. Elton went on. "You see, Daryl and I are what you call integrated with this community. They know who we are." He leaned forward, glaring at Henry. "And they know who you *and* your father are."

Pa's expression hardened. "Word I hear," he said, "is that you shit your pants when you saw the enemy and surrendered before you even got into battle. You have no idea what I would do, what William would do." He looked the sheriff up and down, a pathetic, trembling sight. "You've never had the opportunity to see what men are capable of."

"I believe I have," the sheriff retorted, looking back at him. "I believe I've seen an example just this morning."

"Get to running," Mr. Elton said, no longer in an entertaining mood. "I'll feed and shelter your horse, then I'll give him to Charles to bring back tomorrow once you've had time to cool down."

I think the sheriff realized there was no way out of his predicament and started walking back to town, brushing his arms for warmth.

"You'll be much warmer," Mr. Elton said, "if you get those lazy feet moving."

Henry glared at us one last time before jogging away.

"You didn't have to do that, William," Pa said. He'd told me more than once that Mr. Elton was an army colonel, while Pa got to the rank of sergeant before discharge.

"We're not that far apart in age, Daryl, and you're a great friend, but forgive me for saying I look at you as a son. If only my own children had half the fortitude you've got. Charles is a good boy, but he's young." He paused, looking north toward the trail. "I don't particularly care what happened between you and some man out there. I trust you and your judgment, and that's sufficient for me. Sherriff Henry or his good-for-nothing father gives you any problems, you let me know. They know who contributes to the town common fund—who they get their money for infrastructure from."

"Obliged," Pa said, his eyes shining. "We're off, then." He nodded at Mr. Elton, and we rode for home.

Justice was justice, and Pa had no qualms about how he dispensed it last night. In spite of my questions, neither did I. We spent the remainder of our journey home in silence. I wanted to ask more about the man in the gully, but Pa was glowing and I didn't want to wreck his bliss. Seldom before had I felt the depth of love for this man like I did in that moment.

It was early afternoon when we got home, and the temperature had dropped much lower. The sky was now dumping snow that made it impossible to see further than fifty feet, I'd guess. Pa parked the wagon beside the paddock. As I unhitched the horses, snowflakes bombarded my face like freezing needles sticking into my skin. I began shivering, my coat and hat doing little against the storm. Leading Buck behind him, Pa swung open the gate, dragged open the sliding barn door, then pulled the horse inside. I walked up with Clyde and Fred, putting them in their stall.

"Leave Buck in the aisle, apart from the other two. We'll build his pen tomorrow."

Buck was a generous wage for Pa's labor, and got along perfectly with the brothers—a natural diplomat among strangers. Reward for their behavior was equal scoops of oats. After locking up, I walked to the house, which had disappeared in the whiteout, holding my hat down, my wet hair whipping and stinging my neck and face. As I neared, the orange glow of a lantern in the window beside the front door guided me over the veranda.

"Ma," I called out, pushing the front door open. From Ma and Pa's bedroom, I heard him unbuckling his belt and unzipping his trousers. A drawer opened, and like the sound of a dusty floor mat being shaken, he flapped a piece of clothing in the air before sitting on the mattress—the bed frame creaking—and pulling on another pair of pants, fumbling with his brass belt buckle.

"You're letting snow in!" she yelled at me from her

rocker.

Inside, the fireplace roared with flames, and heat pushed against my tingling, defrosting face. I stepped over Buster, water dripping from the brim of my hat and onto a grey rug her mom had crocheted for her as a wedding gift. I was tempted to disrobe the way Pa did last night, but hesitated, unsure if Bethany was there. I looked around, not seeing her.

"Get those wet clothes off," Ma said. "You weren't raised in a barn. And goddamn it, get off that rug!"

Very well. I disrobed to my underwear in front of the fireplace. The house smelled of ham and split pea soup. "Call me when supper's ready," I said, running up the stairs.

"If you're lucky," she called back.

Stormy days were always shorter, and though it was midafternoon, we were only a few hours from bedtime. I debated turning on a lantern in my room, but the muted light from outside evoked a fine radiance from my alabaster clapboard walls, my walnut-oil-finished wardrobe and trunk, and my unfinished pine table next to the door. Heat from downstairs diffused through the wood floors, and it was too warm to get under the covers of my bed, so I lay down on top of my sheets, resting, staring at the ceiling, and thinking. I rolled onto my side to face the window. The pecan grove had disappeared and all that remained was a square of white— shadows darting fast in random directions, and that crow looking back at me.

"You waiting for something?" I whispered to him, wondering what birds did in weather like this. "Aren't you supposed to fly south for the winter?" I grabbed a pine nut from a small bag I kept on my table and pushed open the sash just enough to fit my fingers through. Freezing air poured inside, and the bird turned his head, darting sideways to face me. He took the nut from my fingers, then angled his neck as if he had his own set of questions about my predicament. "I'm still not letting you in, friend."

THREE

The following morning, I woke, lying in bed, staring at the ceiling. The house was silent but for the hushed snore of Pa downstairs in bed. *You still there?* I wondered, raising my head and looking at the window for the black bird. It was dark outside and impossible to see, though I imagined he hadn't moved. *What would it take for him to fly off, to find his own companions, to make a home for himself?* I got up to check on him and carefully pulled the window open so he couldn't squeeze in. Moving my finger back and forth in the cold air, he gently nipped at my skin, perhaps thinking it was a nut. "I guess we're both still here, aren't we lil guy?" I stayed a moment longer, then felt an urge to go outside and join him. On my way out of my room, I threw a coat over my long johns, put on my hat, and grabbed the bag of pine nuts.

Downstairs, I yanked on my boots, my heels getting stuck like always, so I laced them tight against my ankles,

47

figuring they'd slip on the rest of the way as I walked. The front door creaked as I opened it slowly, so I yanked it hard, and the creak turned into a loud screech. Figured. Pa's snoring stopped a moment before resuming, this time deeper than before. No wonder he woke with a sore throat so many mornings. I exhaled and released my death grip on the door handle, confident nobody was awake, and peeked around outside. The storm was gone, and stars flickered in the dark blue morning sky. I popped my collar, pulled it closed around my neck, and buried my hands in my coat pockets as I walked out.

My cheeks tightened. Wasn't expecting it to be that cold. The sound of sand shaking in a canvas bag caught my attention. Frightened, I looked all around for its source, then I realized it was just my boots dragging in the snow.

A slight crescent of orange peeked over the eastern horizon, casting enough light to brighten my white breath in the frosty air. Snowdrifts piled against every upright surface, leaning like drunkards against the pecan trunks, the stack of firewood beside the house, the chicken coop, the wagon wheels, and the paddock fence. An eagle shrieked from miles away, the crisp air carrying sounds far over the prairie. I walked out to the oak tree for a better angle to see my windowsill, then noticed a pair of footsteps leading around the house—footsteps that didn't belong.

Something caught my eye. Turning toward the pecan grove, a big white bird flew off one of the branches, followed by a flurry of snow dumping onto the ground. I sensed I wasn't alone. A chill ran down my back, thinking it could be a foreign migrant, or another dirty, dangerous vagrant who made those footsteps. For an increasing number of folks there was no distinction. But wayfaring vagrants seldom came off the trail, and though rumors were plentiful, true stories of their harassment were limited. Then I remembered when Ma's older brother, my favorite uncle Walter from New Hampshire, surprised us a year after her miscarriage. I was little then but recalled his smile and caring disposition. He had been one of Pa's closest friends back home, and I grew up on stories of his stalwart service and commitment to others. I know it inspired my pa to be the man of duty he became, which inspired me as well. The chill I felt was replaced by joy, imagining he was out here to see us again.

Before we moved to Kansas, my earliest memory was Walter holding me on his horse, riding fast through the white birch forest outside the Dover family farm. The summer wind blew through my hair as beams of sunlight penetrated the glittering leaves overhead, wrapping my skin with a divine warmth, and the thick green scent of ferns and moist undergrowth was like a meal for my lungs. I remember him holding me tight and safe, feeling an instinct that life and truth were so much bigger than my ideas. We darted through the blurry forest, and I remember a moment of feeling that I should have been scared—surrounded by an infinite, undefinable, and forever unknowable thing—but Walter's hands had held me snug and assured me that love was the rope that reached out of the clouds and down to earth. I knew then that no matter what, everything wasn't just okay, it wasn't just the way it was supposed to be. Things were actually perfect.

"Walter—is that you?" I asked in a loud whisper, remembering his penetrating brown eyes and dark brown hair. I scuttled over to the footsteps, dragging my floppy boots in the snow, and realized they weren't footsteps at all but shadows of small, wind-blown snow caps. The stupid wind tricked me into thinking someone was here. I looked up at the windowsill, the crow now visible and looking back at me. My joy dissipated as a cold breeze blew the hat off my head. It skittered over the snow, stopping against a patch of ice-wrapped barnyard grass. Reaching down to grab it, I felt another gust of wind, and a crashing sound shot out from the barn, taking my breath away.

Terrified, I jumped clean into my boots the rest of the way. The startled horses neighed raucously, banging against the sides of their pen, and stomping loud enough to be heard a hundred yards off. I didn't know Buck's temperament yet, and he could be destroying our barn aisle trying to get out. *What the hell was that?* Something was obviously wrong. I ran to check when suddenly Pa passed me on one side, sprinting barefoot and coatless in the freezing weather.

I entered the barn through the east door and saw Pa wrangling Buck by his bridle, rearing fierce as though woken from a nightmare. But the fact that Clyde and Fred were likewise scared was evidence that whatever happened was no dream.

"What happened, Pa?" I asked.

"Give them other horses some oats, boy. Talk calm to them," he said, trying his best to soothe the new animal.

"Throw some this way while you're at it."

This behavior was entirely unprecedented for Clyde and Fred, especially Fred who couldn't give a shit about anything that didn't directly benefit or threaten his wellbeing. "Stop it, Fred! You're going to break the pen!" I yelled at him, hoping he'd calm, knowing if he did, Clyde would surely copy. Ma walked to the door and watched, her coat bundled tight and Bethany by her side.

"Slide open the barn door, Cess!" Pa yelled. He was no dancer, but I watched him leap and jolt as good as any, avoiding those massive hooves while they blocked Ma's way, the man and animal like partners dancing to a wretched jug band tune.

"How do you propose I do that?" she yelled back, bracing Bethany as Buck continued his tantrum.

He glanced at the door latch. "Go around," he answered. "Yank it open. Ain't locked."

She bustled away while Bethany stayed and watched us. A moment later Ma slid open the door and Pa managed to get Buck outside. Seeing Clyde and Fred weren't yet relaxing, he grabbed a bullwhip, swung open their stall door, and dragooned them both into Buck's company. Outside, and sucking the cold morning air, all three of them finally started to calm down.

"Thought you locked that, James," Pa said, catching his breath. The tones of accusation and anger were unmistakable.

"I did, Pa. I always do."

He scowled at me like never before, gripping that bullwhip tight. "You don't lie to me, boy. Never. Now tell me

51

the damned truth!"

"Why are you so dramatic, Daryl?" Ma asked, her tone condescending. She hurried to his side and took the whip from his hand. "It doesn't suit you."

"I'm not talking about the sliding door," he said, pointing at the east entrance to the barn. "The door was swung wide open when I ran up. God knows who might have drifted in here and frightened those horses."

He milled about, taking account of all his tools and gear to see if any were missing while I examined the door. "Pa," I said, "I'm telling you. I locked it."

Starting above our property, a scant hickory grove curved through the valley around the southwest hillside below the trail, ending beside the barn where a great branch from the last tree reached the granary window. A pile of broken glass sat in the dirt under the window, along with a four-by-eight board that had been left upstairs. The room was small, hardly a granary at all, more of a garret—an uncanny place that haunted my dreams for no particular reason. There was no floor under the window, just a straight shot down thirty feet to where we stood. "See?" I said, my finger pointing down, shaking.

On seeing the glass and board, Pa grabbed a knife from a box under the staircase and dashed up into the pitch-black loft.

"What's up there?" Ma asked him, pulling Bethany close.

We heard him stomping around on the plywood floor, kicking straw that dropped over the edge and on top of the glass shards. He worked silently, and I could only imagine he was assaulting that darkness on the chance of finding a trespasser there. That was unlikely, I thought, given the gap of space they'd have to cross. But perhaps that's what the board was used for—to make their way across the chasm.

"Well?" Ma asked as Pa came down the stairs.

"As I thought," he said, inspecting the broken glass. He picked through it with the knife, then found one piece and held it up for us to see. "There you go."

"What is it?" Bethany asked.

"Blood." He looked up at the window. "A fall like that will leave a mark, broken glass beside. I'll be back." And he darted out the door, returning a few minutes later.

"Where'd you go?" I asked him.

"Someone was here, that's for certain," he said, focused. "Footsteps covered over with snow lead up to the trail." He picked up a piece of bloody glass and inspected it. "It's dry. Whoever hurt themselves here, it was a while ago."

He put the knife back in the box and gathered his tools, sizing up the horse pen. We watched while he squinted, figuring in his mind. "Well, God help whoever that was if I catch them. They'll find no comfort with me. Here, James," he said, shifting on to new business, "we'll add the boards here and put any extra wood over that window upstairs. Leave Clyde and Fred with a little more than half the stall. Buck is a big boy and needs space."

"That's it?" Ma asked. "Really? You're not concerned about this break-in?"

"Cess," he said, glancing at her, then back to the pen,

"my job is to look after this family. You know me. Are you concerned about my ability?" We waited a silent moment for her to reply, but she didn't. "We've all got jobs here," he said, his voice deep and imposing. "Would you please put on some coffee?"

"Pa, are you going to work like that?" Bethany asked, pointing at his bare feet.

As Bethany spoke, Ma rolled her eyes, huffing, "*My* job!" on a heavy, muted breath. "*Coffee…*" We all pretended not to hear her.

"You have a point," he answered Bethany. "I'll be out in a minute," he said to me. "Fetch the tools we'll need."

Leaning against the sliding barn door, I watched him, Ma, and Bethany walk to the house, then gathered the saw, hammer, and nails beside the pen boards, and hurried back outside to the paddock and the company of our horses. I felt uneasy inside the barn, knowing someone was there, the residue of their presence clinging to the air as if they hadn't left. Probably some trail creep, I surmised. Some damned coward, long gone now. In my imagination, I watched myself running up the loft stairs and slashing the straw the way Pa had done.

"What are you doing out here in the cold?" Pa asked as he walked up carrying a pot of coffee and two mugs.

"Nothing," I said, making my voice deep, not wanting him to think I was scared or anything. "You got back fast," I went on, relieved he was here.

Within minutes, we had Buck's pen built and dressed nicely in clean straw and an old zinc-dipped water trough.

The horses continued playing outside, nosing each other. Sitting on tree stumps by the sliding barn door, we watched them, drinking our steaming hot coffee in silence, caressing the mugs in our cold-whitened hands. After a few minutes, I broke the trance and asked, "You think they're still out there?"

Pa's gaze was fixed in the distance, now toward the trail at the top of the hill. "They're always out there," he answered. Reentering the silence, we sat a little longer, my body relaxing and the morning chill slowly burrowing its way back into my muscles. Each sip of hot coffee ran down my insides, tingling and defrosting.

"I'm sorry, son," Pa said eventually. "I shouldn't have gotten so mad at you earlier."

I thought he was going to hit me with that bullwhip. "It's okay," I told him, but resented him calling me a liar. I decided if I wasn't a liar, I had to be honest with him. "Actually," I said hesitantly, pushing through the discomfort of standing up to him, "it's not okay you called me a liar."

"Were you not implying just yesterday to lie to Buddy Burton about those boards?" he asked, his eyes at once curious and knowing.

I sat there for a moment, deciding not to answer until I sorted this out in my mind first. Why wouldn't he suspect me of lying about locking the door if he thought I wanted to lie about how many boards we bought. An epiphany struck me. Technically, he was wrong. I was actually implying to *steal* instead. I sat upright, ready to speak, when I realized that stealing was no better, and possibly worse than lying.

My shoulders rounded, and I curled around my mug once again. Perhaps he observed embarrassment in my face and the recognition that he was right. I was humiliated and felt like flipping inside out and disappearing.

"We learn from our mistakes, son," he said, patting me on the knee. "That never stops, no matter how old you get."

I caught my breath, holding it against the spasm that yanked down hard in my lungs—powerful and overwhelming—while my eyes welled with tears. It's uncertain why I reacted that way, but in the moment, something stirred deep inside, and I couldn't control it. I turned away from him, wiping my face. Instead of looking at his eyes, I stared out at the snow that had melted and refrozen—a white blanket both light and heavy, sparkling in tiny prisms. Pa was brave and honest, forged hard like steel. He was unforgiving yet subtle and refined in his matter-of-fact way. Every part of me wanted to be like him, but as I sat there, that impossibility was glaring. We were different people, no matter how hard I tried. Tears broke free and ran down my cheeks. The image of me sitting beside him was a picture of opposites, the juxtaposition of honor and shame, worthiness and futility. Perhaps he sensed this too. He was a proud man, and though I believed he loved me, not hearing it from him meant it didn't have to be true. I wiped my face again, my eyes dropping to the ground. He never said I made him proud. Pa never lied, and his silence must have been a matter of integrity.

"You know I love you, right Pa?"

"I know, son," he said, squeezing my knee. "I know."

Not the response I was hoping for. "Well, hey," I said, standing up. I walked into the barn shadows, to keep him from seeing me cry, and cleared my throat. "I'll get these horses put up. Don't worry about it. You go in the house and get warm."

After locking up the barn, I grabbed fresh clothes from my bedroom dresser and went to the bathroom, filling the tub from a hand pump plumbed to the well outside. The water was frigid, but not more than I could handle. Whether I liked it or not, I was used to it. Dunking myself quickly, the cold took my breath away, but I forced myself to stay, my arms and legs trembling. I wasn't a sissy, after all. Staring out through the window, my mind drifted, daydreaming.

Summer had been punishing, and we'd rejoiced when it came to an end, the last exhausted flickers of heat clinging to the shrinking day like silent screams of a mute man drowning. It involuntarily surrendered its oppression to a more powerful autumn—a mighty season of decay that prepared the way for the omnipotent juncture of winter, its touch lethal and eternal.

On those hot copper evenings between summer and fall, we sat on the veranda in the shimmering air that radiated from the tips of yellowing grass. I'd sharpen my whittling knife with a stone I kept behind a chair while Pa had waxed on, softened by his jar of moonshine, his stories infused by the ghosts of his secret dreams and veiled childhood. Lying in the tub, I reconstructed his memories in my imagination. I saw his life as a boy in New Hampshire who barely knew his Pa, always away earning money—scraps that never put a proper meal on the table. Pa was a late bloomer, raised and teased by his five older brothers and three older sisters. In time, a growth spurt gave him two inches over his oldest sibling, Roger—a blustering, arrogant boy who directed his antagonism at my father. Their fistfights toughened my pa, and he grew to hate his brother, but when a dark-skinned man from out of town took issue with Roger's unfavorable attitude, leading to my uncle's death, Pa vowed retribution. If anyone was going to kill Roger, it should have been Pa himself. Soon after, he learned the killer was Mexican, and in late spring of 1846, at seventeen years old, he volunteered for the Mexican-American war, misplacing his acrimony on an entire race of people.

As the sun went down and a cool easterly breeze swept away the hot earth-baked air, he told us that it was foolish of him, but a lesson for Bethany and me to learn by. "Never confuse an individual with their group," he had said. "Groups are arbitrary and made up, fluid and always changing. They're constructs of attributes and only exist in your mind, whereas a neighbor is someone you can shake hands with. You'll hear talk of the Natives as savages, but don't believe it. Push any man far enough, and you'll discover what's inside him, good or bad."

In my mind, I watched him outside Mexico City, noiselessly winging his knife like a paintbrush over the throats of his adversaries, fluid and graceful. Never once, he said, did he contemplate his victims' families—their mothers who loved them, their children now deprived of their father's guidance and protection. Such was the nature of justice, he explained to us as the copper sky turned plum, and he sipped on his whiskey. He was an instrument of justice, after all, and so were we, with duties rooted in aptitudes which time and opportunity would eventually reveal. "Be careful," he warned. "Wrong choices have irreversible consequences. In one way or another we all bear those scars."

I stood up in the bathtub and wrapped myself in a towel, staring through the window as deputy Charlie Elton rode his horse up the road towards our house. He slowed, looked around, then sped toward the barn. I threw on my clothes and ran outside.

"He's under treatment," Charlie said, leaning on the paddock fence and speaking to Pa as he brushed Clyde.

"That's no concern of mine," Pa replied. He nodded to me as I walked closer.

"I beg to differ, sir. It's precisely your concern, as it was you he was in the process of taking in peacefully before you took his gun and forced him to walk back to town. If he wasn't walking, he wouldn't have slipped and broke his leg."

"Is that what he told you?" Pa asked. "You all created this problem. If you would do your job, we wouldn't need to do it for you."

"Now that's just the wrong attitude," Charlie said. "An entirely wrong attitude. I'm young, that's true, but..."

"Spit it out, boy," Pa said. "You're wasting my time." He motioned for me to join him in the paddock, so I ducked and stepped between the rails. "Take Clyde inside," he said to me, "and bring Fred."

"Don't insult me, Daryl. I won't stand for it."

"You going to spit it out or what?"

"Dammit, I need you to come with me," Charlie said, raising his voice.

I turned back and watched Pa walk to the paddock fence, put his foot on the rail, and tie his shoe. "What is it you got with him anyway?" he asked Charlie, not looking up. "That snot-nosed boss of yours."

"Here you go," I said to Pa, returning with Fred. Seeing Charlie squirm the way he did caused me to smile at him, something he noticed and didn't appreciate.

"I see your family has a well-earned reputation for disrespecting authority," Charlie said, squinting at me.

"You two like best friends or something? You and Sheriff Hanky," Pa went on. "Play make-believe convict and prison guard when no one's there? Maybe some bare-assed spankings for the bad criminal?" I could tell by the sound of his voice, Pa was struggling to contain his laughter. "I would suppose you two switch roles from time to time, but I don't think that's Hanky's style. Guessing you take all the bruising."

"For God's sake, Daryl, that's enough! Are you coming with me or not?"

"You're a smart boy, Charlie. What do you think?" Pa turned his back on him and started brushing Fred.

"It's *Charles*, for fuck sake! Why is that so hard to remember! You don't get to do what you did to that man and just walk away. I'll be back with Deputy Nathan, need be."

Pa took a deep breath, then walked up to Charlie, face to face. "You dare come to my doorstep and threaten my ability to ensure the safety of my family?" I could see the muscles in his jaw working. "Do I understand you properly? While you're playing grab-ass with the other dressed-up kiddies, I'm doing your job. You should thank me and thank your pa for having the spine to do more than talk. You've tested my patience long enough, little boy. I expect to see you off my property immediately."

His body trembling, Charlie climbed on his horse. "I'll be back, Tuck."

"Make haste, boy, before this gets ugly."

He rode away, glancing back every so often with a scowl.

"You okay, Pa?" I asked.

"Blows my mind that child is a son of William's," he said, brushing Fred's ribs with focus. He loved the attention and squirmed left and right as Pa ran the brush over him, maneuvering so the bristles reached just the right spot.

"So Hank, our hard-nosed sheriff, slipped in the snow and broke his leg?" I asked. "Really?"

"Unbelievable, if you want my opinion," Pa said. He nodded toward the barn. "Or perhaps there was snow on the tree branch he climbed."

"You think that was him?" I asked, but Pa didn't answer, walking inside the barn instead to put away the hairbrush. He yanked the sliding door closed and walked over. "But why? What for?"

"Knowing why anyone does anything takes a smarter man than me," he answered.

Bethany ran out with one of my shoes in hand. She

stopped twenty yards away and held it up, shining it at me and goading me to chase her. "I'm throwing this in the creek," she yelled, then sprinted away past the oak tree and around the chicken coop. Buster was there, barking up a storm and clawing on the chicken fence as best as his fat body allowed. Bethany then disappeared behind the house. Spotting her from his blanket on the porch, Spooks got up and zipped to catch up with her.

"Go on, have fun," Pa said.

The warm sun melted the snow as I chased my sister around the oak tree a few times, then through some of the pecan trees up the hill, but not more than that before she turned and ran for the barn, disappearing into the hickory grove. Covered in mud and exhausted, we lay on the ground under the oak tree, searching for squirrels and birds' nests. We laughed and made fun of each other, wondering what our futures would look like.

"If we live to one hundred, we'll be alive in the 1950s," I said. "Who knows, maybe by then we'll be living in space and have steam-powered robots who do everything for us, so we don't have to do anything. What do you think?"

"I think that sounds perfect," she answered, pulling Spooks close to her side. We stared through the leaves at a faraway half-moon shrouded in sea fog. The face of the hemisphere looked like the plank of a pirate's ship, its light plunging into the blue expanse. "Do you think there'll be creeps then?"

Bethany was strong, and her voice didn't waver as she asked her question. "If there are, we'll get a robot Spooks," I said. "Get a dozen of them. Anyway, I think you're going to get married to a rich guy and have a mess of babies, and all of them feisty sons of bitches like you."

"Watch your tongue, James!" she said. "You're the only son here. By the way, your sort is disgusting, and you'll find me dead before you find me married."

"I'm not disgusting."

Bethany looked at me and rolled her eyes. "You're sixteen, and how many times have I seen you picking your nose in your room, laying on your bed when you think nobody's watching? I saw you. I saw you wiping your finger under your mattress. You think I'm going to marry some guy like you with sticky hands who sleeps on a bed of boogers?"

"You're lying!"

"Am I, though?" she asked.

Sometimes it felt like I was being watched while I lay in bed, and whenever I turned to my door to see, there was no one there. To my humiliating detriment, it turned out I was right after all. "Well," I said, my face burning red, "you shouldn't be peeping like that. You're a peeper!" She looked at me and busted up laughing, so I yanked on her hair and ran away.

"Get back here, you nasty boy!" she said, on my heels already. We stopped running when we saw Charlie riding up the road with Deputy Nathan and two other guys dressed in black suits, all of them on horseback. We ran for the barn.

"Pa," I yelled, standing at the paddock fence. He walked out of the barn, then saw the posse for himself.

"Go back to the house. Take your sister," he said.

Minutes later, Bethany, Ma and I watched from the front porch while Pa mounted Clyde and followed the men toward town.

"You two get undressed right now," Ma said to us. "You're filthy." But I ran for the barn instead.

"I'm not your little boy anymore," I yelled back at her.

"Could have fooled me," she said, hollering. "What do you think you're going to do anyway?"

Her voice faded while I ran through the paddock and dragged open the barn door. There was Fred, his face droopy and lazy, and Buck—this huge, strong horse that I knew nothing about. The smart choice was Fred, but he couldn't be bothered when he wasn't feeling fabulous. That only left Buck, and stories of people getting thrown from unfamiliar horses played in my mind. At least it's muddy, I thought, and the fall wouldn't hurt *that* bad. Looking at him, at his ripped and rippling muscles, fear struck me like a gong. I contemplated Pa's words about giving room for fear. *Move.* I needed to move to rid myself of this feeling, so I mounted him bareback and ran him out of the barn, through the paddock gate, and we were off.

Holy shit, that horse could run. I struggled not to slip off, being wet and muddy, and leaned forward to get out of the cold wind he created, balancing on my forearms while I clung to his neck, pinning my knees to his flanks. The landscape was a blur, and minutes later we were at the doorstep of Mr. William Elton.

His property was legendary, sprawling and massive, spotted with barns and work shacks. "That's some fine riding, son," he said as I brought Buck to a trot, then a stop. I hopped off while he reached up and petted his former property. "Real fine. What's going on?"

"Your son Charlie," I said, tired but not winded. "He took my pa to the sheriff's station with Nathan and a couple other guys I don't know. It's about the man they found by the trail."

"Charles filled me in on what your pa did," he said. "He wasn't too happy about it, either. Times are changing, I suppose." While he spoke, Mr. Elton grabbed a loop of rope off his front porch and lassoed Buck. We walked to the back of his house to a grand veranda overlooking his seemingly unending farmland.

"Do you know what that man did?" I asked.

"Your father will tell me if he wants me to know," he answered. "But I know your pa, and he doesn't do anything without purpose. I'm sure it was just. Here," he said, motioning to a chair, "why don't you stay while I go check on him. Maria," he called in through the back door of the house. His wife walked outside in sandals, a beige huipil dress, and her long black hair in two braids, each resting on a shoulder. She was accompanied by their youngest son, Tommy the Troublemaker, who was my age.

"Honey," Mr. Elton said to her, "would you mind making James something to eat? I'm going to town to check on Daryl. Actually," he said to me, "this gives you and Tommy a chance to catch up. You haven't seen each other for a while." Tommy stood there, smiling at me.

Back before Tommy flunked out of school, he earned the

nickname Guts for gutting a live lizard with a rusty nail during lunch. Smiling, his mouth way too big for his shiny, plump face, he pulled at the little organs and taunted the girls with them, then flicked them down and licked his fingers clean. It was only once we saw the teacher paddling him something fierce, and him still smiling, when we realized that creepy clown grin must be some kind of permanent birth defect. At just four feet tall, he looked like a snowman, his body made of only two bulbous parts—receding old man hair on top, and feeble spidery limbs that stuck out from the sides.

"You two stay out of trouble," Mr. Elton said to us, then went to the barn for a horse and rode off. *Not likely*, I thought, suddenly regretting coming here.

"He's a good boy, isn't he?" Guts asked as he petted Buck, smiling for no discernable reason and staring at the horse with hungry, distant eyes. He looked like a character from a horror story, kid parts and old parts and midget clown parts all mixed up.

"I don't know," I answered. "Seems that way. He is fast."

"Oh, I know it," he said, moving his hand in long strokes across Buck's back from shoulder to hind. "Sexy, right?"

Bizarre. "I wouldn't say that." Maybe Guts's disposition toward this animal had something to do with Mr. Elton giving him up.

"James," Maria said, "do you want anything to eat?" She was a warm and hospitable person, but her Spanish accent was thick, and I sometimes didn't understand what she said.

"No, ma'am," I answered, thinking that her English had gotten better since I saw her last. Looking at Guts, I realized I'd avoided this place for quite a while. "Thank you."

"You wanna play?" Guts asked. He pulled on Buck's lasso, walking him to the barn. "I got a rifle we can play with."

"A real rifle?" I asked, tempted to just go home right then but feeling indebted to Mr. Elton for looking after Pa. What the hell was I walking into?

"Real play," he said, excited. "Bingo showed me how."

Bingo—his real name, actually—was Guts's older brother. He was older than Charlie: a reclusive character that might have been pulled right out of an Ann Stephens novel, brimming with delusions of grandeur and immortality. His ashen skin was a stark contrast to the black clothing he wore from head to toe. He was mythical and spent so much time indoors few people even knew he existed, apart from rare references by his family. I'd only seen him through windows on occasion as he crossed a room inside the house, where he spent day after day, year after year, playing games— according to Guts. *Games*. What kind of a person spends all day inside playing games?

While Guts went inside one of the number of barns, this one exclusively his, I sat outside in the shade overlooking a flat stretch of dead fescue. It ended at a creek beside a wood-fence-enclosed apple orchard where he'd set up a series of tin cans. The trees were ominous, like they were yanked from the earth and jammed back in crown first, their withered, splaying roots dangling in the cold air. After a few minutes, he walked out and handed me a .44 caliber lever-action Henry rifle.

"Your parents gave you this?" I asked, surprised, working the lever until all the bullets had popped out of the chamber one at a time. I stood and aimed at a sparrow flying through the sky. *Click.*

Guts scooped up the bullets and took the rifle from me. "Let me have that thing," he said. "That's not how you play with a gun. Don't be such a chicken shit." Frustrated, he pushed the bullets back into the magazine. "I think I counted fourteen. You see any more?"

"No," I said. "I think you got all of them."

He stood and slammed the lever open and closed, squeezing the trigger between each motion, jacking off several bullets that flew through the air like popcorn, the tin cans reeling off their posts. His face transformed, and for the first time, his perma-smile appeared genuine. "I love this thing," he said, speaking in a tender, childish voice. "Watch this," he said, putting the muzzle on top of his foot. He pulled the trigger. *Click.*

"How'd you know there weren't any more bullets?" I asked.

"I didn't," he said, still beaming with joy.

"You must've been counting," I said, standing up and grabbing the bullet casings off the ground. "Got thirteen here. One's missing."

He studied the ground. "Nope," he said, realizing his luck. He cocked the lever one more time, aimed toward an apple tree, and pulled the trigger. *Boom*. Bark went flying while he fell on the ground laughing.

"You're crazy, Guts," I told him.

"I'm not crazy," he said. "I'm gifted."

"Fine. You're *touched*. We both agree on that."

Two years prior, probably the last time I was here, he about burned down the barn, taking us and his horse, Gummy, with it. He thought it would be smart to build a fire in the loft and fry a skillet of oil.

Six months before that, he almost killed me too. We were riding a few miles from his house when he wanted to see if his horse could clear a ten-foot wadi. It wouldn't have been a problem for an adult horse, but we were on two of his father's yearlings. My horse threw me off, tumbling ahead of him, and I watched the horse land, its front hoof inches from my face. I got up, brushed off, and watched Guts take his turn. He ran his horse into the side of that wadi, tearing open both its front legs—splintered bones sticking out of ruptured skin. The cries of pain that horse made were something I had never heard before or since. We both rode back to his house on my horse, Guts swearing he'd tell his pa what happened and go fetch the injured one. But the instant we saw his pa, he laid on some story about how his horse ran off while he was taking a leak and didn't came back.

"Yearlings'll do that," Mr. Elton said. "They don't know any better."

But people do. Guts left that injured horse to suffer. I was so disgusted with him then, and that feeling bubbled up as I stood there with him again. Enough. I went to fetch Buck, leaving Guts on the side of the barn without a word.

"Where you going?" he asked.

"I'm leaving, Guts."

"You're too scared," he said, fumbling with the rifle. I could hear him loading more rounds. "Not man enough. You're never going to grow up, are you?"

"You got me, Guts. Nailed it." I unlassoed the rope from Buck's neck and tossed it on the ground, then climbed on his back.

"You think I'm lucky, James?" he asked, taunting. "Cause I am. Luckiest boy in town." I kicked Buck, and he trotted away while Guts pulled the trigger one more time. A bullet zipped right past my ear. "That was close," he yelled. "Guess you're lucky too!"

However fast I took Buck getting here, I took him twice as fast back home. I didn't know he was holding out on me before. The sun began to set as he trotted into the paddock. I opened the barn door to Fred's surprise, and he turned his head away as if embarrassed. "Take it easy, Fred. It's just me." Clyde was still gone, which meant Pa was probably at the sheriff's station.

"Hey, Ma," I said, covered in mud as I walked into the house, stepping over Buster. Kerosene lamps were blazing in the corners of the room and she sat reading in her rocker, not looking up. The smell of my favorite meal, Indian mush, hit my hungry stomach with force. The pot cooked in the fireplace, hanging from the chimney crane. I peeked in, seeing Ma had added meatballs, turning my favorite meal into something without rival.

"Yep." Ma's response was curt, and I could tell I was bothering her. Upstairs, Bethany played with her doll, making baby sounds.

"You think we should go check on Pa?" I asked anyway.

She glanced over her book at me, then lowered her face behind it again. "Get off the rug, *Mucky Tuck*," she said. "How many times have I told you about coming in here all grubby?" The sound from Bethany's room stopped, then resumed. She talked to her doll, calling it Mucky Tuck, and laughed quietly. "Didn't you check on him earlier?" Ma asked. "He's fine."

"How do you know?" I said.

"You can see I'm reading, right?"

It was always the same with her. "I'm just saying. You don't know if he's fine. There's a lot you don't know."

She lowered the book to her lap and glared at me, revealing the same New Hampshire toile dress she wore yesterday, and the day before. Crumbs roosted on her wrinkled top like a broad-collared Egyptian necklace. "Is that a fact?" she asked. "And you're the one to instruct me?" She huffed. "I might say there's a lot *you* don't know ... but I wouldn't want to spoil it for you."

I figured there were lots of things she knew about Pa that she never let on, things I wondered if he'd ever tell me. Even if he didn't tell her what he did to that man on the trail, she must have known. I looked at my dirty ma, thinking of that vagrant. "You might want to brush off," I said, wiping my hand over my shirt. "I'm just saying."

"*I'm* just saying," she said, eyeballing my muddy

clothes, then raising the book. "Don't bother me anymore. I'm at a good part. You can go."

My stomach turned when I looked at the pot in the fireplace. I headed upstairs to get cleaned. "Tell me when my meal is at the table, woman."

To my surprise, she followed and persuaded me to remain in my bedroom. "That's no way to act like a man," she said, "if that was your goal."

I stayed in my room, stomach empty and growling, nursing a tender cheek with a bright red handprint.

What a day, I thought, uncertain how this predicament with Pa was going to shake out. After turning my kerosene lantern low, I plopped on top of my bed, dry mud bouncing off my clothes, and lay down. One crooked line at time, I followed the contours of shadow created by the lamp glass across the ceiling. The gnarled pattern charted courses from one side of the room to the other, fleeting stamps laid over an apathetic plaster and lath like our lives over the face of this planet. Once the oil burned out, the pattern would disappear as if it never existed. For whatever time the light shined it made the ceiling interesting, the silhouette meaningful. But shadows weren't chisels, no matter how beautiful the pattern they formed.

Lying there, I felt sad, thinking about how Ma made me feel like I wasn't hers. I wished I was invisible to those feeling—cruel shadows in their own right, hunting for a canvas to bedeck. I wished I was invisible to her. There was only so much oil in that lamp by my wall, and while I could top it off, other cisterns weren't refillable.

I stared at the window into the darkness and the invisible pecan grove. My imagination drifted up to the invisible trail, and the migrants there. How many were out there, escaping, searching for their own invisibility? *Yearning* for invisibility in this new environment of suspicion. I hated to admit a part of me, buried miles inside, loathed that woman. To spite her, I refused to fall asleep regardless of my weariness. Still staring through the window, I got out of bed and grasped the sash, wondering about Pa. Leaving the lamp to burn, I threw on my coat and snuck out the window, careful not to let the crow in.

FOUR

The night was cold, and the half-moon shined bright in a black ocean sparkling with diamonds, sending down a blue glow that glazed the earth. The horses spooked when I unlocked the east barn door. Inside was pure darkness. Smelling it was me, Fred swooshed his tail and ground his teeth, something he and Clyde always did when they knew I would give them oats. I felt my way through the alley and dragged open the sliding door, allowing moonlight to flood in. Buck stood in his stall, grand and impressive, watching me, while Fred licked his lips.

"Here, you drama queen," I said, dropping a handful of oats in his stall. I opened Buck's pen and put a bridle on him. "You're coming with me."

I hopped aboard, and we trotted until passing the house, then I let him fly down the road toward town. The air turned into a strong wind blowing us back, as if a warning to what

74

lay ahead. He stretched his long muscular legs, flexing, clutching clay underfoot, wrenching up clods and hurling them into the void behind us. He commanded his stride around the curves, never slowing down, smashing puddles that exploded in a million drops of mist that moistened the skin below my pant legs. Riding Buck was an extended moment of sublimity, reminding me of the enchanting ride with my uncle in Dover. As we dashed through the night, a night dressed in fluorescent foliage and kindled in remnants of smoky yellow sunlight, I transformed for a moment into something more than myself, something outside myself, something other than myself.

Five horses were tied to the hitching post outside the sheriff's station, one being Clyde and two belonging to Mr. Elton and Charlie. The others were unknown to me. We walked closer, then I climbed off and guided Buck the rest of the way. Clyde recognized me and started fussing. I hoped nobody heard his ruckus as I hurried out of sight beside an undressed window on the side of the long, rectangular building that was lit from within. I wanted to push farther back to where the hazelnut bushes grew, so I guided Buck past the window, seeing him totally cover it with his immense body, prodding him to move faster.

"You stay there," I whispered, wrapping the rein around a branch as if that had any value whatsoever. "Don't move." He obeyed and stood still alongside the wall, watching me as I tiptoed back to the window which was opened slightly. I looked up into the sky and realized the moon was so bright anyone inside could have seen Buck pass. All I could do was hope they didn't.

"Well, am I under arrest or not?" I heard Pa ask, sounding impatient. "We've been doing this for hours, wasting my time."

"Be reasonable, son," Mr. Elton said, speaking to Charlie, I supposed. "Your goals here elude me. Just end this already."

"Sheriff told me to round him up, hold him till he stopped by later," Charlie said.

"It is well past later," Pa said.

"Son, you know as well as anyone this wouldn't be an issue if not for the sheriff," Mr. Elton said. "Since when did law worry about a father protecting his family?"

"I know, Papa," Charlie answered. "We just have to wait. I'm sorry."

"You know about our break-in last night," Pa said, "following an attack on my daughter by some worthless vagrant. Tell me I don't have cause for concern about my family's safety."

I couldn't help peeking through the bottom of the window and saw Pa sitting in a chair, handcuffed, on the opposite side of the station facing my direction. The walls were paneled with wood that glowed a light brown in the lantern light. In the back corner was a jail cell, and next to that was a desk littered with papers. The fancy-dressed fellows sat facing Pa, their backs to me. Mr. Elton was facing away as well, one leg draped over the other as he leaned back in his chair, smoking a massive cigar with an impossibly long cantilever of ash clinging without falling. Charlie and Nathan stood, milling around.

"You're keeping me from my chief duty in life for no good reason," Pa said, his voice growing in intensity. "I'm looking at you, Charlie, and you, Nathan," he said, dead in the eyes. Charlie's lip turned up on hearing his boyhood name, and he mouthed the word *Charles* to himself as Pa went on, "God help you both if anything happens while I'm detained."

"Cool down, Daryl," Mr. Elton said, then looked at Charlie with an expression warning him to back off.

"It's true, all right," the taller suit said with a slight lisp—leaving off his *R*s—his voice breathy. I didn't recognize him. "We got a problem out there."

"So now he speaks," Pa said. "And your mute partner here? Does the dreary Queen Victoria talk too?"

The other suit, a short, heavy-set man, wore a smashed white wide-brimmed hat that looked like a mourning cap. He stood, his mouth downturned, and tilted his head looking at Pa as if deciphering his insult. "There's reports of more confrontations," he said in a surprisingly high-pitched voice. "More assaults, especially in this territory. Families like yours are the most vulnerable, so close to the trail. Governor sent us to spread the warning."

Pa stared down Charlie, his eyes like knives. "*YOU!*" he said in a voice that sent chills up my spine. Charlie looked away and walked off, fumbling with some papers on the desk in the corner, his face turning white.

Deputy Nathan, a new hire in the area less than a year, had been quiet thus far and waited to see if Charlie would say anything in response. He rested his hand on the handle of his pistol, watching Charlie cower over the papers, trying to look busy. Seeing Charlie had nothing more to say, he turned to Pa. "There will be a reckoning for what you did to that traveler on the road," he said.

I didn't know Deputy Nathan that well, and my interactions with him were forgettable at worst, mildly cordial at best, but as he finished speaking, he puffed up like a five-foot-tall meatless rooster, his skinny ribs almost visible through his shirt. Rumor had it, Nathan's long game was to be mayor, then governor of Kansas one day. One step at a time, I suppose. They say perception is everything. I give it to him. He was trying.

"Drifter, you mean," Pa shot back, glaring at him. Just then, I heard a wagon pull up.

"*Chuck!*" I recognized the sheriff's scraggy voice. "*CHUCKY!*" Then I heard a knocking and, "Dammit Doc, give me a second." Perhaps feeling cramped, Buck moved around, jangling the branches to which he was tied, then banged his heavy body into the side of the building with a thump.

"Shh, boy, keep it down," I whispered, wrapping myself the best I could against the cold, knowing for certain those inside heard the noise. *How am I going to get out of here?* I wondered, looking around just as the front door to the station flung open, hitting the wall.

"Back up, Doc. I got it," Hank yelled.

Figuring everyone would focus on the sheriff, I took a good peek inside the station. Mr. Elton and the two suits walked toward the door. As they passed out of sight, Pa's eyes caught mine. His face was stern, and he shook his head as if telling me to beat it.

"Here," Charlie said, running to the front door, his boots clanking over the wood floor.

"You back off, Chuck," the sheriff said. "Give me some space. And tell Doc Joe here I don't need his help. He won't listen to me. Did you get him? Did you get that son of a bitch, Daryl?" Unable to see him, I listened as the sheriff walked over the wood planks, his crutches pounding with each step.

"I got him, Sheriff," Charlie said, oddly proud of an accomplishment that wasn't his. "He's inside."

"Good, good. Very good," the sheriff said, walking into sight, his acolytes following. "You the boys from Topeka?" he asked the two suits.

"That's right," the skinny one said, extending his arm. "Pleased to meet you."

Hank brushed past him, shoving his arm out of the way. "We don't need you," he said, stopping directly in front of Pa and staring at him. "We got things under control here."

"We're here in an administrative role only," the suit said, straightening his jacket. "Governor's orders. I assure you, we want nothing but to make sure word's out about these miserable foreigners. They're dangerous. People need to take precautions against these cockroaches."

Hank huffed and brushed his hand through the air at the man, waving him away. "You're under arrest, you bastard," he said to Pa. "*I'm* the law, *not* you, you coward son of a bitch."

Doc Joe—an unusually ugly man with long whiskers and protruding facial features like an exaggerated sea creature—waddled in, negotiating his porcine belly from side to side to keep from losing his balance and toppling over. The trench coat he wore no matter the weather brushed the floor as he approached the sheriff. "Hank," he said, waving his hands, each finger a kielbasa exclamation mark, "you need to rest. Rest and food—plenty of food."

"That's enough," the sheriff said. "I'm done with you, Doc. Get out of here."

But the doctor insisted, moving closer, then dragging a chair for the sheriff to sit on. "Here, sit," he said. "Let's find you a snack. Charles, do you have anything that the sheriff can eat? Perhaps if you've got extras..."

"For shit's sake, get out of here before I arrest you!" the sheriff said.

The doctor's face turned red and he returned the chair to where he'd gathered it, then exited without a word. His wagon rode off into the night. Mr. Elton and the suits all sat back down.

"How's the leg, Hanky?" Pa asked, smiling, then took a deep sniff. He wiggled his nose, and I could tell he wanted to run his finger over his lip so bad but couldn't. His smile disappeared, and he glared at the sheriff. "I find out that was you broke into my barn last night, and you're mine." The words left his mouth with a tone of satisfaction, as if he were envisioning what he'd do to him. Everyone in the room was silent for a moment.

"What's this asshole talking about?" the sheriff finally

asked, nervous, looking at Charlie.

"Apparently, some kind of break-in," Charlie said, thrusting a paper into the sheriff's face. "See here. Got it written up and everything."

"Aren't you the industrious one," Hank said sarcastically. He shoved the paper out of his face. "Get that out of here. What do I care? Look what you did to me," he said, leaning into Pa. "Turning my own gun on me and putting me on the road in that weather. It's illegal, what you done. Illegal. And you'll rot for it!"

Pa nodded at the sheriff's leg. "Sure you didn't get that falling into my barn last night? Must have been some surprise, learning the hard way there wasn't a floor under that second-story window."

"He's lying," the sheriff said, looking at the government suits. There was something more going on here that I couldn't discern.

"Daryl's no liar," Mr. Elton said.

"It's true," Charlie agreed. "He showed me a handful of glass, some with blood on it."

"That doesn't prove anything," the sheriff said. "Why are we wasting our time on this anyway? I'm booking you for murder, Daryl. You'll hang."

"First I'll rot, then I'll hang? Which is it, Hanky?" Pa asked. He studied the sheriff. "If you're saying you didn't break into my barn, then that's *two* drifters menacing my family and property. This is no place for me if they are under threat. It's time to end this charade—this little boy brigade of manliness—and let me go."

"You'll go when I say," the sheriff said.

"Had over a dozen complaints this week alone," the fatter suit said from his chair. He rolled the end of his mustache between his finger and thumb. "Started innocent, but as the reports got more frequent, the encounters got more aggressive."

"Doesn't give you the right to kill one of them," the sheriff said to Pa. "*Our* job is to enforce, and yours is to obey."

"Fuck you too, Hanky," Pa said. "And who says it ain't my job? This is America, land of the free. And that means free to defend ourselves, goddammit! Since when do you give a shit about some child-molesting drifter?"

"Man's got a point," the skinny suit said, shifting in his chair.

"Times are changing, Daryl," Hank said. "Like it or not."

"Release me, so I can go home," Pa said. I could tell his patience was gone.

Hank ignored him, walking to the desk and sitting down, propping his broken leg on the tabletop. Reclining, he laced his fingers behind his head and winked at Pa. "Get comfortable," he replied. "I own you now."

The skinny suit stood up and asked his fatter associate a question, too quiet for me to hear. "It's clear Daryl's got cause to be home and protect his family in this environment," the skinny man said to the sheriff. "Phillip," he nodded at his overweight partner, "confirmed squaw scalps fetch five dollars apiece. Give the man his money and send him home."

"He'll be lucky to get dinner, let alone a red cent from

me," Hank replied. "That was a white man he carved up out there."

"You've seen the body," Phillip said. "Other than those clothes, which he could have picked up anywhere, there's no way you know that for certain."

Pa admired the Natives, though he certainly would have killed one of them as much as anyone else that laid hands on Bethany. Treating them with disdain for no reason, however, was something he didn't tolerate. "That's enough," Pa said. "That man was no Indian. He was white as you, Hanky—common features with you, now that I think about it. Grimy vagrant, smelling of shit."

Hank exhaled deeply, relaxing. "That the best you got?" he asked. "Wipe them boogers all you want, Daryl. I got the last laugh. We're experienced professionals—civic warriors. You'll learn to respect the law, and I'm the one to teach you."

Pa laughed. "Warriors?" he asked, looking at the sheriff and his deputies. "Ironic your defining experience was being locked up in a POW camp—voluntarily, I might add. Hardly qualified for more than surrendering to the enemy. No wonder you want to take it easy with these drifters."

"I didn't surrender," the sheriff said, lowering his leg and sitting forward on his chair. His face reddened, and his voice cracked. I could tell Pa shook him up. Then Pa took another long sniff, deeper and longer than the first, and asked in a gentle voice if the sheriff needed something to wipe his nose. "Goddammit," the sheriff burst out, standing. "I've had enough of you!"

By this time, my bones were cold, and I couldn't get rid

83

of the shiver. I looked at Buck, contented now and chewing on a stick, and debated heading home.

"How're we gonna resolve this, fellas?" Mr. Elton asked.

"Daryl waits for his trial in that lockup there," Hank said, pointing to the jail cell. "The rest of us go our way for the night." Nobody in the room moved but looked at the sheriff as if he had more to say. "That's it," Hank said, yelling. "Go home!"

The group stood, and everyone but Mr. Elton made for the door. "Don't worry, Daryl," he said. "We'll resolve this quickly. I'll stop by your place on my way home to let Cecelia know where you are."

"I appreciate that," Pa said. "Go on, then. No sense staying here any longer than necessary."

"You ready, Papa?" Charlie asked Mr. Elton.

Everyone but the sheriff exited and mounted their horses, then sped off without catching sight of me. I hoped to talk to Pa, but the sheriff sat back down in his chair and reclined, making himself comfortable. He pulled a bottle of whiskey from under the desk and uncorked it, pulling swigs, watching Pa in silence. Pa shook his head and looked at the ceiling.

"Throw me in the damned cell, then," Pa demanded.

"Not yet," the sheriff said. "Those cuffs probably a bit uncomfortable, I'd guess." Pa just looked at him, then looked away.

After a few more minutes, I could tell nothing was going to change, and was freezing besides. It would be a cold ride home and colder the longer I waited. I unwrapped Buck's rein from the bush and walked to the front of the station, stepping out of the shadow and into the moonlight. Everyone had left, and only Clyde remained tied to the front hitching post. I loosed him, climbed onto Buck, and we rode home, trotting into the cold night. Soon we left town for the open prairie, and I brought the horses to gallop to get home faster.

From far away, the howl of owls rang over the sound of Buck and Clyde's hoofs, crisp on ice-bitten dirt. As we rounded the hillside beside our property, Charlie sprinted past me on his horse, nearly colliding with us, heading back to town. I couldn't tell if he even saw us as he passed. A moment later, the night sounds were replaced by Ma's screaming. My body tensed, and I froze for a moment, doubting whether that was Ma or not. *Just move!* I told myself. Kicking Buck's side, we shot away, Clyde's rein slipping out of my hand. Clyde was a fast horse, but Buck dusted him.

Outside, Ma ran around frenzied in the moonlight, desperate and disoriented, searching for something. "Ma," I said, jumping off Buck and holding her shoulders. "What's wrong?"

She shook me off, glaring, then seemed to look right through me as if I wasn't there. "Where's Bethy?" she asked. Her voice loud and accusatory.

Mr. Elton rode up on his horse, breathing hard, his face concerned. "Your sister," he said to me. "She's gone missing. I did a quick search, but nothing. Charles went to fetch your pa."

I mounted Buck and kicked his ribs. We navigated all

the spots me and Bethany played, but came up empty. Ma stood at the oak tree in the middle of our property, bewildered and crying. A moment later, Charlie rode up with Pa sitting behind him, the horse driven hard and exhausted.

"Cess, what is it?" Pa asked, hopping off the horse and running to her.

"Bethy ... she's gone. I can't find her." She sobbed between words, then doubled over, catching her breath, crossing her arms, and holding her stomach.

"What are you talking about?" Pa asked. "Stand up, Cess. Tell me, what do you know?" I watched him, waiting for his switch to kick in, hoping to see him transform into a single-minded war machine. He had a calm urgency, but perhaps without an established foe, he wasn't the pinpoint of purpose I'd seen in the past. "Give me something, Cess. Did you hear anything? Anything outside before you noticed she was gone?"

Ma straightened her back, forcing herself upright in her nightgown. Her face was washed in tears, her skin ghostly in the freezing blue moonlight. She took a deep breath, paused, and screamed "*BETHANY!*" into the night, sending a volt of vultures out of an Eastern red cedar, high on the westernmost edge of our property. The gigantic birds flapped their heavy wings overhead, the air under their feathers hollow thuds against the black vault, circling us.

"I don't know, Daryl," Ma said. "I don't know." She buried her face in the bend of her arm, sobbing. "I woke up and she wasn't there," she said, raising her head and staring at me. "Where did you take her? Did you do something? Are you trying to get back at me?"

"*Did* you do something, James?" Pa asked.

"No!" I answered. "Is that a serious question?!"

I could tell Pa was losing his cool and growing frantic. "Let's not get ahead of ourselves," Mr. Elton said, his voice reassuring. "Most of the time when kids go missing, they're found nearby, safe. Takes a couple days, sometimes, so let's maintain ourselves."

Pa nodded at his friend, knowingly, and collected himself. "Cess," Pa said, "you go back in the house and lock it up. Double-check she's not hiding somewhere, and make sure all the windows are shut and latched. William, you and Charles scout the trail. Maybe she's there—that's where she was attacked." They rode off on their horses. "James, you come with me."

We ran to the barn, going inside through the east door, where Pa lit a lantern and retrieved two revolvers from a locked trunk beside the staircase. He handed me one, along with a box of ammunition. "You scout around the property as far as the moonlight allows. You're not to enter the shadows under any circumstance. That's where I'll be looking. Ride everywhere. Ride in widening circles around the barn looking for any kind of signs, and if you see something, you holler with all your lungs." As he spoke, he slipped an eight-inch knife into a sheath that was in the trunk too, then ran his belt through the sheath and tightened it against his body. "If I call for you, then you put that horse in motion and get to me as fast as you can. Look at me, son," he said, eye to eye with me and holding my shoulders. "Don't stop and think. Go find your sister. *GO!*"

Back outside, he sprinted to Clyde, who was standing by the closed paddock gate. They rode off into the shadows of the pecan grove. I watched, losing sight of him in the darkness, my eyes continuing up the hill where Mr. Elton and Charlie rode along the trail. It made sense that if something was foul, it would be where the drifters haunted—lingering on the trail, or in that damned grove. I climbed onto Buck, and we were off. We darted around the property, surveying every inch of it out to the fence line and back to the pecan grove, him leaning into his turns, his leg muscles hulking and grooved, pushing earth out of his way while I yelled for my missing sister. With nowhere else to go, I rode up the side of the hill to the trail.

Far off, I spotted a few campfires flickering like stars in the sky—migrants on their journey. The faint howls of owls returned. Mr. Elton and Charlie both rode up on their horses while I scanned for Pa, figuring he rode out for one of those camps.

"You think he's out there?" I asked Mr. Elton. "At one of those camps?"

"There's a good possibility of that," he answered.

"Sheriff expects him back tonight," Charlie said. "Put him in my custody."

"You're not serious," Mr. Elton said.

"Afraid so. If Daryl returns empty-handed, we'll organize a search party. We'll find her."

"Son," Mr. Elton said to me, "you put up your horse and go inside for the night. Nothing more we can do until daylight."

Reluctantly, I barned Buck and headed for the house. "Where is she?" Ma asked when I walked in. She was frenzied, her robe seeming to levitate off her body, her hair untamed, her eyes demanding. Every lantern in our home was lit, as was the stove and the fireplace. "I'm heating some water to give her a warm bath. What's taking so long? Does your pa have her outside?"

I didn't answer. I didn't know what to say.

"I asked you a question, James. Don't you give me that attitude from earlier, or I swear to God I'll tear you limb from limb. Where's *BETHANY?*" she screamed in my face, tears bursting forth.

My body trembling, I forced an answer. "Pa's looking for her. I looked around the barn and the house, everywhere he told me to, but she's not there. He's looking for her. He'll find her, Ma. Don't worry. She's coming home. He'll find her."

"Where were you? Why weren't you here before?"

With so many little nips, bit by bit she picked at the irrational, built-in affection a boy has for his mother. I felt sorry for her, but my affection had become shabby over time, like the frayed wool of a sweater that no longer warmed. "I went to find Pa at the sheriff's station," I said. "Something I told you we should have all done before."

"This isn't my fault, boy," she said, flicking her tongue. Her eyes were wild like a woman possessed. "Most likely, your sister went off looking for you. You're the cause of this—once again. *What's your game, child?*" She paused, staring at me, her eyes growing black. "Anything happens to that girl, and you're the one to pay. God help me, you better pray your pa brings her back unharmed."

My mind returned to the nymphs I'd seen before encountering that creep on the trail. All of God's creation were peace personified, like steam condensed on glass—otherworldliness you could literally touch with your finger. The memory of that purple sky fixed itself in my mind, and it's all I could see standing there now. I looked around at the stove, at Ma's nightgown, at the dining table, the tapestries, the glowing balls of lamplight. Not at the brightness, but the shine that floated out of those lamps and painted everything in the room. It was a shine that let me see under the surface of all those objects, finding not just beauty, but a *oneness* and a properness that was impossible to violate.

"What's wrong with you?" Ma asked.

Her eyes were squinted, puzzle-solving, and her voice brought me back to the moment like waking from a dream to the memory that Pa was looking for Bethany and that Ma's disdain for me didn't matter in the least. It was flecks of ash, the remnants of whatever destruction occurred within her soul, flittering out her mouth on the wind of her hostility. My chest warmed the way it did when Bethany and I played earlier that day, laughing. My sense of something greater gave me the courage to consider the worst. Whether alive or not, I knew on a deep level—though still not believing it—that Bethany would be okay. That she *was* okay and everything was the way it was supposed to be. I had a role to play here, but had no idea what it was. I did know, however, that time would reveal all of our fates.

"Nothing's wrong," I answered.

Outside, I heard a horse walking toward the house, and we ran out. I expected to see Bethany nuzzled in Pa's arms. But it was just Pa. Ma and I watched as he snapped the reins, staring straight ahead and riding in silence. Clyde glanced up at us with understanding eyes, then back at the ground before him. A short way behind was Charlie on his horse.

"Heading back to the sheriff's station," Pa said as he passed by, emotionless. He seemed broken.

"You're not," Ma said.

"It's too dark. Nothing more we can do at this point. I'll be back at daybreak." He turned Clyde toward the road to town and trotted off, Charlie nodding at us as he passed.

The following morning, Mr. Elton rode up with Guts and Bingo, each on their own horse. I couldn't believe my eyes—it really was Bingo. Guts looked at me, his perma-smile donning a grave seriousness I hadn't expected. Must have been his eyes I heard, speaking in silent tongues, his gaze deliberate and stern. We gathered around our veranda, along with other townsfolk, as Charlie escorted Pa back from the sheriff station. Ma, offering hot coffee to everyone, shook her head toward Pa as he approached on Clyde, indicating Bethany was still missing.

"There's a chance she's hiding somewhere," Mr. Elton said to everyone. He sat like a magisterial man-of-the-people atop his horse, in his tattered charro hat and regal green mantle cape flowing over his imperial frame. "Our best case.

However, it's incumbent we pursue every possibility, which means scouring this land for any clues. The bulk of you," he said, "comb these hills and every crack of earth. Daryl and I will ride west of here along the trail, doing likewise."

"I ain't one for kicking rocks," Bingo said, his horse flinchy, hoofs popping like corn in a hot skillet. He wore a long black trench coat and hat with a black lasso tied beside his black saddle. The deep voice he put on made me chuckle when he spoke. "As discussed," he continued, addressing William and then the rest of us, "Tommy and I are riding out, east. Won't return until she's found. Mark my word on that."

"Grateful," Pa said to him. He wore last night's sleepless angst in crumpled clothes and unkempt hair. "William and I—and Charlie, I guess—will ride west of here, further than I went last night." I could see he was exhausted, again absent for words as he looked at this community who admired him. His swollen eyes glistened, and he appeared lost in thought. I wondered what ran through his mind as I watched him acting so unlike the tenacious self I'd only ever seen. It was a moment of uncertainty for us all, watching my invincible hero transformed into flesh and blood.

Each group of horsemen circled their animals, yanking the bridles, and dashing up the hill to the trail, departing out of sight in a puff of dust. The rest of us watched, then sauntered up the hill, a hushed murmur rising from the townsfolk as they walked, speaking in low voices that there but for the grace of God might have gone their own children, victims of violence by brutal foreigners. In coats and scarves, they formed human chains, hand in hand, and walked the hillsides, through the brush, through the unmelted snow drifts, through icy creeks, and through flat and barren land, refusing to accept that a little girl could disappear without a trace.

At first, I joined the others, one body in a line of dozens kicking through the frozen grass, flipping stones with my feet as if she had shrunk to the size of a mouse or lay buried in the stone dirt with only a patch of skin showing through. The back of a hand, or maybe a big toe, but there was nothing, no sign of her at all, no hint of a sign, and no indication of a hint. She was just gone.

The apathetic expression Ma had worn till now was like humidity in the air, an invisible, pervasive texture that one generally got used to with time. Even Pa lived in the dank more and more as Bethany and I got older. But Bethany was something else to Ma, exempt mostly. Ma stood at the edge of the trail on top of the hill in nightgown and overcoat while I searched down below with the other townsfolk. I caught her eyes a few times staring at me, her expression interested in our effort, and part of me took heart that our relationship could be repaired. But after some time, I grew unsettled by her presence. I stopped my hunt beside a dry sage bush on an angle of loose dirt and stared up into her full flaxen eyes, taking off my hat. Her nightgown flapped in the breeze, her unbrushed hair like fire in the eastern sunlight.

I could see her expression changing shape one fragment at a time, entranced as if stuck in a memory from long ago, or captivated by a revelation rising into the light of awareness, assembling itself as it slowly floated up. I watched her eyes droop, then squinch, then protrude, look away, and finally become wide and loathful, undeviating as they tunneled into mine. My hair stood on end for the first time in my life, and curiously, I filled with a vague sense of doom. Without words, she told me plainly what she thought. If there was any doubt before, she now blamed me entirely for all of this.

The gentle wind was icy as it tousled my hair, the shrubs whistling softly, the muted murmur of searchers in the distance. Ma stood unmoving in the cold breeze, each moment another burst of enmity. Eventually, she walked away. Leaving the dispersed chain of townsfolk, I walked up the side of the hill and down through the pecan grove toward the barn. It was ridiculous to think Bethany might be hiding from us in there, tucked cleverly behind a loose board or under a pile of straw, places that had been checked a dozen times already, but I'd check a place a million times if there was the possibility I was wrong.

Ma stood on the veranda outside the house, watching me as I passed. I pushed my hat down on my head and darted my eyes elsewhere. A ways from our barn was a massive evergreen magnolia tree growing at our property edge. The leaves shimmered and jostled in the breeze, but my entrenched anxiety grew stronger. Deep inside me was something demanding attention, like a memory shrouded in heavy fog, remembering its existence for the first time ever. *Was it a memory*? It felt like it, but the feeling was vague and far away.

When I was younger I wanted to be a botanist. Trees were my favorite. I sat under the oak tree within a wedge of roots and read books on dendrology like they were fantasy tales. Then at night in my dreams, the trees became ancient, undiscovered men stuck in porch chairs made of clay, their joints creaky and painful. Old men who sat around and reminisced on a yore so distant nobody could understand it. But their faded memories were real, despite the yellowing. I walked on, gazing at the magnolia. A wonder of nature. I saw nothing and could only sense its movement, but what I felt inside *was* a memory, sending tiny bubbles to the periphery of my awareness.

Sweat beaded on my head and I felt my heart race. A sense of inevitable, unstoppable panic swelled in my body. That magnolia tree was the most beautiful thing we had on our property. In springtime, its white dinner-plate blossoms flourished, and Bethany and I would break off as many as we could reach and scatter them around the barn, even using webs from banana spiders to stick them onto Fred's back. Those were fun memories, and I suppose it shouldn't be a wonder Fred became such a prima donna. He loved the smell of those flowers and marched around with his head held high, ignoring me and Bethany for as long as that dreamcoat didn't fall off. I would not look back at Ma no matter how bad I wanted to, but I focused on Bethany instead, and those flowers, and all our memories. My heart yearned for Ma's forgiveness despite the callous that built over my chest. *What did I do, Ma?* I thought. *What did I do?*

Below the tree branches was where Pa buried our brother Benjamin. He died as a miscarriage, younger than me but older than Bethany. I rarely went to his grave anymore, marked with a cross made of wood. Something about it was unsettling and I suddenly felt guilty, like I'd disregarded him. Like I was a bad brother, and in some illogical, backward way, the consequence for my neglecting his gravesite was his passing. Tears filled my eyes as I considered my negligence of Bethany, leaving her alone with Ma in spite of her attack and the break-in. I slowly came to believe that I did something to cause her disappearance too.

Pa and I assumed Bethany was kidnapped, carried off somewhere down the Santa Fe Trail since it made no sense she would run off in the freezing night, though Ma was mistrustful of me. I longed she could hear my thoughts as I passed her on the veranda, screaming in my head that I didn't do anything to Bethany, and why couldn't she be a regular ma who just loved her son, and that's it? I heard her spit in the dirt, and couldn't resist looking at her any longer. She leaned on the porch rail, turning her head to follow me, her eyes filled with a rage that crushed my heart.

The musty barn was perfectly silent when I pushed open the east door, dusty shadows casting sidelong over the dirt floor and rough-hewn wood. I walked in, glancing upstairs at the loft, then at the cartons of tools, rope, and wire under the counter along the wall. The dust stuck inside my nose as I breathed. "You here, Bethany?" I asked, as if a glittering beam of sunlight might point me toward her hiding spot. Fred and Buck neighed at me as I rounded onto the aisle—a hint? I entered the stalls and kicked up the straw, hoping she'd be crouched there, her hand muffling her laughter. "Dammit, Bethany ... show yourself!" I demanded against all common sense, knowing she wasn't there but pretending otherwise and seeing myself as a lousy actor at the Wanderlust Drama Stage. Even Ma's performances were better than mine in that barn. "We're not playing around! Ma and Pa are worried, and you got the whole town out here looking for you. Think what you're doing to our folks, after what happened to Benjamin."

I waited for her to tell me Benjamin's death was my fault as I walked back to the staircase. It dawned on me there was one place I hadn't looked yet, gazing up the stairs into the pitch-black granary. But Pa would have looked there, I thought, disgusted at myself for letting fear override certainty about Bethany's safety. "Come down here," I said, yelling into the darkness. She knew how much I hated that space. "Don't make me come up there." But of course she would, if she were there.

At the top of the stairs, I stepped into the shadows, trembling, gathering my bearings by feeling the walls and railing, splinters poking my clammy palms. My shoes ran into piles of straw, which I kicked about, grateful even if I were to kick Bethany just to find her there. But she wasn't. I sat down in the middle of that black, the center-place of my nightmares, feeling energized for entering what I never thought possible. A thin ray of sunlight pierced a crack in the barn siding, illuminating a small spot on my crossed leg. The dark I entered wasn't just physical, but imaginary too, since I had populated the physical with apparitions of my fears, those two overlapping, blending, and becoming indistinguishable. My fear was a conjuring, discovering no murderous migrants and no molesting creeps in the rafters of our barn, invented all along only by myself. The point of light that cut through the darkness moved, shining on my eye. I squinted to keep from blinding. *If fear was a conjuring,* I pondered, *what else was?*

The first time I saw Pa cry, he addressed me and Bethany, stopping us while we gathered eggs from the chicken coop. He'd just gotten word that his ma passed away back in Dover. "This is a hard lesson about valuing life," he said. Grandma was a godly woman, if not religious. She was also a hopeless alcoholic, destitute with grief since the passing of my grandpa. Pa later confessed a guilt for not trying harder to get her sober. "Do everything you can," he said, wiping his face dry, "to protect and cherish life." A philosophy he applied to every righteous living creature he encountered, man and animal alike, regardless of race.

Was there redemption? Realizing the answer was at hand, my body tingled. Bethany's disappearance was no wound that would heal over time but was a *hard lesson.* I overcame the darkness I feared in the granary, a darkness I realized was *me* all along. And I knew by overcoming myself in the granary, I could overcome the darkness on the trail, too. Redemption for my sins—known and unknown—might not yet be available, but it certainly could be. Like an unseen door, suddenly revealed and opened, there seemed the promise of *possibility*, where before there was only black. My calling was clear, and I ran out of the barn to the ridge at the top of the pecan grove, straining to see Pa's return.

FIVE

After hours of waiting in the cold, my hands pushed to the bottom of my coat pockets, Pa, Mr. Elton, and Charlie finally came into view. From a distance, their horses looked tense and exhausted. They trotted slowly from the west along the ridge of hills, the men's shoulders hunched, their arms dangling at their sides. I took off my hat and waved it at the group, hoping they found Bethany. The sun behind their backs concealed their faces. They continued riding, stoic, but I could tell something lay in Pa's lap. *Was it her?* Whatever it was, it wasn't moving. My mind raced. *God, don't let that be her. Where was Spooks?* I wondered, looking around, surprised I hadn't thought of that before. We never looked for him! Pa drew close and brought Clyde to a stop by my side, and I realized it was his own wounded arm in his lap, slinged in a jacket. He carefully climbed off his horse.

"You all right, Pa?" I asked.

"It's nothing—just took a spill, that's all."

Mr. Elton and Charlie stopped their horses beside Pa, all of them dusty and exhausted. The skin around Clyde's red eyes was puffy, and he breathed deeply through his mouth. All three horses turned their heads to look at the stream that ran through the pecan grove while a few townsfolk, including Miss Peggy, our widowed neighbor, and her four young boys, ran over for any news. Ma walked up the hill from the house dressed impeccably in a billowy coral-colored skirt, white blouse, and white knit sweater—her first clothing change in a while. She approached, solemn.

Pa's face looked smooth, like the fissures of age had disappeared, and a serenity—or a defeat—took over. He looked at Ma, who was standing quietly to the side. "Nothing," he said. "We found nothing out there. I cannot do this again, Cess. Not after Benjamin."

Ma stood quietly, her arms crossed. She peered far off toward the setting sun, shaking her head slightly, seeming to be deep in thought.

"You're all right," Mr. Elton said to him. He and Charlie climbed off their horses, and Mr. Elton asked Charlie to take all three horses to the water. More townsfolk hurried over for news, a crowd gathering.

"Did you see anything?" Mr. Samuel Burton, Buddy's father, asked. "Any signs whatsoever?" He was rounder than he was tall and distinctively Greek in appearance. Among other quirky adornments, he wore a strapless chintz dress which he mysteriously attributed to a Scottish ancestry.

"Let's keep looking," Mr. Elton said to everyone. "She's

not at any of the encampments west of here out to fifteen miles. It's unlikely she'd go quietly in the night if she was taken, so our best prospect is to find her near the house, perhaps injured or unconscious. Let's recover this child of God and make our community whole again. We're counting on you and are grateful for your help."

"Before you all go," Pa said to the group, "I want you to know how much your work means to me." I could see Pa was moved, and I connected to the emotion he must have been feeling. He was an abiding man like I was determined to be, but such a tragedy has a way of turning hardwood into pulp. "I'm grateful," he said, fighting to keep tears from spilling down his face.

"Could have been any of our young'uns," said Phyllis Roush, a neighbor raising five children on her own, all with fair skin, jet black hair, and high cheekbones. Story had it, her husband was an Ottoman immigrant who worked the coal mines in southeast Kansas most of the year, which explained why so few folks had met him. But Pa told me in confidence her husband was a Native, and until the attitudes of enough Kansans had changed, it wasn't safe for them to live together. She knew Pa's respect for Indians and his support for her and her family. "You've always been there for us, Daryl. We're here for you. You got a fight, you've got me on your side."

"That's a fact," agreed Wes Furrough, a prosperous, no-nonsense farmer who moved here from Atlanta before the War and whose wife and children kept a storefront in town to sell his produce. "Our children are the best of us. Give up on that, and might as well give up on everything. I know I'm speaking for most of the town when I say you need us for anything, we'll be there no matter what."

"Well," Pa said. He was at a loss and could only watch as the crowd dispersed, returning to their hunting grounds along the hillside. He turned to Mr. Elton. "Thank you, William," he said. "How about we grab a bolt of whiskey and ride east next."

"You're in no shape, Daryl. And besides, my boys ventured that way earlier." Seeing my pa overwhelmed with emotion, he squeezed his shoulder. They exchanged glances, nodding sharply, their lips stiff. "Can you walk down this hill?" Mr. Elton asked. "Or should we get you back on that horse?"

"No," Pa answered. "I'll walk. The bouncing of that horse has caused enough pain." He slowly unwrapped the jacket, a garment he didn't ride out with but must have found on the trail. Unpeeling it from the top of his forearm, a shard of bone poked through the skin, which was both stained and bruised purple. "Look at that, dammit."

"Hey, Samuel," Mr. Elton yelled. Mr. Burton turned and saw him waving, and as graceful as a deer, he sprinted over, tugging his sweaty dress away from his skin. "Doc Joe out here?"

"Ain't seen him," Mr. Burton answered. He glanced at Pa's arm. "I'll round him up."

"Appreciate that, Samuel," Mr. Elton said. "We'll be at the house." He nodded his head in the direction of our home. "Let's go, Daryl. Let's get that bolt."

Suggesting a moment alone with her husband, Ma

looked at Mr. Elton. "All right then," William said. He joined Charlie at the stream for a moment before they walked the horses down the hill toward our house.

"What is it, Cess?" Pa asked.

She looked at me as if I wasn't welcome either, but I wasn't going anywhere. "Where is she, Daryl? Tell me the truth," she said. "Is she dead?"

"There is no way of knowing that. Don't get ahead of yourself," he answered.

"Well, where is she, then? You were supposed to be the best back in the war. Why aren't you bringing that now and finding her? Instead, you go and get all busted up. What good are you now?"

"I won't be lectured, Cess. I'm doing my best. We're doing what we can."

"It's not good enough, Daryl." She grew angry as she spoke.

"You think I don't know that? Just stop, please. You're not helping."

"I'm not helping?" she asked loudly, causing some folks to stop and look at us. "For God's sake, Daryl, neither are you! Do we need to recruit the sheriff for this?"

"You're kidding, right?" he asked, amused but irritated.

"At least he's young and energetic," she said, looking Pa up and down. "Virile, and strong."

He took a deep breath. "He's none of those, Cess. When will you let go of your idea that the frontier sheriff is always the hero? Get your damned head out of all those books. Hanky is a loser. A dinky broke-dick coward who threw his hands up at first sight of the Confederates, then shit himself."

Pa's comment drew Ma's outrage. "You watch your mouth, Daryl. He's our sheriff. Where's your respect for superiors?" Some folks gathered up again, looking our direction.

"Superior," he said, shaking his head. "We're done talking. Give me a hand, son." He raised his good arm to wrap over my shoulder. "You walk beside me, close."

We stepped carefully downhill, avoiding mud and the patches of ice that endured through the sun. "Don't you dare walk away from me, Daryl," Ma said, but neither of us acknowledged her.

Grunting quietly, the protracted lines of an arduous life returned to his face. "Are you tired, Pa?" He looked at me with sagging blue eyes, closed his lips, and nodded softly. He was a strong man, but his age showed through. It was clear he was in no shape to get back on the trail, his legs wobbling as we stepped over rocks and tree roots down the hill. Huffing past us to the house, Ma held her skirt off the ground, flipping it smartly with each step.

"I'll be fine after the doc sets this break, son, and William and I will be back on the trail. Don't you worry about your sister. We'll find her, and God as my witness, she'll be safe and sound."

Ma stood at the porch rail as we approached, scowling, staring directly at me. "If you didn't run out, she wouldn't have gone looking for you." Her voice was sharp, carrying over the landscape, and I assumed audible to everyone out there. Mr. Elton's wife, Maria, stepped outside the front door and put her hand on Ma's shoulder.

"Take it easy, Cess," Pa said. "There's no need to start a fight. Not now. This wasn't the boy's fault, so don't go making it such." He walked onto the veranda, the boards squeaking with each step, and sat in a rocking chair, exhaling. Maria disappeared into the house, then reemerged with a tray and four glasses of lemonade.

"You men thirsty?" Maria asked.

"Don't you know it," Mr. Elton said, already sitting on the porch. Charlie had remounted his horse and seemed insecure, like he sensed he wasn't welcome. I could only imagine how dumb his task of chaperoning Pa must have felt.

"You are a doll," Pa told her. "You are a lucky man, William, my friend."

As she passed, Ma grabbed one of the glasses and threw it on the wood floor, shattering it at my feet. "It was *his* fault the last time," she said, staring at me and nodding her head in the direction of Benjamin's gravesite. I wasn't alone in my thinking. "Do you know what he's been doing while you've been out looking for Bethany?" she went on. "He's been in the barn, playing with the horses. Don't give me that shit that he had nothing to do with this."

I suppose her words should have hurt more than they did, but they didn't. I'd grown accustomed to the distance between us, and to be honest it was refreshing to hear why she'd pushed me away all this time. Maybe she'd seen the way I avoided Benjamin's grave and came to the same conclusion I did. Of course it didn't make sense, but what did? Was *sense* the best people could do, anyway, struggling for more than survival, and maybe even a taste of happiness once in a while?

Pa and Mr. Elton took their glasses of lemonade and drank, ignoring Ma, their bodies sinking down into their chairs as Maria handed the last glass to her son, Charlie. Mr. Elton motioned for his wife to bring out a bottle of whiskey.

Reluctantly, Pa broke his stare into the distance and looked at Ma. "I will not argue with you, Cess," he said, wiping sweat from his brow onto his shirtsleeve. "But I will tell you that is no way to treat your child. I understand your frustration, but you will not make my son a monster. He is *my* boy and forsaking him is forsaking me. Collect yourself, woman."

I watched as Ma stood there, brewing at his upbraiding. She crossed her arms, shifted her weight to one leg, and made a short *hmmph* sound as if she'd just proved a point. When Maria returned with another glass of lemonade and the whiskey bottle, Ma grabbed the liquor from her and took a pull, choking it down. It ran over her chin before she took another and then handed it back to Maria. She passed me the lemonade and offered the whiskey, looking at Pa for consent. He nodded, and she topped off my glass with just a splash of the good stuff, then topped off the other glasses.

We all rested a moment in silence drinking our spike, the breeze cold, and patches of still-frozen dew on the brown blanket of winter grass, iridescent in the golden sun. Perhaps it was the liquor, but Ma took sympathy on Pa's broken arm, approaching him with a gentle manner. She unwrapped the jacket, inspected his injury, and then fetched water and cloths from inside, causing Pa's scornful eyes to soften. He loved her, and no amount of disagreement would shake that.

"How about I go look for her?" I asked, breaking the trance we all seemed to be under.

"How about you stay here and not disappear on us," Pa answered. His eyes told me he had no tolerance for the topic, and the idea was out of the question. "You will not raise that suggestion again, and if you get anxious to do something, you finish the repairs on our fence, or spend more time with Tommy getting familiar with a rifle. If Bethany was abducted, it was by a drifter. All the more need for bolstered defenses around here. In fact," he said, eyes squinting, "I am making that your duty."

Doc Joe and Mr. Burton pulled up in a wagon. The doctor stepped out carefully on his short legs which were otherwise concealed by his long trench coat, then hurried to Pa's side like a levitating walrus.

"What do you think?" Pa asked him.

"Could be worse," the doctor answered, eyeballing the glass of lemonade. He poked softly on the skin surrounding the puncture, then noticed the bottle of whiskey on the table between Pa and Mr. Elton. "I suggest you take your fill of that now, and we'll commence with setting this bone right."

Twenty minutes later, after Pa was sufficiently drunk, Doc Joe had Mr. Elton and Charlie hold his shoulders, while in a single motion, he pulled on Pa's hand and squeezed his forearm together. Ma watched, leaning on the doorway, while Maria occupied herself inside the house. The bone slipped under the skin and back into position while Pa merely looked on. Seeing there was no bleeding, the doctor opted against stitches but cleaned Pa's arm and wrapped it in a bandage. "We'll splint this, but I'm not going to cast it for a few days, week at most," he said. "Need that to heal shut, no infection, beforehand."

"We'll be on the trail later," Pa said.

The doctor studied him a moment. "You won't, sir. Not if you want to keep that arm."

"Goddamn an arm if I can recover my daughter."

"I quite understand, Daryl," the doctor said. "You venture out, allowing that cut to get infected, and I can promise you that infection will spread to the broken bone, and that arm will be amputated within the month."

"Arrange to take the arm now, then," Pa said. He grew unruly on hearing anyone tell him he wouldn't do that on which he set his mind, something I'd seen in him before. "And you get that look out of your eye," he said to me, fully angry at that point. "It belongs to a father to protect the lives of his family."

"It doesn't, Pa," I replied. "You told us yourself, life was to be protected, imposing no conditions. Does it belong to a father? Or does it belong to every person?"

"Don't you backtalk your father," Ma said to me with vitriol, still in the doorway. I didn't look at her but kept my eyes on Pa during an awkward silence.

"Taking your arm now will only move the risk of infection closer to your heart," Doc Joe said. "Put you in greater danger of death." His words were innocent, but his tone stern and castigating, and though he appeared a lunkhead at the sheriff's station, he demonstrated a respectable temper for anyone telling him his profession. "Would you prefer I arrange to take your heart?"

Rebuked, Pa turned away, peering furiously into the distance. "Where the hell are those Topeka boys?" he asked, shaking his head. "They can take this back to the governor. Let him know we need help finding Bethany."

Mr. Elton took a drink of his spiked lemonade. "No telling," he said, unbuckling the frog closure on his cape and settling lower into his chair. He removed his hat, showing the wrinkled bald spot on top of his head—an island surrounded by shiny, blond waves. "Charles mentioned them moving through town, not staying. That right, son?"

Charlie nodded agreement from his horse.

"Why don't you get off that damned horse already," Mr. Elton said.

"It's my job, Papa," Charlie replied in a firm voice, then looking away again.

"Just the same," Pa said, scowling. "Figured they would be all over this." Along the trail at the top of the hill, we watched another neighbor, a Russian immigrant named Boris, chase one of Miss Peggy's small sons. The two of them were playing and laughing, reminding me of how Bethany and I would kill time on long boring days. "I respect you," Pa went on addressing Mr. Elton, "and your boy for what you are doing to help us. He's a good boy, you've got. I give him hell, but he's young. And Maria, God bless her."

Charlie turned his head slowly to look at Pa, hearing his

words, and his hardened face softened. He climbed off his horse and joined us on the veranda where we stayed a while longer, none of us moving but locked in our thoughts, staring out into nothing as the sun dropped onto the horizon. Noises from inside the house suggested Ma and Maria were making supper, while the chirping of noisy blue jays reminded me that no matter what, time marched on. The otherwise calming thought filled me with fear, knowing if Bethany was kidnapped, she'd be moving farther and farther away from us at every moment.

"Hey," Miss Peggy yelled at us from the top of the ridge, her voice crisp as it carried through the winter air down the hillside. She waved her arm back and forth, something in her hand. "Hey, y'all! We found something!"

"You want to see!" Boris called down to us in his thick accent.

We all looked up the hill, Pa and William standing out of their chairs, frozen with surprise. *A sign! Whatever she found—maybe it's a sign,* I thought. Anything...

"You stay here," Mr. Elton said to Pa.

He, Charlie, and I ran up the hill, immediately joined by Ma and Maria. Miss Peggy's oldest boy stood with Boris while her younger three ducked in and out of her long, poofy skirt, clambering through her legs the way Spooks used to do with Bethany. A small group of neighbors gathered around.

"Stop that, boys," Miss Peggy said, swatting her hand to shoo them. She handed a torn swath of clothing to Ma. "You said she was wearing a red toile nightgown."

Ma took it in her hands just as Pa walked up behind her.

"What is that?" he asked. Out of breath, the doctor approached as well, his face red and gleaming with large globules of sweat, his overheated body seeming ready to collapse.

"It's from her nightgown," Ma answered. She appeared deep in thought and handed the fabric to Pa. "Look at the seam stitch. I do that on all my clothes. It's gotta be hers."

"Where did you find this?" William asked.

"Buddy found it over there in the brush by the stream." She pointed at a dense section of bush on the backside of the hill, a small brier beside a rock not far from where the creep who attacked Bethany had camped.

"I didn't think much of it, nope, I didn't," Buddy rattled off. From the back of the crowd, he shot me a dirty look, then moved his way forward, accompanied by his father, Samuel. "I like numbers," he went on, staring at his pincers. "Noticed the stitch, it's a nice stitch, two by two by two. You got a nice rolled edge there. I square lumber nicely too, plus I like hot cocoa."

"Oooh! That does sound delicious," Doc Joe agreed, licking his lips while he caught his breath. "With a dash of peppermint extract and those little marshmallows..." he said slowly, savoring every word, eyes closed and tapping the fingertips of each hand together in front of him. The lunkhead had returned.

"They're so cute, aren't they?" Samuel, Buddy's father, asked the doctor. A giant sweat spot stuck his dress to his hairy, lower stomach just over his crotch. The chintz in that region was now unforgettably see-through, showing a mat of rough and tangled pubes. I looked away while everyone else stared at him and the doc, jaws open, befuddled they were having that conversation.

"You did good, Buddy," Mr. Elton said finally, rolling his eyes at the doctor.

"Very good," Pa agreed. "You should be proud of your boy there, Samuel."

"Very proud," Ma said, then looked at me with icy eyes. "I might even have some marshmallows for you." Doc Joe and Buddy appeared to jump in place like schoolboys, subduing their smiles.

"Not you," I whispered hard at Buddy, giving him a piece of what he gave me at the lumber mill.

"Why would that patch of fabric be down there, though?" Charlie asked. "What's it mean?"

For God's sake, I thought, *you're the deputy! Shouldn't you know the answer to that question?*

"I hate to say it," Pa said, "but I think that's some of the best evidence we've got that she was abducted and didn't run off on her own."

"She hated the trail," I added. "No way she'd come up here or over the hill on her own, especially at night."

"Come morning, we'll ride out again." Pa addressed William. "You go east. Take your son, as where that fabric was found suggests she might have been eastbound. I know your other boys went that way, but they're not experienced like you. I'll go west, knowing most traffic along this route heads that direction." He stopped talking and looked at Doc Joe. "Don't give me any shit about it, you hear?" He raised his broken arm. "If this gives me any trouble, I should be able to find help."

We wrapped up, and Mr. Elton called all the other townsfolk to gather around, whistling with two fingers, louder than any steam trumpet on the Kansas Pacific. The crimson sun filled the sky with blood as it set. "Get on up here," he said. "We're calling it a day." Ma helped Pa back to the house, Charlie following some steps back, while Mr. Elton explained the findings of the day and their plan for the next days. "We need anyone who is able to continue searching the property until Daryl and I return from our expedition. It won't be long, I promise."

The plan was forming in my head faster than I could keep up. I would venture out in the early morning hours, taking Pa's place westbound on the trail. His instinct was to go west, and that's where I'd go. The search would begin after fifteen miles, as far as Pa and Mr. Elton went today, so I'd have to go forty miles at least to have any chance of catching up. It would be tough on any horse, and while I adored Clyde and Fred, I thanked God for Buck. He could probably do it. I'd take Ma's stash of money and bring Pa's bedroll and some dried meat and bread.

Despite the tragedy, I was excited at the idea of returning to Pa with the prize of his daughter in hand—his sweetheart—and hear him tell me how grateful he was to be my father. How he could never have earned the right to be my pa, but that it was only by grace. I knew he loved me, but he never said it. I wanted him to say it.

I left Mr. Elton and came down the hill. Hearing me

walk over the squeaky veranda, Pa called from inside the house. "Hey, son?"

"I'm here, Pa," I answered, stepping over Buster as I walked in. The kerosene lamps were lit, and he sat in Ma's rocker, resting, her food crumbs haloing his feet on the ground while she warmed corn cakes at the stove. Outside I could hear Mr. Elton say goodbye to Charlie, who was sitting on the porch.

"Get a fire started, then fetch the supplies I'll need for a short road trip. Put them here," he said, pointing beside the fireplace, "so I can see everything."

"Yes, sir," I answered. What luck! I didn't have to hide my efforts to prepare my ride! "You want me to get a horse ready too?"

"Go ahead and do that," Pa said. He's gonna pick Clyde, that's his favorite horse. "Fix Clyde up. Feed him extra tonight, so he's got time to digest. And son … I know this is a difficult time, but we'll get through it. If the worst should come to pass, we've gotten through it before. I suppose we could figure out how to again."

"I know, Pa." On impulse, I looked at his arm. He must have seen me looking since he took his other hand and carefully rubbed over the top of the bandages.

"Where is that son of a bitch!" Hank yelled from outside. I heard a buggy slide to a stop in front of our house.

Pa stood up and walked to the door while I stepped outside. Charlie was on his feet, his arms fumbling as if he was supposed to be doing something other, tripping over his words to explain everything was under control. Hank looked at him from his personal buggy, fit with purple canvas and a gold crown embroidered on the back.

"I don't give a goddamn!" he told Charlie. "You had one job. It's been hours, now it's time for him to return."

"What's this about?" Pa asked.

"You've had your time to search for her. I'm taking you back to jail," he said.

"Like hell you are," Pa said.

Ma came to his side, resting her hands on his good arm, watching. "Just go," she said to Pa quietly. "We don't need any more drama today."

"Son, fetch my revolver," Pa said, staring at the sheriff. "This dispute between us ends tonight."

Charlie eyeballed the sheriff, then addressed Pa, saying, "Don't be hasty. You're not searching tonight anyway. First light, I'll have you out."

"You won't, Chuck," the sheriff barked at him, still sitting in his buggy. "Not my fault you didn't find her. You owe a debt to justice, and I'm here to make sure you pay."

"James," Pa said, "I gave you an order. Move."

"Stop, Daryl," Ma said, her voice pleading now. "You said yourself she's probably eastbound, and William's boys are searching that route already. Plus, your arm. Think, Daryl. Don't be rash."

I could tell the sheriff wanted to say something, but he stopped himself. "Just get in," he told Pa. "Chucky, you follow on horseback if this bastard tries anything."

"Go, Daryl," Ma begged. "No more drama, please."

Pa looked at her, then at me, his defiant expression

dropping. I could tell he was thinking hard, maybe calculating every angle in this situation, his only concern getting Bethany back safe. "You let me ride tomorrow," he said to the sheriff. "Charles in tow to keep watch, and I'll come with you peaceful tonight."

"You'll come with me regardless," Hank said, then spat in the dirt.

Pa looked at Ma one more time. He bent over to kiss her forehead, but she moved away. "Go," she whispered softly.

"Mr. Elton is an exceptional scout," Pa said to me. "He'll find her. You stay here with your mother and keep her safe." He grabbed his coat and got into the sheriff's buggy, the two of them riding off into the twilight with Charlie following behind.

Ma and I dined quietly that night, the lamplight shadows zigzagging over the interior of our home. Surprisingly, she wasn't hateful toward me, but unfeeling instead, as if my presence made no difference in the universe. After dinner and without a word, Ma got up, went to her room, and blew out the lantern. She fell asleep while I was still at the dining table, light from the fireplace flickering through the front room.

I gathered what Pa would have for his expedition, bundled it in a pile on the table, left a lantern burning and the front door open, and then went to the barn. As I walked, I gazed overhead into the starlit night, listening for Bethany, only hearing night sounds. "Where are you?" I asked quietly, desperate.

Lighting the lamp by the east door, I carried it inside. A

donut of light surrounded me, throwing hard, radial shadows off everything it touched, and a sharp apathetic blackness outside its range. The horses were quiet, and there were no noises except for my crunching footsteps on the dirt floor. Without my consent, my imagination filled the shadows with villains and hooligans, stealth beings dodging the lamplight in the nick of time as I shined it about. I swung it to where the broken granary glass had lay on the ground, startled by random flashing moths. Then I held the lamp up toward the loft, broad beams of light like long timbers tilting awkwardly about. There, just hours ago, I was so confident, empowered against my weaker self, brave in the same darkness I'd face out on the trail. But now I was terrified again. Riding into the vast wild to find Bethany was not the same as sitting in a barn attic.

Against the silence, I heard a gust of air and a quick series of loud slapping sounds. I swung the lamp around, frantic to see what it was. Someone was in here! My fears were right! I ran into the alley as fast as I could, to be near the horses, and dug in a box on the ground beside the hay bales for a knife. The lamp light bounced violently. I tried steadying the lantern, hoping I didn't cut my hand open as I thrust it to the bottom of the box, digging. My heart raced. *Hurry*, I thought. *Hurry!* Again the sound rang out. Fuck it. Unable to find the knife, I stood up slowly and turned to face the sound, shoving the lantern ahead of me. Clyde lay on his side blowing out a long puff of air, his lips flapping and slapping each other. "You fucking animal!" I yelled, trying to catch my breath.

"What the *hell* are you doing, Fred?" He stood over Clyde, straddled him, his front legs beside Clyde's stomach and his hind legs beside his back. "Get off him, go on!" I walked to the rail and waved my hands, trying to shoo him off, but he didn't budge and just looked at me with a dopey expression. "Buck, do you see this? Do you see this rude display of dominance?" But Buck took no notice of his barn-mates, instead just watching me.

A handful of oats got Fred to move, while Clyde remained idle, exhausted. His bloodshot eyes were heavy, showing only when he pulled them open. It was good he'd rest tomorrow. I don't think he was conditioned for such long rides anymore. I walked into his stall and knelt beside his head, petting his nose. "I'll miss you, boy. But I'll be back soon. Bethany and I will both be back soon."

I yanked a rectangle of hay off the bale and tossed it in Buck's stall. "You're some horse, Buck. Well, we'll see what we run into out there, right? Tell you what—you cover me, and I'll cover you. We'll bring each other home in one piece. Deal?" He gobbled his food while I spoke, glancing at me once in a while. I threw him a handful of alfalfa, then more hay. "You eat up," I said. "We've got an adventure in front of us."

A tiny flame flickered silently from the lamp outside the front door to the house. In the soft moonlight, faint shadows of wavy lantern glass danced on the wooden table where it sat, equally serene. I traced them with my eyes for a moment, then looked up at the bright white moon, and my own shadow cast over the veranda, before going in the house.

That night, I waited in my bed for morning, eager to leave, my mind a whirlwind of thoughts.

At first sign of light, I pushed on my hat and tiptoed downstairs. The house smelled fresh like wild herbs had blown in on a frigid air, knocking the fatigue off my bones, replacing it with excitement. Red embers smoldered in the fireplace, sending dark smoke into the chimney, and in the pristine ambience, I wrote a note on my old school chalkboard, telling Ma I'd gone to find Bethany.

Before leaving, I grabbed my telescoping brass monocular, a gift from two Christmases ago; the pipe of money from the sink; and Pa's rifle and pistol from the wall above the mantle. I loaded ammunition into a pillowcase, then gathered the supplies under my arm and exited the house. On my way, I pocketed the sharpening stone from behind the porch chair. The morning was clear and dusky, brilliant stars still shining overhead, crickets chirping softly as if to say I'm not alone. I looked back at the house, forgetting to close the door, pondering how open doors direct our paths if only we'd walk through them. "I'm coming, Bethany," I whispered. A moment later, Ma walked over, her eyes drooping and strands of hair slipping from her nightcap. I could tell she didn't notice me as she closed the door.

It was cold and tranquil, and the earth was covered in frozen dew that crunched as I walked to the barn. I could hear an occasional owl hoot and some far-off coyotes. "You ready, Buck?" I asked, buckling his saddle and strapping down the supplies. His body was thick with brawn, tensing into granite under my touch. "I know you are." Leading him outside, I hopped on his back, pushed my hat farther down on my head and cinched the chinstrap. Then I took a deep breath, the cold air tickling the bottom of my lungs, issuing a thick white cloud as I exhaled. We walked across the property behind the house, away from the bedroom windows, up the hill, and onto the trail. High above our property, I looked around, seeing no campfires for miles. Buck and I could have been alone in the universe, just us and my goal to rescue Bethany.

"I have faith in you, boy," I said to Buck, petting his neck. I kicked his ribs, and we were off. His massive, rippling muscles were like metal gears under my body. Leaning forward, I gripped the reins tightly as he moved with grace and precision through the icy air, faster than I'd ever ridden before, water pushing from the corners of my drying eyes.

SIX

As we rode, I recalled some years prior when Pa brought me a few miles west along this trail, the old Lt. Simon Bolivar Buckner route from Ft. Leavenworth, Kansas to Santa Fe, New Mexico. It was a primary route west used by countless migrants before the Transcontinental railway opened last year in 1869, and still popular among regular folks without means to afford a train pass. A few stagecoaches used this route, but they were uncommon, mostly traveling the route south of Leavenworth from Kansas City to Wilmington. And of course, folks moving their merchandise of turquoise, obsidian, and Navajo blankets from the west to the east coast——mostly Mexicans and citizens of the southwestern United States.

From what Pa told me, the best a suited horse could ride in one day was forty miles, *maybe*. Forty miles is a long way. If Bethany was taken by a small party of horse riders, it'd be less than forty miles, for sure. But that made little sense to me. What was more likely, I figured, was that she was nabbed by someone with a wagon. Maybe spotted outside looking for me, like Ma said, seen by someone from the trail who wanted her—for God knows what purpose. Tied up and muzzled, then thrown in the back. My mind drifted down dark avenues. *Focus*, I told myself. *Gotta find her*. All right, so if she was in a wagon, they'd only make it ten to fifteen miles at most. The trail was ill-maintained, which was fortunate. Wheels can only knock so much on knotty ground before they're thrown clean off a wagon. If it was pulled by a few strong horses, they might be able to get farther than Pa and the Eltons rode yesterday, assuming the wagon was in top shape, but it would still be difficult.

As I considered all these things, I began to doubt the direction of my pursuit, determining she was probably taken east after all. Pa said they rode fifteen miles, and it would be lucky if a wagon made it that far. Besides, I had no sense of distance if it got more than five or so miles, so how would I know if I'd gone far enough? Pa and Mr. Elton had a solid sense of distance, and based on how far they rode, if she was taken this way, they would have caught up. An impulse rose within me that demanded I turn around and head home, that this was a foolhardy mission best conducted by those with more experience and that I was a damned idiot to think I could do it. *No*, I told myself, stopping that thinking any further. There was too much at stake. Not just for Bethany, but for me too. I turned my attention to details on the trail, tucking them into my memory and using them to piece together helpful ideas.

Some distance outside Ft. Leavenworth, the first rays of sunlight penetrated the dark morning sky behind me. The ridge we'd been riding put us in a shallow valley between a range of wide low-lying hills with a scarcity of trees. Living in a wooded area, it was odd to see so much vacant land lying open with nothing to hide. Diffused sunlight penetrated a faint mist like glowing, wispy cotton unrolled over the earth, and patches of snow glistened like sequins on a lace scarf. All across the rolling prairie land, the blanket of squat brown grass was spotted black with the traces of campfires. The ground was bare, owing not only to the time of year but to the damned prairie dogs that ate the grass which horses would have fed on. I considered pulling Pa's rifle and doing every horse and oxen along this trail a favor should one of those rodents show himself, but there wasn't time for tangents. My goal was singular.

Cresting a short hill, I saw ahead of me an old man leading four oxen west, pulling a large wagon. Galloping beside him, it was clear the wagon load was quite heavy, the wheels creaking with each turn, hammering the ruts in the dirt road. Three young women in ankle-length wool day dresses and pelerines walked alongside the animals, each with a stick in hand, reminding them of their course. They looked at me with no change in their expression, then returned their attention to the trail. The old man, short and olive-skinned, tipped his hat in my direction.

"Bethany," I yelled loudly, studying the reaction of these folks. They looked at me like I was crazy, their eyes squinting and their mouths curling.

"Whatza matta with you?" the man asked. He spoke just like Dominic Ameche, one of the regulars at the Wanderlust Drama Stage back home. "Shoo! Go away!" he said, moving his hands as if he could brush me down the road.

"I'm looking for my sister," I said. "She was kidnapped."

The man pushed up his dirty white sleeves, the cuffs already folded back. He looked at one of the women, then at me. "*Vaffanculo!*"

My patience was thin, and this guy could have been a creep himself for all I knew. "I said she was kidnapped. What, don't you speak *English*?" I rode like this, pestering that poor man for another five minutes before I realized I was wasting time. At the rate these people were going, Pa would have seen them yesterday and already checked them out.

I drove Buck hard to make up ground, and in a few miles, heard the sound of his breathing take on a slight hiss. His mouth was dry. We slowed down and galloped another mile or two under the bright blue sky, dotted with sharply edged clouds. I wondered if the giant was up there, watching me. It wasn't long before we descended a broad hill that led to a narrow creek crossing, shaded by a line of red maple trees, the first gathering of trees I'd seen yet. Their branches reached through the low morning sunlight, and soaring, gangling shadows painted the hillside ascending across the creek.

"Drink quick, Buck," I said. "We got ground to cover."

"You didn't pay for that, boy," a stern voice called out

from behind me. I whipped around and saw a skinny young man, maybe twenty-five, wearing a puffy shirt and pants that stopped at his knees. He snickered into his fist. "Nah, boy. I'm just playing," he said, walking through the water along the shore. I looked around and saw no wagons or anybody else with him, but a blanket and an empty circle of rocks behind where he first appeared. All of a sudden, his body straightened up, his smile disappearing. "But serious question, do you have anything to eat? I'm hungrier than a, I mean, I'm hungrier than a … " I stared at him, curious what he'd say next. "You know what I mean, don'tcha?"

I put my hand on Buck's neck as he drank, slurping with barely a breath. "I don't know what you mean," I said.

"But you didn't answer my question," he said. "Well, technically you did, but I'd hoped you'd favor the obviously more important question of the two. So what'cha got?" he asked, kicking the edge of the water as he stepped onto dry land in split boots laced around the calves with rope to keep them from falling off. "This here water's cold!" he went on, faking a shiver. He snickered again, this time less dramatically. As he got within arm's reach, I could see his eyes were crooked, and he had a long scar along the side of his face.

"How long you been out here?" I asked him.

"Oh, I don't know. Reckon a week or maybe even two? No wait—months, not weeks. Shit, *years*? You lose track when you're so hungry." Rubbing his concave belly, he walked around the backside of Buck, eyeballing what I'd packed. "Travelling light, I see."

"Not going to be out long, couple or three days is all," I said. Looking ahead, the creek was maybe ten feet wide at most and no more than a foot deep. We could be sprinting off in no time if this guy turned funny.

"I get it," the man said. "Need to get out of the house, get away from your Pa. He's probably a hateful fucker, putting you to all sorts of punishments."

"No, he's not like that," I said. I petted Buck again, hoping he'd be finished drinking by now.

The man walked around the front of Buck, then back to me. "I said the same thing when I was like you. Told myself the same lies he told me." He stopped talking and looked me up and down. "Well, maybe," he said, nodding with understanding. "I wasn't packing for a couple days when I made my split. Anyway," he went on, his voice growing somber, "you got any food?"

I hopped off Buck and made an effort to look busy, tending him while he drank, then tightening the saddle strap, adjusting the reins. "If you've been out here a while," I asked, "did you happen to see anyone suspicious pass by?"

He laughed. "Look at me, boy. I *am* suspicious!" He put me at ease, and I didn't know what it was about this weirdo, but I liked him.

"Here," I said, reaching into a saddlebag and pulling out a couple bread rolls, "take these. They're all I've got," I lied, "but we're good until the next town."

He took the food in filthy, stained hands, and the gratitude in his eyes told me more than any words could say. "Suspicious, huh? That the real reason you're out here?" he asked.

As he spoke, two elderly Native women approached down the trail from the west, walking slowly alongside a donkey pulling a wooden cart, whose contents were covered by a blanket. I moved out of their way, yanking Buck to take his drink a few feet downstream, watching these women. Their thick hair was pulled in a braid down the back, imbued with rigid white strands like straw that shot out at random angles. Their faces were kind, with deep cracks in their soft brown skin like ancient, weathered fresco paintings.

"Good morning," I said to them. They both smiled at me, saying nothing. "My sister was kidnapped," I continued, raising my voice and glancing at the man. "Have any of you seen an eight-year-old girl that looked to be held against her will?" I grew sad. "She actually just had her birthday a couple weeks ago. February eleven."

The women said nothing, I assumed not understanding what I'd asked, and the man looked off into the sky as if watching the last few days in his memory. "Suspicious is a good word for a kidnapper," he finally said, finishing the second roll. "You got any more food?"

I watched the women pass by and continue on their way. "No," I said, my gaze arriving at the man. "If you don't want to help, then fine. Let's go, Buck." I climbed on his saddle and gave him a gentle kick. He raised his head and splashed across the creek, then trotted up the trail and out of the spindly shadows.

"That's a beautiful horse," the man called over to me "I don't know. Maybe I've seen someone like that."

He's playing games, I thought, looking back and giving Buck another bump with my boot to get on.

"Yesterday," he hollered. "In the morning. Only got a glimpse, but it was a man driving his horse, pulling a little box wagon." I stopped and listened, turning my ear his direction. "Something like a circus parade wagon, but wasn't any animals painted on the side. Heard a girl calling out from inside but couldn't make out the words."

I hurried back to the man. "What color was it? The wagon?"

"White. It was white, but soiled," he answered, looking at his hands. "I was sleeping, and he was riding so fast over this busted dirt, the sound of everything inside bouncing around woke me up. I hurried to wave them down, see if they had any food to share, but just as fast that wagon was out of sight. A cloud of dust."

He could surely see how important this was to me. "What's your name?" I asked him.

"You can call me Carl," he said.

"Well, Carl, thanks for the information. I gotta go now, catch up with that wagon."

Carl's eyes opened wide. "I'm coming with you," he insisted. "Ain't nobody pay attention to me out here, and you've been a good neighbor. I'm helping get your sister back."

"Sorry, Carl, you'll slow me down. Buck here's strong but carrying two bodies won't work."

A smile crept over Carl's face. He raised his fingers to his mouth and whistled, to which a tall black horse stepped out from behind a line of laurel bushes near Carl's encampment. He walked over slowly, his limbs long and skinny.

"That old boy doesn't look so good," I said.

"He's good. Don't worry about that. Let's go."

I considered asking about the stuff he was leaving behind but didn't. I'd spent enough time here, and if that wagon could keep its pace, I probably wouldn't catch up to it for another full day of hard riding. "I'm just saying, if your horse can't keep up with Buck here, then thank you for your willingness to help, and I wish you the best on wherever life takes you."

Before I finished my sentence, Carl hopped on his horse and sprinted westward, up the slight hill, and out of sight. That horse didn't look it, but he could fly. I snapped the reins and yelled for Buck to make haste. He darted through the dust cloud left in Carl's wake, and I'll be damned if it wasn't a mile or more before Buck fell into stride alongside the other horse. Looks certainly were deceiving.

"I caught up to you," I said, yelling at Carl as our horses ran side by side.

"No," he yelled back. "I slowed down for you." Whipping the reins, his horse again shot out in front of us. I couldn't believe how fast we were going. Finally catching up to him again, Carl winked at me with a sly smile, reminding me his horse had Buck beat, no problem.

We rode over open prairie and long, low, undulating hills. The monotony of vast sky and boundless, flat landscape caused me to recall happy days in our house, nostalgic for their return. Not far off the trail, we passed a party of soldiers dressing their bison kill, each man to his task—cutting out its tongue, stringing strips of meat to dry on the back of their wagon, hammering and splitting open the large bones, and scraping the marrow into a bowl.

We passed families and their horse-drawn prairie schooners, chased by excited pet sheepdogs that had to be swatted away from snipping the horses' feet. We passed parties of ones and twos, some of them appearing destitute and depressed, while others seemed delighted. We passed graves and hand-tied crosses pounded into the dirt, a string necklace hanging from the top branch of one cross, the pendant reflecting the sun, blinding me.

Ahead were some small ponds tucked in the shallow recesses of the prairie, edged by short shrubs of foxtails. The bright sun wasn't hot, and a breeze dried the sweat that beaded on my hairline. My hands ached, squeezing those reins. Both our horses needed a break. I brought Buck to a trot and steered him to the nearest water hole. After wetting his mouth, he ate on the nearby bushes.

"Your horse surprised me," I said to Carl.

"He's the only good thing I got from my pa. A little like me, I suppose. Doesn't look like much, but he'll surprise you."

"That's a fact."

Carl hopped off his horse. "So what's your plan? Besides getting your sister back." He picked a foxtail and popped it in the corner of his mouth.

Bringing her home was my way of proving I was no

coward, making amends with Ma for whatever perceived role I had in Benjamin's death and persuading Pa I was a worthy son, good enough to earn his pride. "Get her back is the first thing," I answered.

"Right," he said. "Then what?"

I hadn't thought of after. "I've got some ideas, I suppose," I said.

"None too good, I trust," Carl said, his sly smile returning.

I knew exactly what he meant. "Downright evil," I said. "Whoever did this might have done it before or do it again if I don't stop them."

"Justice," Carl said, nodding, his eyes lighting up.

"Exactly."

"By God, we'll bring justice, then," he said. Whatever his pa imparted on him in his younger days was a clear influence—a motivation—even still. I grew emboldened by Carl's support, feeling a kinship with him already.

"The way I'm figuring," I said, "this man's coming wrath will be the most difficult trial of his life."

"Sure you can muster that?" Carl asked. "You ain't the biggest fella. How old are you anyway?"

"I'm sixteen and just might have a trick or two myself. Circumstance steers people down all sorts of paths. I find my sister's been abused or hurt in any way, and we'll see what road I end up venturing down. Suppose we won't find out until the moment's upon us."

Our horses relaxed, their shaking legs finally settling. "Your horse got a name?" I asked.

"I call him Carthon. He used to be Wayne, but that name's ridiculous. Changed it when we started our new life together. Carthon's supposed to mean guardian. That's what he's been for me." Carl paused and drank a handful of water. Wiping his mouth, he stood up and looked at me. "I never did get your name," he said. "Suppose it could be Carthon too."

Here was this guy, a stranger, willing to jump right in with me to save my sister. He looked like nothing—a scrub, trash blowing in the wind. In fact, he looked like what I figured most people on this trail looked like—creepers and degenerates. Funny I'd only seen one example of my expectation thus far, everyone else the forgettable family and soldier types, yet he's the one by my side.

"My name's James. How old are you anyway? You look about twenty-five."

Carl laughed into his fist. "That's a good one, James. I'm seventeen. Suppose this life in the wild piles on the years."

Damn, I thought. He was just a year older than me. Could be me standing in those raggedy boots with black-edged teeth if it wasn't for circumstance. "I'm glad I met you, Carl," I said. "I'm real glad. We settle this whole affair, and I want you to come back home with me. My pa is good people. We'll take you in."

Carl thought for a moment, his skin flushing, then turned his head and splashed his face with water.

"Anyone that lives out here on their own must be pretty smart," I said while he brushed his clothes with wet hands.

"Smart?" he asked, his voice cracking. "I ain't smart."

"Well, clever then, I guess. You got a way about you. Something different—in a good way." I studied him a moment. "Can you read?"

"Of course, I can read. What difference does that make?" He looked at me and took Carthon's reins. "We should get going. Got a few more hours of daylight."

"You're right," I said. With that, we mounted and headed off.

The landscape was unchanging. The undulating hills hypnotized me, pinning me square against my thoughts the way heaven and earth pinched me to this trail. So much blue sky and so much brown prairie, and my sense of time just disappeared. We could have been riding for days like that, the sun and earth locked in their orientation, eternity just one long barren afternoon. We passed other families, most keeping to themselves, but no wagon trains a hundred-parties deep that I'd heard organized to keep the savage Osage Indians away. We passed a few camps with a few wagons and a few travelers stirring cast iron pots over fires, resting on blankets, re-shoeing horses, while kids chased each other. Their sounds infused the air, carrying long over the unobstructed terrain—shouts and laughs and commands and barks and hammer-strikes and dinner bells, all deconstructed elements of life itself. How they magically fit together, like floating pollen grains that somehow found each other in an interlocking whole and assembled this diorama, was inexplainable. And what gravity held them in place once each piece found its home in the greater puzzle? God only knew.

Looking up, I thought the sun must have moved by

now, but I found no evidence and concluded that hours were in fact minutes, and minutes in fact seconds. Carl rode with the same determined countenance, focused on the trail, resolute in his attention. Noticing my glance, he nodded and winked, then snapped the reins and buried us in a cloud of dust.

I recalled my fears in the shadows of the barn. How powerful an imagination can be. It creates whole realities based on nothing but conjuring. *Conjuring* ... The word lulled me deeper within. My thoughts—like fragments of a fractured ice sheet—calmly drifted away, revealing an intimate, ghostly abyss underneath. A glimmering, deep-blue jewel. It summoned me to enter as I stood over it, mesmerized, and soon I found myself floating in a dreamlike place beyond my sight. The sun slumbered beneath the blanket of earth in an upside-down world, shining purple on red leaves that grew from azure trees. Though blind, I followed the infinite sky above as it tapered into a tiny cavern that collapsed to a man-sized cave. I imagined myself standing there, looking in, and seeing nothing—objects extinguished by the dark of the transformed sun that in the end made all things invisible. Within the cave was silence and black, but there was life in it, and while I couldn't enter the shadows, I pressed my body against the last ray of midnight violet sun at the threshold of this ecumenical womb, sensing its fetus, realizing logic and expectations made the rules that delimited my potential for knowledge. To my surprise, I realized fear wasn't the only conjuring, and in fact I never had seen the right-side-up world.

"Hey," Carl yelled, expelling me from my reverie. Ahead were circled wagons, maybe a dozen, making camp for the evening. I was shocked to notice that the blinding sun had passed down in front of us and perched below the horizon, its glow fading like a lantern low on oil, the cold air getting colder. Carl brought his horse to a trot, both of them breathing out white smoke.

"Yeah," I answered, slowing Buck to the same pace.

"We should get settled," he said. "It'll be dark soon, and they probably have water."

"Good idea," I said. "Follow me."

I nudged Buck, and we trotted off the trail over low grass and soft soil, pocketed by prairie dog burrows, toward a wagon beside which stood a group of five men. The dark gathered quickly as we approached, and one of them lit a lamp, holding it up to us, their five faces pressing into the light from the shadows.

"Can we help you?" a man asked. He appeared to be a family man, tall and traditionally dressed. Over his shoulder, around a large fire in the center of the wagons, sat women and children.

"Good evening, sir," I said. "My name's James. Me and my friend Carl are looking for water and wondered if you all didn't by chance happen to make camp by a stream or pond. Our horses are thirsty."

"We did, son," the man said. He held the lamp for a closer inspection of me, then Carl. He rubbed his chin, studying us, then withdrew the lamp. "We got room enough for you, but not your friend here."

I looked at Carl, who appeared used to this kind of treatment. "Like I said, he's my friend. He's hit bad times, that's all. Who among you hasn't?"

"You got some tongue," another man said. He was short with a broad face and a wide-brimmed hat.

"We're just looking for water, maybe company to spend the night with. We haven't seen any Osage, but that doesn't mean there ain't. I'm happy to offer my protection of you all in exchange for your accommodation of us."

The short man scoffed. "Protect us?"

"That's enough," the tall man said to him. He held up the lantern, revealing the little man as a dirty creature himself, coated with thin patches of mud from dust and sweat. "Tell you what," the tall man went on. "There's a stream just outside the circle of wagons over there." He pointed across the campfire and past the farthest wagon. "You get your horses refreshed, tie them up with ours, then come find me and we'll sort things out. My name's Hugh."

"Thank you, Hugh," I said.

Carl and I walked our horses around the wide circumference of wagons, twelve in total. The sunlight faded to speckles, the last crescent of corona slipping into the clay, leaving way for the brilliant full moon overhead. Between that and the large, roaring campfire, there seemed plenty of light to get the horses watered and settled for the night. As we rounded the furthest wagon, I heard the stream babbling through the rocks.

"Over here," Carl said, releasing Carthon, who made haste for the drink. About twenty yards downriver were a few Buckeye trees where a handful of horses were tied up. I let go of Buck, and he followed Carthon, drinking by his side. Carl and I both drank as well, and washed our faces and arms.

"You think they'll let me stay?" Carl asked.

"I think so. No reason not to." This was a good omen, I believed. Contrary to the malevolence I assumed would characterize the trail, all I found was hope. "He wants us to tie our horses with theirs. That's not nothing."

"Maybe so they can steal them. You think of that?" Carl asked. I didn't answer, not wanting to ruin my emotion. "Nah," he went on. "I got a good sense. They seem all right."

"We leave early, though, you hear me? If you're with me, I'm leaving early," I said. "I'm not giving that kidnapper any more time than he's got already. I'm not living with him getting away on my conscience."

"Hey, you over there," a female voice yelled out. It was raspy and deep, and I expected to find a large woman on the other end of it. This slender woman with a graceful step glided in our direction, her long hair bouncing from shoulder to shoulder. Her boots kicked up the hem of her dress, revealing her long johns underneath. "What the hell you two doing near our camp? Beat it. Find your own squat." She untied a ribbon from her wrist and pulled it around the back of her hair, binding it into a ponytail. Even in the low light I could see that her arms were strong but gentle, and as she approached, the moonlight revealed the most beautiful girl I'd ever seen. She was unlike the girls from school in Leavenworth. Her features were more angular, her skin a shade darker.

"Hugh told us," I said.

"Hugh told you what?" she demanded.

I stared at her, enraptured by an item of beauty the likes of which I could never anticipate. She was stunning—I almost couldn't believe she was real.

"How long you two been on the trail? You dehydrated or something? Losing your mind?" As if by instinct, Carl turned away and knelt by the water again, scrubbing at his hands. "You deaf? Or dumb?" She paused. "Or *both*?" I didn't know what to say. "All right," she continued, "you quench your thirst, then get the hell out of here. I'll wait for you to leave, and if I see you back, I'll cut a hole in you both with my forty-four caliber." She swung her hip holster around from her back, revealing a Colt Army 1860, and rested her hand on the grip. "No amount of stream water will soothe that void."

"I was going to say," I managed to get out, "that Hugh told us to get our horses refreshed…"

"You've done that," she interrupted, impatient.

"And then tie them up."

"You can do that elsewhere," she insisted.

"And to find him," I said. Carl looked back at me as I finished the last sentence.

"What does he want with you?" she asked.

"I asked if we could stay with you all for the night. I offered my protection in exchange for…"

"In exchange for what, exactly?"

Remembering my purpose on this journey, I too ran out

138

of patience. "Never mind," I said, walking next to Carl and drinking some more. "You don't need to worry about it. My discussion is with him, not you. Be on your way, now."

"Suit yourself," she said, turning and walking away. "I'll have a word with my pa before you're able to convince him of whatever plan you're up to."

"Ain't no plan," I yelled as she got further away. I was furious now and slapped the surface of the water. "Simply trying to find my sister who was kidnapped on this route. Is that so hard to understand, or are *you* dumb?" Without turning to look, I heard her footsteps stop as if she paused to ponder my words. "Don't go judging people before you know their circumstance." The sound of footsteps resumed, eventually fading to quiet.

"Some people," I said to Carl. "Got no fucking compassion. You know, I actually thought that girl was the most beautiful thing I'd ever laid eyes on. Gospel truth when they say it's skin deep."

"She don't know us," Carl said. He yanked a handful of grass and fed Carthon, petting his neck. "You get used to it— getting judged for no good reason. It's all right, friend. We'll find your sister. They can't stop us from laying our heads down right here where we're standing, and we'll be on our way bright and early like you said."

"Why are you doing this?" I asked him, genuinely curious. The thought crossed my mind that he might have ulterior motives. "I mean, you barely know me."

"I can tell you had a good life. Not sure you'd understand," he answered. "It's too late for me and my family. They made their choices, and I made mine to leave. But if I can do anything with my life, I aim to. You got any more food, by the way?" He smiled and paused a moment, then continued while I rummaged through my saddlebag. "We got the same goals, you and me, but different targets. Your purpose is exclusive. You got a bullseye in mind, saving one person, someone you know and love—your sister. Whereas me, I got no bullseye. If I can save anyone from the kind of life I had, then that's my bullseye. I don't need to know them. Wish someone would have did that for me. I'm old now, like you said."

"Not old, but you look older," I said, tossing him an apple. He caught it, giving me a look that told me he remembered the lie I said earlier, and fed it to Carthon.

"Weathered, then," he said. "My point is, however long I got before this weathered vessel finally crumbles, I'm going to do something good with my time."

As Carl finished talking, we both heard footsteps approach from along the bank of the stream. Shade concealed their presence, but on turning to face them, they stepped out into the moonlight. It was Hugh, accompanied by the beautiful girl, who must have been his daughter, who left our company a moment ago.

"Evening, gentlemen," Hugh said. His voice was heavy, and I was pretty sure he'd heard most of what Carl had said. Addressing Carl, he continued, "I'm sorry for the way I treated you earlier. You never know who you'll run into out here."

"I'm sorry too," the girl said, addressing me, her voice

tender and genuine. "I can't imagine what you're going through."

"You've asked us for nothing but company for the night," Hugh said. "No reason we can't accommodate. This fiery lass is my daughter, Katie. Remind me of your names?"

After a formal introduction, we followed Hugh and Katie to the large orange campfire in the center of the wagon circle. The dirt crunched under our feet, and the smell of smoke and grilled meat opened my dusty sinuses, causing my stomach to growl. There were a number of families here as I looked around, each with the standard prairie schooner. Off the back of one, a man constructed a makeshift metal repair shop with spools of wire strung on a rope, an anvil sitting on a two-foot-high log of tree trunk, and an assortment of hammers and boxes of nails laid out on the tailboard. Beside another were three older women—sisters, I guessed. They were wearing gingham dresses—one red, one white, and one blue—each stitching their own cloth with needle and thread in hand. Another wagon had two banjo players, older teenage boys, sitting on the ground and leaning on the wagon wheel, plucking and tuning their instruments. A few women and their children were at the fire preparing their suppers. And along the perimeter, a group of six men illuminated by two oil lamps walked from wagon to wagon checking on everyone, rifles at shoulder arms.

Hugh introduced us to the women around the fire, matrons of the families he'd linked up with on his pilgrimage west, their heads held high in spite of their obvious poverty. Listening to their stories, I was shocked at their honesty and moved for them by sympathy. They were indebted to Hugh for his leadership on the prairie, his always seeing that the families were fed, and the wagons in good repair. The women echoed one another's stories; each family had sold most of their possessions and invested all of their money in this journey and a shot at a better life. Life in the east was worse than starting over, they all said, so they were contented with their choices. They were resolute, God-fearing folks, inspired by a dream and grateful for the future. The future, they all agreed, was where the promise lay.

"Ask us how we're doing in thirty years," a heavy woman said, holding her hefty daughter on one knee. This was a sweet and doting family, I could tell already. "This apple of our eye will have a family of her own, and her kids might profit by the sacrifices we're making now." She kissed her girl on top of her head.

"We do have one man, Theodore, getting over consumption," Hugh said, nodding to a man sitting back from the fire. "Perhaps when we're done here," he said to Katie, "you can take him and these boys along with your brother for a short walk." Katie looked at me and smiled for the first time, swinging her hip holster back to the rear. Turning to face the wagons, Hugh called out, "*Jessie!*"

A young man ran over, his features glowing in the firelight. Brawny, he stood a good six feet tall, unshaven for a week or two, pants tucked into his boots, and wearing a narrow-brimmed, light-brown Stetson hat.

"Jessie, this here is Carl and James. They're staying with us for the night, offering their assistance pulling guard. They won't be with us long, just a few hours before they're back on the trail." Hugh cleared his throat. "James's sister was kidnapped, and they're hunting down the man who took her." I could see Hugh's eyes were glistening as he glanced over at Katie, then at me. "We'd help you find her, James, if we could, but you can see we've got our hands full." He smiled, pushing his shoulders up. "Plus, I trust you two determined young men are more than capable. You'll find her. I know it." He turned back to his son. "Jessie, go get Theodore on his feet. He needs to open those lungs of his. Take him for a walk, and while you're at it, each of you grab a horse. When you're back, we'll have a plate of food ready for you."

On the mention of food, Carl looked at me with a big smile. "Yes sir, Mr. Hugh," Carl said, even before Jessie could respond.

"You got it, Pa," Jessie said, then jogged off to one of the wagons.

"Theodore's come a long way," Hugh said. "Surprised he made it this far, but he got over the worst of it. Not in the clear, but he's getting there."

"He kin of yours?" I asked.

"No," Hugh answered, thoughtful. "Just a fellow soul on a common road. And you," he said to Katie with strict concern in his voice. "You take it easy. Understand?"

I walked over to one of the iron pots on the fire and looked in. "You like stew?" a woman asked, stirring her concoction with a long wooden spoon and smiling up at me with warm, tired eyes. "My husband's favorite, but I still

143

make it. Reminds my son of his pa before he died. Don't worry about us, though. My brother's traveling with us."

"Sorry to hear that," I said.

"I'm happy to share with you boys if you like," she said. "By the sounds of it, you'll need the energy tomorrow. Find me when you're back from your walk, will you?"

"Is there anything I can bring you while we're out?" I asked, moved by this woman but knowing I had nothing to offer.

"You're a sweet boy," she said. "You bring your appetite, okay?"

Theodore, a tall old man with gray stubble along his sharp jawline, sat ten yards back from the fire on the edge of the light. The shadowed ridges of his windpipe showed past his open shirt collar, and his elbows and knees were wider than his skinny limbs. I thought a gust of wind could have blown those matchsticks of his apart, watching him fight intense pain and spasms in his breathing to get on his feet. He was a tough knot of wood.

Carl and I unwrapped our horses' reins from the tree branches while Jessie and Katie grabbed a couple of the bigger ones in their group. We all kept pace with Theodore along the dirt shore of the stream where he wouldn't slip in the dust.

"That's a beautiful horse," I said to Katie. She guided a large tan horse with a dark brown mane and tail.

"Thanks," she said. "His name is Blue. He's got blue eyes. Not the most creative, I know."

"It's okay," I said. "He's gorgeous. Blue is a strong

name. I like it."

She reached up and pet his neck as we walked. "He's my little boy. I'd defend him with my life."

"At least those kind of little boys aren't so irritating," Theodore said. Maybe it was the pain, but his voice carried venom in it. He pushed himself along, his back arched, using a long branch for a walking stick. We crested a short hill under the bright moonlight, surrounded by barren prairie for as far as we could see, then walked down into a shallow valley, the sounds of our camp disappearing in the distance.

"You're getting stronger," Jessie said to Theodore. "We've walked a mile or more, maybe. You got some tenacity."

"You'd be surprised what you can do," Carl said to me, "when you want to."

"That's right," Theodore said. He coughed, squeezing his walking stick, then pursed his lips and forced himself onward.

"Sure you don't want to turn around yet?" Katie asked him.

"I'll let you know, young lady," he answered, short-breathed, with a subtle blend of appreciation and indignation in his voice.

The night sky was brilliant, taking *my* breath away, millions of stars overhead sparkling in all the colors of the rainbow. "What do you make of all this?" I asked Theodore.

"What's that?" he said.

"All this," I said, pointing at the sky. "I figure you've been alive the longest here, have the greatest insight."

145

"You want me to tell you the meaning of life or something?" Any note of courtesy in his voice was gone, apparently not interested in this line of discussion.

No, I thought, *I guess I don't want you to tell me the meaning of life.*

After a few quiet minutes, Theodore answered, "Look. You're no different than any gadget. You got gears that need oiling, and eventually the parts wear out. You're young, so I'll give you the benefit of the doubt that you ain't some imbecile. Though you might prove me wrong … There ain't no meaning of life. You want to ask what's the meaning of *a gadget*? Okay, that's a question. Gadgets do things. In other words, do things with your life. That's it. That's the fucking meaning, genius."

What an asshole. "How about all those stars?" I asked, feeling indignant. "Doesn't that suggest something bigger than us?"

"That's horseshit," he said, then spat in the dirt. "Shouldn't have given you the benefit of the doubt. Okay, Jessie, I'm ready to turn back. Getting tired of this all of a sudden."

Screw you, old bastard, I thought. He could rot for all I cared. We turned around and headed back along the stream.

As we walked, I noticed far off points of light ahead of us, moving back and forth, up and down, against the canvas of starlight, along with small patches of black that blotted out the stars. "What do you think that is?" I asked.

"*Oh,*" Theodore said abruptly, holding up his arthritic hands. "Michael Faraday here has a question. Quiet

146

everyone, mastermind at work."

Jessie looked at me and rolled his eyes. *Good*, I thought, *it's not just me*. High clouds rolled in fast—balls of cotton in front of the bright moon with holes like a loose-knit sweater. The clouds grew thick as more pushed into the sky, closing the gaps and hiding the stars. "I'm betting we walked a solid two miles," Jessie said, grabbing a lantern from his horse's pack and lighting it. "Can you make it back, Theodore?"

"Have this know-it-all keep asking me questions," he said. "That'll keep me moving. You got anything else, sport? Ask away, little boy. You might just see me running."

Fuck you, I thought. Instead of this dusty bastard, I tried to focus on what I'd do when I found the white wagon, going through the steps in my mind. Load and carry both weapons, fill your pockets with rounds. The revolver holds six, the rifle two. Bring Pa's bowie knife from the saddlebag, maybe see if you've got skills to match his. Make a stealthy approach, go on foot, leave Buck tied a safe distance back. Carl will be there to help. He can approach from the other side. Haven't seen him with a gun, so stay in eye contact, signaling if either of us sees anything. Hopefully it's only one drifter. Carl said there was only one rider on that little wagon.

It was dark where Jessie's lamp didn't shine, and we all slowed our pace to keep from tripping. Nobody talked as we walked back, focused, Carl and I steering our horses through the cold stream under the trees, each step splashing, wetting my pant legs. Besides, I don't think anyone wanted to talk— Mr. Chipper ready to brighten our moods at the slightest remark. Gradually, between the splashes, a faint screech of a faraway owl grew louder and louder. Overhead, the clouds finally pinched away the moon's pale light completely, and walking in the amber glow of Jessie's lamp reminded me of the barn and the villains and hooligan hiding just beyond.

"You hear that screeching sound?" Carl asked me.

"I do. It's just an owl." I wasn't sure it was an owl, but I resolved not to be afraid.

"That ain't no owl," he said. "Trust me. I know what an owl sounds like."

"It's nothing, you big baby," Theodore said. "You think it's the *boogy* man? Need mama's warm, wrinkled teat for a mouthful of milk, and tuck you in with a lullaby?"

"Don't talk to me like that, you toothless son of a bitch," Carl said. "I'm surprised you can hear anything, saggy ass poopy pants."

I couldn't help bursting into laughter, drawing Theodore's glare. Jessie and Katie seemed unconcerned with the noise, so we kept walking, the sound eventually fading back into the still night, punctuated by Carthon and Buck's splashing hoofs. The stream curved away as we ascended the final short hill that led down to camp on the other side.

Standing on the ridge overlooking the bivouac, we all stopped, straining to discern what exactly was different. It was so dark, but something ... *something* was different. As my eyes adjusted, the wagons seemed undisturbed, their canvas bonnets flickering in the campfire light, but the campfire—it was ... small. Way smaller than we left it. I looked for the horses tied up by the stream but didn't see any.

The shrieking sound, which I determined to be an owl,

returned and we watched—frozen—as figures, black against the night, rode horseback through the camp, their arms swinging and waving, bringing them down against more figures on the ground. As fast as I could, I bashed at Jessie's lamp, smashing it to the ground. We went pitch black. The distant fire was dim, but I saw shades of gray and made out silhouettes of all the people down there. They were lying disorganized in the center of the circle, their bodies piled on top of the campfire, a dozen bodies like firewood heaved on the dying orange embers.

Katie gasped, and I could hear her dress rustle—raising her arm perhaps. I imagined her eyes wide with panic.

"Let go, floozy!" Theodore yelled, and I could hear him shake his body. "You ain't my type, skinny bitch." I guessed Katie grabbed him, and he didn't like it.

Without a word, Jessie hopped on his horse and charged into the shadowy fray, screaming, riding to one wagon, and managing to pull something from its side under the bonnet. He charged around the wagon and into the ring, taking aim and firing a rifle at two other riders before getting clubbed from behind by another rider and falling to the ground. The one with the club got off his horse and beat down on Jessie with it, ringing out the sounds of bones smashing and tissues bursting. I heard Katie lurch forward, yanking on Blue's rein, her long johns swishing.

"Don't go," I said, stern but quiet.

"Look at that! I have to go!" I heard her sniffles as she cried, and thought she might have been wiping her face.

"They'll kill you," I said. "Wait."

149

"Wait," Carl reiterated in a hallowed voice that would quiet a storming sea. The sound was a gentle hand on our hearts, holding us in place. He was unflappable in his response, unfazed as he watched. "We have to wait. When they leave, there might be some people we can help. But not before they leave."

Theodore must have figured out what was transpiring. I heard him drop to the ground and weep quietly. Our eyes continued to adjust, seeing better, and Carl, Katie, and I stood in silence for maybe thirty minutes, watching as some hidden pilgrims were routed and murdered, then dragged on top of the campfire. Shadowed figures pillaged the wagons, taking only what each could carry on horseback. I thought about the gentle woman at the stewpot. I thought of the doting family and their hope for the future. I thought about Hugh and his kindness in shepherding these separate families. I thought of my purpose on the trail—to save Bethany—and how I was instead watching a slaughter before my eyes that I made no effort to stop. I hated myself for the hypocrite I was. A coward still. A boy. Worthlessly standing beside a woman I'd started to fall for who just lost everything. *Justice*, I thought, contemplating my mother's gushing affection for me and my pa's gushing praise. *My life is my reward.*

After the last shadowy figure appeared to leave, we waited some more, lying on the dirt and looking at the sky. The whole thing was so unbelievable. It was so easy to pretend it didn't happen. The night was freezing, and we all shivered, scratching our way under the loose surface of earth. Above us, the clouds began to thin, islands of gossamer floating in the heavens, moonlight glowing brightest through the narrowest depressions. So much ugliness in the world, yet so much beauty—blue and white arrays of cheetah patches, the shiniest stars traces of sparkling minerals in the animal's fur. I wondered if Theodore saw this, and that he might understand my question now.

I asked him if he wanted to ride to camp on my horse, but he declined, preferring to stay on that short hilltop. "You all go," he said. "Tell me if you find my wife, Lottie. Bury her, please, then come get me."

Carl, Katie, and I mounted our horses and rode down. The fire cracked and popped in loud, startling bursts, burning an unusual fuel. We stayed on horseback to scout the area, the brilliant moon unobstructed at that point. When we were confident there were no attackers, we dismounted and walked from wagon to wagon, finding only dead bodies.

It had been five and a half years since Pa and I unknowingly rode out to the aftermath of the battle of Westport where hundreds of Rebellion soldiers lay dead on the ground. Clyde and Fred clopped along slowly, pulling our wagon of handmade furniture for the Kansas City market through the fallow battleground, the faces of fallen and contorted men staring at us, their expressions frozen in terror and fury. Most were killed by rifle fire, but a number were slashed open, their insides spread over the brown grass and dirt. Those images haunted my dreams, the men speaking to me from their sprawled positions until they had no more to say about the fragile nature of life and faded from my nights. Like me, Katie and Carl were old enough to have experienced the horror of that war, a perverse and revolting preparation for what we encountered as we walked among the wagon circle.

"This is Theodore's rig," Katie said.

Carl and I walked to the wagon, and the three of us stood over the body of an elderly woman with no visible injuries, her face serene and lovely. Maybe she died from a heart attack. She had a lamp, which I lit and placed on the ground near her.

"Have either of you found anyone alive?" I asked.

They both said no, Katie looking at another wagon across the circle, which I guessed was her family's. Carl walked to the next wagon where the makeshift metal repair shop was set up and returned with a long-handled shovel.

"I'll bury Lottie," he said. "I'll bury her right here where she lays. Shouldn't take me long. If you want, you can get Theodore."

I looked at Katie, who was still fixed on the other wagon. "Katie, I'll get him. You do what you need to." We watched her cross the ring past the fire and stop beside a wagon, holding her hands on the side of the bonnet, her head fallen to her chest. "I'll be back," I said to Carl.

At the top of the hill, I found Theodore, his expression transfigured and all that malice he harbored gone. He actually looked happy, lying on his back, eyes open to the stars, ready to apologize for his narrow-mindedness. Well, not that last thing. "Theodore," I said, hopping off Buck and standing over him. "You ready to go?" He didn't move, and it was then I realized his eyes weren't blinking.

We spent the remainder of the night, sometimes by ourselves and sometimes with each other, contemplating what we experienced. Much of that time, Katie mourned her parents and sister. Their lifeless bodies lay huddled next to one another, perhaps as Hugh endeavored to protect them. Her low words were indiscernible from where I worked, though I heard her sob, and occasionally hyperventilate. She combed her family's hair out of their faces, caressing their hands in hers, and removed her parents jewelry, putting it in her dress pocket. After some time, she stood up and spoke above the cracks in her voice, forcing the words out. "I took you all for granted," she said. "And I can't get you back. I should be with you there. God, I was so selfish for not rushing to help you. For not doing *something*." She paused, weeping, and took a deep breath. "I'm sorry. Ma, Pa, I'm so sorry I didn't do more. Please forgive me. I vow, in whatever capacity I've got, to atone for my fault and resist wickedness with a passion the likes this world has never seen. God willing, I'll cross those who did this to you, and I'll rip their souls from their trifling bodies."

I imagined my own response if that were my family, and gritting my teeth, had to walk away to keep from hearing Katie any longer. My heart broke, but I wanted to stay strong and do what I could for these folks. I wouldn't break down in front of Katie or Carl.

Carl continued to bury the dead, including Theodore, who I brought down from the hill. Katie joined us, and I cried while dragging the scorched bodies of these strong women and their children off the campfire, sorry for the loss of so much tenderness and divinity. Not all of the dead were burned, though, and we planned to bury those ones last. After helping me, Katie returned to her family's wagon, where she held successively, her father, her mother, her baby sister.

The morning sun opened on the eastern horizon like a yellow daisy over the gore—beams of light radiating like petals through a hazy sky, the charred skin snagged in weeds, the pudding innards spilled on rocks. I looked around at the camp, piles of earth where bodies had been buried, and piles of bodies where the earth had yet to open, knowing I had to leave to effect my own purpose on the trail. I gathered Buck, who was tied to a tree by the stream, then joined Carl and Katie.

"It's that time," I said, drying my eyes. Carl wiped the sweat from his brow with the back of his arm.

"What's that?" Katie asked, lines of sweat and tears cutting down her gaunt face through dirt and dried blood.

"It's time I head out. I've got to save my sister."

"Give me a second," Carl said. "Let me rinse off. I'm coming with you." Leaving an open hole in the earth, he jogged to the stream, dunking his arms and head underwater.

"What about all this?" Katie said.

"You're welcome to come with us," I said, "but I've got to leave now."

She turned again toward her family, tears trickling down her cheeks. I imagined holding her as she grieved, lowering her head into my shoulder, caressing her body. I imagined her hair smelling like flowers, her skin silky under my warm hands, and touching her round lips with mine, feeling her breath on my face. "I just don't know why ... why does the world have such evil?" she whispered, her voice sending a chill through my body. "We need to bury them."

"I'm sorry, Katie," I said, looking at her sister, unable to stop seeing Bethany's lifeless face on her dead body. I prayed Bethany wasn't lying somewhere likewise, my resolve to bring justice on her kidnapper hardening even further. "Some people deserve it, but not them. Not your family or any of these folks."

Katie looked at me, standing in silence, our eyes wide and understanding. I had fallen in love with this girl who I barely knew, and her expression told me that she cared for me and didn't want me to leave. I didn't want to leave either. The urge to take her in my arms was strong, and I believed she felt it too.

"I've got my sister," I said. "She's still alive—God willing."

As I spoke, Carl returned with Carthon. "We ready?" he asked.

I turned back to Katie, waiting for her decision.

"I'll bury them in that hole Carl dug," she said. "Shouldn't be long. I'll catch up to you on the trail."

"No telling how far the kidnapper might have gone with her," I said.

"I'll keep on, and I'll keep a lookout for you. Your horses are unmistakable," she said. "Trail ends in Santa Fe, right?"

"Hope it doesn't get that far," I answered.

Carl gave her a hug and climbed onto Carthon. "Thank

you, Carl," she said, reaching up to hold his hand. "You're a good man."

"You going to be all right?" I asked her.

She simply swung her hip holster back to her side, smiling through sorrowful eyes. I stood there a moment in nervous silence. Carl must have sensed I wanted to speak privately with her. He flicked his reins, and Carthon trotted out to the trail.

"I'm a fool, Katie," I said, taking her hands in mine. "Life is short, and I don't give a shit so I'll just say it. I love you, and I want you to come with us." I looked at the bodies of her family on the ground behind her. "But I understand why you can't. Promise me you'll get on the trail and look for us."

"I will," she said, tears running down her cheeks. She squeezed my hands.

God, she was so beautiful. If only I could erase the pain. Do something to make her feel better. Her anguish was mine, as if we were a single being. "I'll be looking for you," I said, "same as your looking for us, and we'll meet up soon. I want you in my life. The three of us will bring my sister home, and we'll stay together in Leavenworth. You'll see, it'll be good after all. It can't *not* be good, with us together."

She wiped her tears with her sleeve and leaned forward, resting her face alongside mine, wrapping her arms around me. I could feel her hands on my back as she squeezed and her eyelashes on my cheek as she blinked. A tear from her eye wet my skin. Her warm breath tickled my ear, then she kissed me on the cheek. After a moment, she pulled back, staring into my eyes, face to face. I glanced at her lips. "I'll be all right," she said. "I'll see you soon."

SEVEN

Carl and I rode into a cold front that tightened my skin and sharpened my senses. We said nothing along the way. The butchery was so unnecessary, and those images would live in my memory forever. The gamey smell of fresh death clung to me like when Pa and I killed a pronghorn late last spring and he had me dress it by myself. Blood covered me to my shoulders and stained my arms a shade of earth red, leaving a stench that lingered into my dreams while we slept that night under a willow tree. I woke, retching, my body unadapted to the raw waters of the garnet river that flow on the boundary of life, encircling it, creating an isle that shelters every knowing creature from the vast insentience beyond. What lay out there in the borderland was terrifying, believing that when the waters emptied from my own moat, I'd be forced into that nether region, forever roaming a damnable land of empty shapes, meaningless patterns, and darkness. I mourned the loss of those good souls, but more than that, I pitied them.

My skin crawled as we advanced down the trail, and I wanted to scrub clean, to scour away the residue of what we experienced. I felt alone and yearned for Katie to join us soon, missing her presence more with every gallop. Life was so bleak, so fragile, so easily taken. Would it have been better if those families had never existed?

Spellbound, the undulating prairie returned my psyche to that deeper place I had ventured into the day before, gliding blind under an unseen and unmarked ocean—a liquid underworld: the precise and phenomenal at its shores demolishing overhead. As we rode, we passed the same pilgrims and migrants as yesterday—not literally the same, but folks in the same wagons, cooking the same food, wearing the same clothes, using the same oxen, performing the same tasks along their same journeys. They were all so similar, as if by plan. I looked at the ordinary world, no longer seeing it but seeing this plan, this underwater current pushing everything along, knowing the creatures may all be disparate, but the water was not. I was a creature, too, I reflected, and my autonomy—my belief in individuality—an illusion. With the tide at our backs, all of this, all of reality known and unknown, was united and singular, indivisible, precise, purposeful, and perfect. In truth, there was no borderland. Having held my breath, I inhaled the water, feeling a oneness with the prairie and its inhabitants, a oneness with Carl and Katie, and all those murdered folks, knowing we were each integral to the whole of reality. It wouldn't have been better if they never existed—that was impossible. They couldn't *not* have existed.

"Hey!" Carl yelled over. "Hey, James, can you hear me?"

I looked at him, disoriented, forgetting for a moment where I was and what I was doing. He rode his horse near mine and pulled on my reins, bringing both horses to a trot.

"You need to wake up!" he said. "You're falling asleep. You're going to get yourself killed like that."

"What?" I asked him, unsure what he was talking about.

"Man, you're closing your eyes."

Our horses slowed, then stopped. I rubbed my eyes and looked around, then back at the trail behind us which snaked into the horizon like a molten crevasse through stubbled and brown-crusted wilds. The dust of our foray swirled over the dry grasslands in a turbulent breeze, lining my nostrils, causing me to cough and realize how hungry I was.

"That was a long night," Carl said. "I'm exhausted too."

"We can't stop," I insisted, pulling Buck's rein out of his hand. I hopped off my horse and dug through the saddlebags, fingering bread crumbs along the bottom, my stomach turning and growing nauseous. "Just for a minute to get something to eat."

"You got more food?" he asked.

"Nope," I said, kicking a stone. This part of the trail was desolate, where the vegetation grew low, and there was no sign of water or other people. "How long have we been riding?"

"Couple hours, I guess," he answered.

Winter days were short, and the sun was already high in the southern sky.

"You ever been this far?" I asked.

"On this trail?"

"Yeah," I answered, too tired to make fun of him for his stupid question. He looked at me with inquisitive eyes.

"Maybe we should get some sleep," he said. "We need to be ready to do whatever we have to when we finally reach your sister."

I imagined every minute of her captivity as an increase in her maltreatment. This was my second day on the trail and her third. Every delay that pushed her further than a day's ride from my presence not only increased the odds I'd never find her but stole her freedom in exchange for the luxury of whatever excuse prevented me from riding.

"Ain't got the luxury of sleep," I told Carl.

"Ain't luxury if we roll up on her kidnapper and watch him get away still."

"I'll figure it out," I insisted. "If you want to nap, you're more than welcome to, and I'll bid you farewell."

"Don't be a boor," he said. "You want to ride, we ride." He walked Carthon in a circle, pulling on the reins and causing him to rear up. "And don't you ever question my loyalty. That's questioning my character. Nobody questions my character." He stopped Carthon and lined him up along the trail. "Now if you're man enough, we got probably twenty or thirty miles before reaching the Kansas river. Stay sharp, won't want to snooze on this journey."

He made one final circle on his horse, then kicked

Carthon's ribs and snapped the reins, "*Ha-yah!*"

I was buried in a cloud of dust, wholly blinded and stumbling to walk Buck out of the veil to where I could see something. Tripping on the edge of the trail, I caught my footing before falling on my ass, twisting my ankle. My hand wrenched down on the bridle rein as I fell, which I could have sworn was a branding iron, burning a red mark across my palm. Buck was a strong horse, strongest I'd ever known, but the force of my weight put a strain on his neck. He whined in pain, turning his head this way and that.

"I'm sorry, boy," I said, watching the billowing dirt behind Carl's tracks gradually fade. As far as I could see were stretches of rolling, desolate prairie. The unobstructed sun cut through the cool, breezy air and heated my skin, beads of sweat gathering under my collar and hairline. For the first time, the stark dormancy of the wide-open space affronted my sense of calm. Buck looked at me, his neck tender. Riding fast like Carl wouldn't be easy on him, so I led him by foot for a mile or so, shaking off my own injured ankle, hoping his discomfort would mellow.

As we walked, I made a mental inventory of all the gear I packed: a fire-starter, a couple pairs of underwear, canteen of water, monocular, the guns and pillowcase of ammo, a hook and fishing line, a blanket, and a heavy coat. I also carried two knives—my whittling knife scabbarded on my belt and Pa's wartime bowie knife, sharp as a razor, wrapped in a flannel cloak at the bottom of the saddlebag. It was a piece of art, like the workmanship it brought into the world. In the hands of my father, a master craftsman by all accounts, it was precisely the right tool. The ten-inch blade curved at the end like smiling lips, and the five-inch wood handle, indented ever so lightly by the iron grip of an unyielding slayer, was soft and stained deep in the lifeblood of its victims.

Pa's reputation was legendary. I would sneak into his room when he wasn't home and go through the square chest of memories on his side of the bed, supporting that broad cold steel blade in one hand, squeezing that silken wood handle in the other, imagining the sticky juice would rise to the surface. I gazed in the steel, seeing the reflection of my eyes, imagining his deft hand glued to this weapon in the thick of bloodshed, each new donor endowing a part of themselves to the slaughter of their own compatriots.

Buck and I approached a strip of cottonwood trees stretching to the south and down a shallow valley created between a hopscotch of low brown hills that extended for miles, each hill rolling into the next like waves over a knotty shore. These giant timbers scattered in the gulch—solitary deities towering over short grasses and sedges, spotted with middling mustard plants, mocking the baldness of that rolling land. I, too, felt minuscule as I looked at them, their bare branches leading my eyes into the blue heaven above, an even more intimidating giant which washed me with a new and general anxiety, an angst for the looming mystery just past the boundary of my intellect. Instantly the stories of stampeding bison herds, bands of attacking Indians, tornados, and raging prairie storms gave rise to visions transposed over the landscape. Looking around, I saw each of these as I contemplated my aloneness in the middle of this unknown expanse, no indication of neighborly life other than the unremitting trail that merely pointed in abject silence. Not even a bird cawed its presence to break the spell I was under, and an overwhelming urge to get the fuck out of there washed away any remnant of my earlier dream of peace and wholeness.

I mounted Buck imperatively yet gentle as I stood in the stirrup. We spent enough time shaking off our injuries, and I hoped Carl was waiting for us someplace we'd be able to reach before nightfall. As we rode over the gulch and past the disordered assembly of cryptic, bark-clad heralds, I knew on a deep and irrational level that I wasn't riding away from whatever lurked in the shadows of my ignorance but toward it.

Buck was timid to run, though I encouraged him, and gradually he gained speed. Soon enough, we bolted along the Santa Fe Trail, his head bobbing up and down in rhythm with his stride, perhaps emboldened by overcoming his own fear of pain. And wasn't that the same for all of us—finding courage when realizing it's the fear of pain, rather than the pain itself, that restrains us.

A mile or so on, we entered a country checkered with immense brown fields enclosed by evergreen hedges. More creeks crossed this territory, giving rise to tree groves and long prairie sandreed grass, which swayed in the gentle wind. Over the next few miles, we gradually descended and rode toward a sweeping forest of ash, cedar, hackberry, and other trees I didn't know. We entered through the crisscrossing shadows of ceremonial elm branches, and our dirt trail transformed into a meticulous and splendid tapestry. I saw Buck's hot breath in the cool, woodland air that smelled of pine oil and sage and a faint trace of moisture, suggesting we might be close to the Kansas river. The branch shadows enveloped us as we bolted along, imparting a sense of peace that gradually bloomed into an overflowing sense of oneness with the transcendent, a palpable feeling and not merely an abstract idea. I laid my hand on Buck's injured neck and imagined his pain flying away like glitter in the air. I imagined myself one with him, the pulsing of his muscles pumping the blood in my own body—our souls infusing each other with a single awareness, a single purpose, a single, widening perception of the world.

Throughout, sunlight filtered through the branches, sparkling off rocks and snow patches with all the colors of the rainbow. Looking into the network of caressing arms woven overhead, my heart seemed to melt and flow over the surface of every object around me. My beating heart expanded with the life of these august trees, this perfect prairie ground, and every hidden animal in this dwelling. We ran for two or three more miles through these woods, wordless, united with the spirit that lay just past the flesh of perception—seamless, continuous, solitary in the communion of life.

Slowly, and against my tacit desire, the sound of rushing water dissolved the enchantment I was under. The Kansas river must be big, I pondered, watching in my imagination as it pushed me out of my dream, my senses returning to the surface of things. The forest grew thin, holes opening wider and wider in the tapestry of shadows around me until I finally emerged from its embrace and into the full afternoon sun. I estimated maybe eight hundred yards ahead was the shore of the river, its audible cascade of whitecaps gleaming like twinkling stars against the gray canvas of water.

I rode again into an expanding prairie, less barren, with signs that others had frequented this district. There were side roads cut off the trail that meandered out to vast patches of dirt, each stained by the black marks of campfires. I passed broken wagon wheels, grown through by shrubbery, and discarded wagon bonnets, frayed and weathered, then reached a wood-carved sign pointing west to *Papin's Ferry*.

Built on the river's shore was a large wood beam dock and a rectangle raft of the same material large enough for a Conestoga wagon. A stretch of rope extended overhead from one shore to the other, and that rope was threaded through an eyelet tied at the end of another rope, secured to the raft. It was clear the attachment was meant to keep the raft on track and from drifting downstream. Each end of the raft was hinged so that a flap of wood would overlap the dock, leaving no space to fall between and into the river during boarding or disembarking on the other side.

I brought Buck to the river for a drink, close enough for me to size up the operation before engaging what appeared to be the only person there—an overweight man in a tattered wool suit reclining on a chair, rifle over his lap, and hat pulled down over his eyes. No wagons or camps in sight and no sign of Carl.

"Excuse me, sir," I said, walking Buck by hand up to the edge of the dock. The man didn't move. I watched him for a moment. He gasped, erecting his body in that overworked chair and started snoring. "Sir," I said louder, "are you awake?"

The man slowly opened one eye, the only eye I could see under his hat. His lips flattened, his cheeks swelled to orange-sized spheres, and with a single flurry, he deflated those massive face pockets, his lips flapping against one another, spit flying over his shirt.

"You woke me up," he said with a German accent, pushing his hat back to reveal his other eye. The umber skin of his face was loose and wrinkled and spotted with irregular-shaped, hazelwood moles. A particularly unattractive man.

"Has anyone crossed here today?" I asked. The bags under his eyes seemed to fold inside his face and hang as flappy jowls from the sides of his jawbone. I could tell I was bothering him.

"Who's asking?"

"I'm asking, sir," I answered. What a dumb question. "Figured that was plain enough."

"I'm no tard, you know." His eyes narrowed to slits, and as if wriggling through a hole in a fence, with great exertion, he shimmied left, then right, then left again, scooting up on his loud-creaking chair. God help him if that damn thing broke.

"Sorry," I said. "I don't know what a tard is."

"Now you're just goofing me," he said, scratching one of

the spots at his temple. A thin rivulet of blood snaked over his rutted skin and dripped on his shirt collar, unnoticed. "Scram, rudo."

Rudo? What the hell was a rudo? "Look, I'm not trying to be rude if that's what you mean. I just want to know if anyone's crossed today, that's all."

"You gotta pay," he said, looking at my pants pockets as if he could see through fabric.

"For a simple yes or no answer?" I asked. This guy was pissing me off now. I studied the river up and down, a hundred-foot-wide blanket of surging, perilous flood. "Look, I said, I know somebody's passed today, so tell me how much to cross."

The man perked up. "Ten cents."

"Ten cents to cross…" I said, half questioning. Curious now how shady this man was, I went on and asked, "How much were you gonna charge me for an answer to my question?"

"Well, ten cents," he said, "obviously."

Obviously. Where the hell was Carl? He had to have passed, but I doubt he had any money. Maybe some he lifted from one of the people last night?

"Everything's ten cents," the man finished, proud of himself. Probably proud he didn't forget the one price he charges for anything and everything—a simple figure for a simple mind.

"Fine," I said, hopping off Buck. I rummaged the saddlebag for the sink pipe and pulled it out, sticking my finger inside. "You got change?" I asked, expecting to pull out a bill but feeling nothing. I looked inside—the pipe was empty. Fuck. Now I was in a pinch.

"No change," he said. "Ten cents."

"You know," I said, "this here pipe is worth more than ten cents. You could sell it for twenty, easy."

The man settled back in his chair as if bartering had become a boring enterprise. "Gimme the money or get lost," he said, pulling his hat to block the sun from his eyes. Slowly, he stuck out his blistered tongue and blew it at me like some frustrated toddler. "Grrrr," he went on, pretending to be a bear, I supposed, yanking the corners of his lips way back to his fried-egg ear lobes, revealing an ungodly collection of black and jagged clumps that hatched out of inflamed gums.

"Where's my ten cents?" he asked.

I rummaged my pockets, pretending there was anything inside but pebbles and loose thread. "I don't have ten cents. Look, I'll tell you straight. My sister's gone kidnapped, and I'm riding with a friend, a grubby fellow on a skinny horse. We're tracking her down, gonna rescue her from whoever took her, locked her up in that little white wagon."

"White wagon, you say, eh?" the man asked. I could tell he wanted to say more but held his words.

"Why don't you just spit it out? I can see you want to say something."

The man leaned on his rifle as if he might stand up but merely shifted his weight to the other side. "Maybe there was a guy who crossed the river earlier, matching that description. I'm not saying there was—that'd cost you. And maybe I did see a little white wagon too."

169

"I swear to God, if you're bullshitting me, I will cut you. I'll cut you so fucking deep you'll flip inside out."

This time he did more than lean on his rifle. He raised it to his shoulder and aimed it near my head, then winged it with a flash over the river, pulled the trigger, and dropped a bird in flight five hundred yards away. "Say that one more time?" he said, dropping the stock of the rifle to his elbow but keeping the muzzle in my general direction. "I don't think I heard you right."

"I just need to get across the river," I said, "that's all. Swear to God, just trying to save my little sister."

The man finally stood, balancing his rotund barrel body on those two bratwursts that seemed to start at the knees, shooting an inverted "Y" out of his ass. Unsteady, he pulled down on his coat and leaned the rifle on his chair. "Okay, okay," he said as if he were surrendering on a battlefield. "I remember your friend. He paid your transport, asked me to tell you he would wait for you on the other side."

"What's with all these games then?" I asked, pissed off. "Why are you fucking with me?"

He just stared as if I hadn't said anything. "Tell you the same thing I told him," the man finally said, nonchalant. "That wagon you said, a white one. It came through earlier this morning."

"And?!" I asked, excited and furious. I was close. They weren't going to get away.

"And what?" He stared at me for a second and must have realized I was waiting for him to go on. "Oh. Well, and that's it."

"Let's hurry, then," I said. "Come on, old man, *move!*" Buck and I rushed to the far end of the raft. The man lifted the end of the ramp, and with a long stick, pushed us off the shore and into the river. We crossed slowly, the raft banking in the swells and water splashing over the bord. Seeing Buck get skittish, I held his rein in one hand and petted his neck with the other, studying the far side of the river and following the trail as it cut through a patchy forest of tall barren trees, yearning to see if that wagon wasn't in sight somehow.

"Did you hear anything?" I asked. "Anyone inside the wagon?"

"Nope," he answered, shoving the long stick to the bottom of the river and pushing off, "that wagon was beat—ain't got too many miles left in it. I said to the man, 'go find a wheelwright before it's too late,' and he grunted at me."

"No sign of anyone else? I mean, you only saw the driver?" I was desperate for something more, afraid Bethany was knocked unconscious or even dumped along the trail. Could I have ridden right past her and not noticed? I felt my heartbeat quicken, my muscles tense, and pinpoints of sweat covered my skin as my attention drew down to a precise angle, cutting away superfluous details of my surroundings. I reached inside the saddlebag for Pa's revolver, ensuring it was loaded.

"I didn't see nobody else," the man said. "If you aiming to take him out, be ready. Big guy, looked strong and not too friendly either. Hid his eyes. When I lowered the ramp, he raced away."

I didn't figure a kidnapper'd be friendly. We approached the opposite shore, and I walked Buck to the back of the raft while the man anchored. No telling how far away that man was by now. Hopefully, his wagon broke down. Staring down the trail, I wondered what was Carl doing, and if he'd try to rescue Bethany himself.

As Buck and I stepped off the raft, a voice, faint over the rushing of the river, drew my attention. Looking over the water, there was Katie on the other side, waving at me, sitting on her horse. I waved, exhilarated to see her.

"That girl there," I said to the man as he raised the ramp again. "I need her. Can you bring her over?"

"Ten cents," the man said, shoving off into the swells. A cold, grainy mist blew off the water at me, forming drops that ran down my face. "Your friend only gave me twenty."

"But she might not have any money," I said, raising my voice. "She's with me. Come on, mister." The man floated farther away.

"'Come on, mister' won't put food on my table, kid. Ten cents." His voice faded into the whitewater.

"There's your payment!" I shouted, throwing the pipe at him. "*Asshole*! And I ain't no kid!"

Anxious to get moving, I mounted Buck and rode a hundred yards down the trail, still in sight of Katie, looking for any signs of Carl or the white wagon. The forest grew thick in the distance as tree trunks filled empty spaces, the curtain shutting after a couple hundred yards and nothing visible past that distance. If the wagon was broken down on the trail, we might have to ride close before seeing it, jeopardizing our advantage of surprise.

Buck paced in a circle, trotting a little further down trail, then back again so I could keep an eye on Katie. The boatman anchored onshore, dropping the ramp, and I watched Katie— still on her horse—ride onto the raft. The man threw his hands in the air, seeming to tell her to get off. He reached in his pocket and pulled something out, holding it between his fingers. A dime I assumed. He showed it to her, shaking his head no, and pointing off the raft. I could tell Katie was getting angry, and when the man pulled up his long stick and whacked Blue with it, I watched as she swung her holster to her hip, yanked out the pistol, and aimed it at the man's face. He dropped the stick and turned toward his chair, where his rifle was. He scrambled to it across the raft while Katie yelled at him. I could hear her distant cry, telling him to stop. But he didn't. In a single motion, he swept up his rifle, chambered a round, and spun to face her just as she pulled the trigger of her gun, blasting a hole straight through the man's nose and blowing off his hat, along with a section of skull from the back of his head. He fell over off the raft and rolled down the shore, his torso bent into the water, his face submerged, and the water washing over the gore.

Perhaps surprising herself, Katie stared at the man. I glanced down the trail again, more anxious than before, but I couldn't leave Katie. She looked over the water at me, her face clearly white even at that distance. *Hurry up*, I thought. Katie looked back the way we rode from, not moving, but simply staring. I wondered if she recalled the violence we watched last night—exposure to mankind's brutality imparting on her a power to access that same aspect of human nature. Perhaps she remembered her family and the injustice they suffered, and forced restitution into the world against this man in accordance with her vow. I stared at her, jealous of her strength, hoping I'd have a similar power when we finally caught up to the man with the white wagon. Katie hopped off Blue, grabbed up the long stick, then pushed herself across the river.

"What are you looking at?" she asked, nearing the shore.

"I told you I'm in love with you," I answered. I was ecstatic that she kept her word and sought me out. Maybe this meant she felt for me the way I felt for her. Her eyes squinted, staring at me with a curious look. "Don't you love me?" I asked.

She smiled, mounting her horse, but didn't answer. Blue jumped off the raft and waded through the water's edge. Standing on dry land, he drank from the river. "Well?" she asked. "Where's Carl?"

I looked at the dead man on the other side of the river, then back at her. "The white wagon is close, crossed here earlier today. Carl got a head start. We'll catch up to him. You all right?" I asked.

She swung her holstered pistol behind her back and yanked on Blue's reins. "Let's go, boy," she said to her horse. "I'm good. You?"

"I'm good," I answered as we trotted down the trail. I took a moment to study Blue—how he moved. He seemed young, his joints fluid, steady, and capable. "Blue's a quick ride, it seems. Is he fast?"

"The fastest," she answered. "Surprised?"

"Constantly," I said, my thoughts returning to Bethany. "Some people ... monsters."

"You saying I'm a monster? For what happened back there?" she asked.

"Not you," I said. "Thinking about my sister, that's all."

"There's a scale needs balancing," she said, determined. "And we're the ones to do that."

I recalled maybe seven years ago, when I told my ma that I stole back the marbles that Guts stole from me. "You're no better than him," she said to me. She didn't get it, that protecting what was yours was important, and I refused to feel guilty for it.

"He took mine first," I said, defiant.

She scowled at me. "You're nothing but a rotten thief and a damned thug. You'll return those marbles, along with an apology."

Like hell. She thought I was a thug and a thief for taking what was mine, and it was then when I realized that age had no claim on wisdom. They say fight fire with fire, and I say fight evil with evil. Be willing to do what your opponent is willing to do, and bring the wrath to him which he dispenses. It became clear to me now, as Katie and I rode the trail together, that our culture had grown decadent, insisting that goodness had no use for evil. Pretending we were better than others for not committing to our goals, no matter the cost, was nothing more than weakness.

"So, have you seen anything? Any sign of the white wagon?" Katie asked.

"Nothing," I said. "I got faith, though."

Katie and I rode farther on, up and down low hills through the forest, looking out for Carl and the white wagon. Soon, the forest thinned, and the town of Topeka emerged through the gaps of the trees.

"Do you have any money?" I asked Katie.

"I got a few bucks."

"Hungry?"

"That's polite of you," she said, smirking, "offering me a meal at my expense."

"I'm broke, that's all," I said. "Gave Carl some of the food I counted on for this trip, got nothing left."

She looked at me, silent. Finally, she burst out with a laugh, relieving my worry that I offended her somehow. "Yea, let's get something," she said. "But what about Carl? How are we going to find him?"

"I have no idea," I said. "I guess he'll have to find us. We'll just stay long enough to grab some food, then get back on the road."

The trail swung in a long half circle around the western side of Topeka. We rode until the route turned south again, and seeing it didn't lead into the city but merely traced its perimeter, we slowed our horses and crossed over onto Fourth Street toward town. We trotted through the outskirts first, past shanty, falling-down houses where shirtless kids with distended bellies chased dogs or one another, their mothers watching from porch rockers, or while splitting firewood, all of them pausing to observe our entrance. Gradually, the homes grew newer and taller until we reached

Kansas Avenue.

"We need to see the wheelwright," I told Katie.

She looked at me, puzzled. "What?" she asked. "Those are legs," she said, pointing at Buck, "not wheels."

"And here I thought they were wheels, this *whole* time."

"I'm hungry, James. I need food."

"Just a quick stop, I promise."

Kansas Avenue was a main street—dry, dusty, and smelling of horse shit. Figuring a wheelwright would put his business by the greatest traffic, we turned south and walked past several businesses, mostly brick buildings, but the older ones built of wood. There was a mercantile, a dry goods store, a livery, a post office, and finally the wheelwright. A few folks milled around town, but not as many as I expected to see for the state's capital city. Perhaps Katie and I looked out of place. Friendly tips of my hat went unreciprocated, strangers' eyes suspicious. It seemed our arrival was not welcomed.

"This place a little off, or is it just me?" Katie asked.

"I get that feeling too," I said, looking at her seriously. "The town, not so much. But you? Definitely."

She put on a goofy smile, the sides of her mouth pulled high to the corners of her squinted eyes. "A proper companion, you are then, to a gentlewoman of my sort."

The sun leaned west, casting cold shadows over the street and storefronts. After tying our horses in front of the wheelwright's business, Katie grabbed a jacket from her saddlebag and put it on before we walked up the creaky veranda through the aroma of hickory sawdust and quenched metal. An older man with a potbelly and leather smock hammered a flat steel tire, matching its angle against a wheel felloe. His shop was a mess of tools, wood scraps, workbenches, sawhorses, and anvils. The man finally noticed us standing there.

"Howdy," he said in a deep voice that matched the dark-brown hair combed low over his forehead and across his eyebrows. "You need something?"

"Howdy," I said—probably for the first time in my life. "We're looking for a busted-up wagon, a white one, dirty. I was told the wheels were damn near falling off and hoping you might have seen it."

"That's right," the man said, running his fingers over the bend in the metal. "A man of few words, but he paid. You belong to him or something? Kin?"

"No," I answered, "nothing like that. We just need to catch up with him." I looked at Katie, my mind filled with images of violence. "Have some business with him."

"Urgent business," Katie added.

"Urgent," the man repeated. "Well, you won't have a hard time reaching him. He said he was in a hurry and couldn't wait for his wheels to get repaired, so I sold him new ones. But they don't fit right. He takes his horse to a canter even, and they'll fall off."

"Thank you, sir," I said, optimistic. "By chance, he tell you which way he was going? I know he's going toward Santa Fe, but wanted to make sure he didn't change his mind or anything."

Still focused on his task, he answered, "No, I don't

reckon he changed his mind. Said he had business of his own. Meeting someone coming a long way here. A trade of some sort. You'll find him on the trail, that's for sure."

I could tell by now I was taking more time from this man than he wanted to give, but I couldn't help asking, "You get sight of the inside of his wagon?" I asked. The man turned his back and grabbed a file from a bench, then scraped the edge of the tire with it, grinding loud. It didn't matter. We'd catch the kidnapper—that was good enough.

"Let's go back to that dry goods store," I said to Katie as we climbed our horses.

A sign on the entrance read *Clarabelle's Cottage*—a funny name for a store selling beans and flour. Flanking the door and running up the sides of the building were columns that framed two high arched windows on either side of the entrance, above which was a triangular-shaped transom window encased in decorative stone, which pointed up to a second and third story. Must be some kind of hotel or something. We hitched our horses near the tar-lined trough out front and walked inside.

A slender, middle-aged man in round-wire spectacles and a white apron stood behind a long counter positioned in front of an arched window. The counter was a glass display case for pistols, pocket watches, and peppermint sticks. Behind him, along a rack no taller than his medium stature, were countless labeled jars of everything from pickles to peppercorns. He stood watching us, his beady eyes protruding past tight eyelids magnified by his glasses, his mouth a puckered blemish that faded into the rest of his pasty face.

"Good afternoon, sir. Not Clarabelle, I assume," I said, trying to lighten the mood. "Looks like you've got a little of everything here."

"I'm Mel," he said, his voice nasally, glancing at the ceiling. "Clarabelle is my partner. Lots of traffic through here. So you see, I'm terribly busy. Do you need something?"

"We're in a hurry too," I said. "We're riding the trail and need something that won't spoil. You got any gumdrops?" Katie shot me a look. "Okay, no gumdrops. You got any dried meat or fruit?"

I stood at the counter while Katie turned and walked further into the store, looking among the shoes, balls of yarn, and bolts of fabric. The store was beautiful, I had to admit— organized and dusted, and smelling of lavender.

"I've never seen a store with two floors, let alone three," Katie said, looking over at Mel. "What's up there?"

He stared at her for a moment, then rolled his eyes, ignoring her question. "We do have dried meat and fruit. Hard cheese too, if you're so inclined, though I'm partial to the softer varieties."

"I always liked cheese," Katie said, carrying a pair of shoes with her as she walked over. "How about you?" she asked me.

"Let's get cheese, then," I told her. "And some meat," I said to Mel.

He simpered, fanning his fingertips over the collar of his cardigan, his magnified eyeballs suggestive through his spectacles. Grabbing a small paper bag, he flicked it open with one hand, then took the lid off a cheese jar with the other.

"What takes you out on the trail?" he asked, filling the bag piece by piece. "Two youngsters like yourselves—your parents must be worried sick about you."

Katie looked at me, irritated at the man's assumptions. "We're not little kids. You have children?" she asked him.

"No. No kids. God forbid the thought!" He put the bag on the counter and filled a second bag with meat, squares of jerky, and pieces of dried links, glancing at me briefly as he did so. "I've been told my sausage is the best in the county," he said, shaking a thick, uncut piece at me before dropping it in the bag. "The cheese is good, but if you see any mold, just cut it off. It won't hurt you." He finished with the meat bag and put it on the counter. "Here we are," he said. He looked at Katie over the rims of his glasses, his eyes carrying a hint of judgment, observing the shoes in her hand.

"You're quite snooty, aren't you?" Katie asked him.

He studied her up and down, cocking his head to the side with an insinuating grimace. "I'm no fan of little girls," he said. "Entitled brats, the lot of you." He huffed. "Discriminating. Not snooty, for your information. Are we going to have a problem?"

"That all depends," she said, glancing over at me.

"There's no problem," I said to her. "We're good. Right?"

Katie was irked, but backed down. She put the shoes on the counter.

"Um-hmm," Mel chirped, as if satisfied he won this

contest of wills. "Will you be buying the shoes as well, young man?" he asked me.

"Why do you assume he's doing the buying here?" Katie asked him.

Ignoring her, Mel took a breath and brushed his apron with his hands, pushing off any wrinkles, then nudged his glasses to the bridge of his nose. At this point, his attitude about Katie was starting to piss me off. "Heading east or west?" he asked me.

"I don't see how that makes any difference to you," I answered.

"Well, there must be some reason you'd leave the comfort of mommy and daddy, especially this time of year."

I looked at Katie, shaking my head. What an asshole. "Is everyone in Topeka like you?" I asked him.

This caught him off guard. "What is that supposed to mean?"

"Chatty, I guess. You talk a lot. How much for the meat and cheese?"

"Three dollars, altogether," he said.

"You're crazy—three dollars for meat and cheese?" I asked him.

"Meat, cheese, and that pair of shoes," he said, pointing.

"We're not buying the shoes," Katie said.

"Very well," the man answered. "Seventy-five cents, in that case." He held his hand out in front of Katie, palm up, waiting for her to hand over the money.

"What's that for?" she asked him.

"Don't be a cunt," he said, "please." His voice was

whining and thick with disdain. "You uppity tarts test me every chance you get, don't you. Spoiled little devils, living a coddled life. Mind you, you're just a baby. I blame your disgusting parents for the way you've been brought up. Judging by you, they should be downright ashamed of themselves. Tell them that, on behalf of civilized society, next time you see them." Leaning on the counter, he brought his face close to hers. "If I have to spell it out for you, this is the part of the transaction where you give me cash, then get the fuck out of my store."

Katie looked down, pensive, then up at me with glossy eyes. The man's words struck a nerve with her. "You take my name down," she said, looking back at him, "charge interest as you see fit, and take up payment with my disgusting parents, as you say." I could see she was holding herself back, itching to lash out against this man.

"Enough games," Mel said. "Time to leave."

"We should go," I said to Katie. "We're wasting time."

"This guy is a bastard," she said, notching up her holster belt.

"Don't think about making trouble," the man said, watching her. He untied his apron and walked around to the front of the counter. His build was even more petite than I suspected. "Law around here doesn't play. Now get the hell out."

He grabbed Katie by the sleeve of her jacket, twisting her arm behind her back and shoving her toward the door. She yelled out in pain, and for a moment, I saw her eyes look into mine as if asking, wasn't I going to do anything?

"You too," he said to me, grabbing my long-sleeve flannel shirt, "you snot-nosed little shit. And here I thought of asking you for company later. I'm a damned fool."

Once his hand made contact with me, a swell of anger broke inside, and all my anticipation for meeting the kidnapper filled my limbs with strength and my mind with focus. I knew I didn't want to hurt Mel, but he had to stop. I pulled my whittling knife and pushed the tip under his chin. He let go of Katie, and his eyes opened wide as I punctured his skin, his warm blood trickling over my hand.

"You're going to let us go now," I said with calm and determination. He tried using his hand to push away from me, but I grabbed him, and whatever jerking he did only drove the blade deeper. "I'm going to skewer that tongue of yours if you keep this up."

He let go of my shirt, so I stepped back from him, taking the knife out of his chin. Before I knew what she was up to, Katie smashed a clay jar of cinnamon over his head, splitting the jar into pieces and buckling his neck in an awkward angle. As the shattered pottery fell to the ground, broken edges cut his skin, and brown powder rained over his face, sticking in the slashes. The man's eyes vibrated in his skull, unable to focus on anything, and he dropped to the floor, gasping for breath but only sucking in that fine, choking dust.

Katie and I ran outside and loosed the horses while a well-dressed man and woman stopped and watched, having witnessed the scene through the window. I was tempted to offer explanation to these spectators and make them see it was self-defense, but I realized that impulse was a choice. An ingrained habit. I saw with clarity that reasoning was a story we made up to get our ways—a strategy to manipulate others' perceptions, and nothing more. The universe was bigger than the capacity of man's ability to think, and avoiding a pitfall of my past, I rode off—stoic and bold. It didn't matter what those strangers thought of me, or us, or anything for that matter, and I felt powerful being able to disregard them so thoroughly.

Our horses sprinted down Fourth Street, and we hopped back on the trail south. Once we got going, Katie looked at me and smiled, then held up the two bags of food. I looked at her feet, seeing her wearing the shoes from the store.

"When'd you have time to put those on?" I asked her, surprised.

She just winked. Her smile made me forget everything in the world but her. I knew I wanted to spend the rest of my life with this girl.

"What are you slowing down for?" Katie asked as we rode away from the town, taking the opportunity to grab a piece of cheese. She looked at it, then at me, and popped it in her mouth "Not bad."

"I thought it'd be smarter to ride slower to keep from running into the kidnapper. I'd rather spot him from a distance and strategize our approach."

Our horses trotted through a forest of dogwoods, and as the sun lowered, so did the temperature. "Why is it so cold here?"

Katie glanced sideways, incredulous. "It is winter, you know," she reminded me.

I pulled a jacket from my saddlebag and put it on over my flannel. With the setting sun, the sky overhead turned orange, though its light didn't penetrate onto our region. The shadows of trees gradually swallowed the gaps where the sun had shined, leaving us to ride along a solid dark path, the ambient glow above fading. The soil here was peculiar too—harder, less spirited if that can characterize something as lifeless as dirt. It jumped differently off our horses' hooves, and the sound of their trot was more oak, less fir. As we progressed, we passed campfire smoke that wove through the knitted dogwood limbs and low over the snow-patched ground. It filled my lungs with the stinging fragrance of smoldering wet wood.

"You can find dry wood out here," I said. "Why would anyone burn wet wood if they had a choice?" Something about it didn't sit right with me. "You see any camps around here?" I asked Katie.

Finishing another piece of cheese, she held up her finger, telling me to wait a minute, then finally swallowed. "Probably can't see them through the trees, that's all. Plus, who knows how far away those campfires are."

I grew edgy. "I don't know," I said, slowing Buck's pace even further. "Smoke doesn't smell like that, if it's that far away." The trees were thick where we were, but there had to be some sign of a cutoff or side road. "Give me a piece of that meat anyway," I said, the smoke stirring my appetite. "Think it's the white wagon?"

Katie looked at me, fastening the top buttons of her jacket as a cold wind scuttled dry leaves across the road.

Overhead, the sky turned dark blue; we didn't have much time to make camp ourselves. "Maybe," she said. "Maybe not. Whoever it is, where the hell are they?"

We continued riding, listening for any sounds of people, the light fading further until we advanced under the glow of the stars. "Are we going to ride all night like this?" Katie asked. "Suppose we should go back to town, sleep there, then come back out tomorrow?"

A long day of riding wiped me out worse than Buck, who did all the work. I could tell Katie was tired too, and I'd been thinking of sleep for a while. "We can't," I told her. "I can't risk him getting to Council Grove. It's too big of a place. Can't risk Bethany like that. Let's just keep going for a while and see if we don't find something. Just for a little while."

"That's fine," she said, smiling. "I'm with you, Mr. James. You never did tell me your last name."

"It's Tuck."

"James Tuck, huh?" she said. "*JT*."

I hated when people called me that but held my tongue. "My Pa said he named me after his Pa, the best man he'd ever met—though he didn't know him that well, truth be told. He hoped I'd be like him, I suppose, starting me off right out of the gate."

"Out of the *womb*," Katie said.

"Right, I guess. Hadn't thought of that, but yeah."

"And are you? You anything like your grandpa?" she asked.

I shrugged. "I never met him. He died when my pa was young. He was killed by a drunk who wanted his money, and that was that. The guy fled town, and the sheriff did nothing about it. Just let him go. That lazy bastard said it was out of his jurisdiction, and the rules on that were black and white."

"And that was that," Katie said, shaking her head. "My pa always said sheriffs are good at the letter of the law, worthless at the spirit. Justice is more than just terms on a contract. It's good you're out here for your sister. Family ought to be the ones to bring justice when one of their own is hurt."

"You think we'll ever know who did that to your family last night?" I asked her.

"I'm sure it was the Osage," she answered. "Who else could it be?"

Of course she was right, but I didn't want to think an Indian tribe, or any tribe of folks, would be so merciless against individuals based only on their group. Fear tightened my skin as I thought the campfire smoke might be coming from an Indian tribe similarly inclined toward us. "My pa always taught me the Indians were good people—people like anyone else doing what folks would do if foreigners moved in and tried to take everything that was theirs."

"He taught you not to judge them?"

"Not to judge anyone, based on their group," I said. "Some folks ain't made to be friends, no doubt. But folks aren't tribes. They're individuals. If you think about it, we've never met an Indian before. Individuals who happened to be Indian, but not *an Indian*. One person can't embody all the vices and sins of an entire group's history, so if all you see when you look at an Indian is their group, then you aren't seeing reality at all. You're looking at a made-up symbol of your own thinking, and hating that symbol is hating your own delusion. Besides stupid, that kind of self-centered thinking only leads to perdition."

Katie looked at me with a puzzled expression. "And?" she asked. "So what?"

"I'm just saying, identifying someone by their group is one thing. Judging them by it is something else."

Katie shook her head at me, uninterested in what probably came off as preachy. "Say what you will," she said. "I want those individuals dead, then."

We rode on, the smell growing stronger. Soon, gray smoke was visible, lacing the air, though the flames were still hidden behind the thick pattern of trees. "Let's take a look," I said to Katie. "Quiet."

She and I dismounted and walked on foot, leading our horses off the trail over shallow dogwood roots and through patches of ice-encased scrub. Overhead, through a mesh of twisted shadows, remote stars burned cold and futile. I brought Buck beside me, knowing his ability to navigate these woods was better than mine, and pulled Pa's revolver from the saddlebag.

"Just in case," I said to Katie.

"Don't you hesitate," she said to me, looking at the gun. "If we run into danger, take any opening and give them hell."

Soon, the glow of firelight illuminated the tree trunks ahead of us. I cocked the gun's hammer, gripping it tight. There were voices speaking English in Indian accents, but I couldn't make out the words.

"Indians," I whispered to Katie, my heart pounding fast. "Let's go back."

I turned Buck, his feet crunching the ground, hoping they couldn't hear us. We weren't that far off the trail and could sprint for town if need be. I grew dizzy in my apprehension and imagined footsteps racing on our flank. Buck and I took a step forward, away from the camp, and a shirtless Indian boy dressed in denim, boots, and a Stetson hat emerged from the darkness. I yelped, unable to contain my surprise.

"Looky, looky!" the boy said, seeing the gun in my hand. "You done bring got me no howdy partner?" He held his hands up, suggesting no ill intention, then twisted his wrists left and right, flashing his spread fingers like hand fans, raising and lowering them as he began chanting and dancing.

"*Why these folks be don't be feared,*" he sang. "*Be get be cool we're not like you.*" As suddenly as it started, the boy stopped cold and stared at Katie and me. "No warmth? Put that back before you hurt someone."

What the hell did he want? "We're just leaving," I told him, taking a step forward. The boy put his hand on Buck's nose and stared into my eyes. His face was round, scarred around the chin by acne, his eyes narrow and intimidating, reflecting the flickering light behind me. I squeezed the revolver's handle, my muscles twitching, waiting for him to do something that would justify my shooting him. But there were others—he wasn't alone—and I had no idea where any of them were in the darkness. Whatever was about to go down, we weren't going to get butchered like Katie's family last night.

"Take it easy, JT," Katie said softly. Her voice trembled, a mixture of terror and fury. "But need be, you *damn* well take it."

The Indian boy glanced at her, then returned his eyes to mine.

"*James?*" a familiar voice called out.

Carl? I thought, tempted to release the tension I'd bottled inside of me, but uncertain what was going on here exactly. "Is that you, Carl?"

I didn't take my eyes off the Indian boy as Carl ran over, his boots missing their long laces. He threw his arm around the boy's shoulder. "Been waiting for you," he said to me. He spoke freely, relaxed. "You met Harry, good. Come on now, let's get out of the darkness."

Harry continued to stare at me, almost glaring, then broke into a loud cackle, doubling over. "I did got you, son!" he said to me, almost shouting to be heard over his laughter. He took off his hat and covered his face, laughing into it as we walked to their camp.

After last night, I admit I was surprised to find Carl in his company. Katie was nervous and elbowed me to give her the gun. "Osage?" I asked Carl, certain he knew what I was really asking.

He didn't answer, eyeballing the gun in her hand. "Don't worry, Katie. They're good people—certain of that."

"*You* might be certain…" she whispered.

"They?" I asked.

Another Indian boy was at the camp, probably eleven or twelve years old, and looked like Harry but wore a ratty knit scarf around his neck. A few feet from the campfire were two shelters made of tarps that were slung over the ropes from Carl's boots, tied between the trees, and three horses were secured behind the shelters. The younger boy watched, apprehensive, as Katie and I approached.

"Arthur," Harry said, "you don't be no friendly. These folks Carl knows told us about." He turned to us. "You your horses with company or no doesn't matter. Tie them there if you want," he said, pointing at the line of woods facing the open side of the campfire.

"Ain't he something?" Carl asked. He walked to a felled tree trunk beside the fire and sat down. "I love the way Harry talks—gets me all tingly inside." Then he laughed into his fist the way he did when I first met him.

"How'd you know we'd find you?" I asked Carl.

"Well, you first told me you were hunting for suspicious," he said. "I knew if you caught up, burning wet wood in this abandoned stretch of forest would stand out." He tapped the side of his head with his finger, smiling. "Clever, like you said."

I tied Buck and Blue to a tree next to Carthon as Katie grabbed the bags of food and sat down on the log next to Carl. "You disappeared," I said to Carl, keeping my eye on the Indian boys. "Thought you might have left us."

"Come on, James," he said. "Can't get rid of me that easy."

Katie offered Carl a piece of dried meat, which he took and gnawed on with his back teeth. "It's okay," he said to her encouragingly, probably recognizing her anxiety remained.

She looked at Harry and Arthur, who stared at Carl as he ate. "You want some?" she asked.

They came over and each took a piece of meat, then sat on the ground in front of the fire, eating.

I sat down next to Katie. "Any luck finding the white wagon?" I asked Carl.

"Not yet—got detoured a little bit getting these brothers put together. Was planning to find the wagon, then wait by the trail for you to catch up."

Arthur whispered into Harry's ear, then they both stood up. "We get sleep now," Harry said. He came over to me and shook my hand with a firm grip. "You good fun, easy bait. Carl said good man." Staring at me as if reading my soul, he said, "I see you. Good man."

"Well," I said, "if Carl likes you, so do I. Good night, Harry." Smiling, he tipped his hat at Katie, and he and Arthur went and lay down in one of the shelters that looked so comfortable it could have been a feather bed.

"How'd you meet up with them?" I asked Carl. I pulled the sharpening stone from my pocket and held it firm, sliding the edge of my whittling knife across its flat surface, checking its razor edge every so often with my thumb.

"It's a long story," he said. "Later. Anything new?"

"Wheelwright in town said the wagon is going this way," I said, "and he's not going fast. Should be easy to catch up with him." I looked at Katie. She rubbed her eyes and yanked on the ends of her ponytail, forcing the ribbon up closer to her head.

"We should get some sleep," she said. "Just a little bit."

"I can't," I said. "If something happens to her, then that'd be on me. I'm not going to live with that kind of shame—for what? Sleep I could have gotten any time?" I was exhausted and could barely focus my vision at this point. I sheathed my knife and stared at the shelters, unable to get the image of me lying down in one of them out of my mind.

"Are you still hungry?" Katie asked me, holding up a piece of cheese. I took it and ate it, bite by bite, chewing slow for want of energy.

"Get some sleep," Carl said. "When you wake up, we'll ride. I promise." He didn't seem to be tired at all, though Katie was already falling asleep. "Katie," he said. Her eyes bolted open. "You can sleep on my roll. Go ahead."

"You sure?" she asked.

"I'm sure," he said.

"Goodnight, then," she said and walked to the other shelter.

The fire popped as it burned, the flames causing a crinkling sound like fizz that dissolved the fortitude of my disposition. Maybe an hour or two of sleep wouldn't hurt. "All right," I said to him. "Will you wake us up?"

Carl nodded. "Don't worry. We'll get your sister."

I got up and untied my bedroll and blanket from Buck's saddle, then put them beside the fire. "What are you going to do?" I asked him.

"I'm good, really," he answered. And he seemed fine, so

I lay down and stared into the flames as they lapped the cold black night. Carl threw some more branches onto the fire and sat back down on the tree trunk.

As I mellowed down, I realized something was chewing at me since earlier in town, and despite being so tired, I couldn't fall asleep yet. I made such a big deal about those people who watched me and Katie in the shop and didn't stop to think about what we did to Mel—if he was okay, or how that'd affect Clarabelle. His neck bent something awful, and it'd be a miracle if he wasn't hurt real bad. He was an asshole who shouldn't have laid hands on us, but there's no way that justified the injury we dispensed in reciprocation.

Here I was trying to run down justice by rescuing my sister. All my bluster about bringing a cold steel fate to anyone opposing justice, yet perpetrating such a grossly disproportionate act. I recalled a willingness to drive that knife straight through Mel's face. I would have killed that man for shoving me and Katie, and realized I had been exactly the person I claimed to oppose. Contemplating this, I grew confused and dizzy, the line between real and imaginary blurring once again. I studied the outline of the orange flames as they extended into the shapeless night and strived to stay sharp in my thinking. This was no storybook tale, and I was no hero fated for triumph.

What am I doing? I wondered. *Why am I really doing it? To control my parents' perception of me?* I loved Bethany and would do anything for her, but I felt shame for my endeavor to rescue her, realizing my intentions were corrupt. Not only that, they led me down paths I purported to reject. I was such a hypocrite, pretending to be righteous. My stomach turned as I watched the fire, but I held down the meat and cheese. I held onto the bedroll, guilt-ridden, squeezing for something to clutch.

EIGHT

A few red embers of campfire smoldered under the pile of ash, their light peeking through unstable channels in the remains of what were once tall strong dogwood trees. Staring at it, I couldn't help but seeing the votive stand from the back of Blessed Martín de Porres Catholic Church in Leavenworth. I'd only been once, with Mr. Elton and his family, years ago. All those small red glass cups in that immovable black iron rack, a montage of people's hopes and prayers, flickering silently. I was transfixed, mesmerized by the fire and glass.

"Go ahead, *mijo*," Mrs. Elton had said to me. Her accent was thick then, but I had no trouble understanding. She must have noticed my fascination. I turned and looked up at her, seeing the large stained-glass rose window high on the wall behind her, glowing in sunlight. "Tell God what you need while you light one." In my heart, I knew all I wanted was to be united with that power I sensed infusing the universe, but

I hadn't the words to say it. I grabbed a long stick, igniting it from a burning candle, and brought that flame to the wick of another candle with only a feeling in my chest, a wish that exceeded my vocabulary. "Have faith, *Jaime*."

Carl lay on his back tucked into the corner of the felled tree trunk, seeming content. It was still dark. Weeds snapped under the shifting weight of the horses. The Indian boys snored in their dew-coated shelter, the sound childlike, innocent. They were the fading lullabies to a soon-deceased chapter of my life, as I envisioned the violence I'd wreak on Bethany's kidnapper. A proportional response for what he'd done. I felt comfortable in this one intention, yet surrounded on all sides by self-doubt and contrition.

Already awake, Carl turned his head to me, smiling, his eyes and that pink scar reflecting the red glow. "We're gonna get that son of a bitch," he said, his eyes slightly crossed. What an ugly mutt, but I loved this guy. We *would* get him, and we'd get Bethany.

"Hey, Carl," I said. "Can we count on Harry and Arthur?"

"We can indeed," he answered, offering nothing more.

An early morning mist materialized as the first hints of sunlight brightened the surroundings. The forest was thick here, and the trail was totally concealed. I checked on the horses while Carl roused Harry and Arthur from their sleep. The horses looked strong, well-rested. I gazed into their eyes, like those of prophets, seeing my reflection in the white shimmer of their irises. Did they know what we had planned?

"Katie," I said, kneeling on one leg outside the shelter where she slept. "Time to wake up."

She sat up and pulled back a flap of shelter canvas, looking past me into the distance. Her face was puffy, and she appeared exhausted, as if she hadn't slept at all. I couldn't imagine dealing with the tragedy she witnessed and wondered if she lay awake all night.

"How are you doing?" I asked her. "You get any rest?"

She glanced at me, then back in the distance. It may have been wrong of me, but I couldn't help staring at her face, her eyes, her lips, the way her hair wrapped behind her ear, her neck, and the little indent that sat at the top of her chest bone. She looked over my shoulder to the boys getting their gear packed, and to Carl, relacing one of his shoes with their shelter rope. My eyes followed the folded-down collar of her long johns to the top button of her white dress, patterned in a small green floral print. A line of small buttons, in the shape of flowers too, holding the two halves of her dress together down to her waist.

"Oh, you know," she finally answered. Her raspy voice was more hoarse than normal, and she tried smiling, but it didn't work. She reached out and grabbed my hand, squeezing firmly. As she did, an earthquake went off inside of me, and the whole world disappeared but for her. Gritting her teeth, her bottom lip quivered. I wanted to ask her if she'd be okay or if she needed anything. Did she need more time to rest? If I had the power to alter time, I would have, and given her a lifetime of healing before returning to my mission. Though if time were pliable, how many things I'd change…

Each fragment of life fit into the next one so perfectly, I recalled the sense that everything was exactly the way it was supposed to be. But now, the idea that it was splendid for Katie to be racked with grief, having watched her family get butchered, seemed so ridiculous. The trail had certainly given birth to some powerful delusions.

Water dripped from the edge of Katie's shelter canvas, and the mist floated around her like smoke. Her penetrating eyes locked into mine. "You look different, JT," she said. Her voice was sympathetic, as if it weren't her who was suffering.

I stared at her—her big, beautiful eyes, her soft hair that glowed no matter what time of day, her supple, electric skin—dumbfounded how such a magnificent creature could be real, let alone enter my life. I hated the name JT, and cursed my teachers in youth every time it came out of their mouths. But when Katie said it in that enticing, magnetic voice of hers, it was magic.

"You still with me?" she asked. "JT? You okay?"

"Yeah," I said, tingling inside. "I'm good."

"Go on, what is it?" she asked.

"What do you mean?"

"You're gawking at me, that's what I mean! You're obviously thinking something. Spit it out." She looked down at her hand, which I still held, and traced the veins on the back of my hand with her finger.

I turned around and looked at Carl, seeing him and the boys securing their gear to their horses. Feeling overwhelmed, my eyes welled with tears. "We're going to get

Bethany today," I said.

"I know that, JT." She reached up and wiped the moisture from under my eyes. "You're a man of purpose, and you won't rest till it's done. I can see that much." She took my other hand as we both stood up, then stepped close to me. I felt her light, warm breath on my face.

"I was hoping when this was done," I said, "that we'd stay on together. We're a good pair, in my estimation." Her eyes turned into doorways where I floated past the glimmering white, over the gold-sparkling cobalt, and into the midnight cosmos of her soul.

"We are a good pair," she agreed. I studied her lips, noticing them swell slightly, turning a shade brighter. She squeezed my hands, then she closed her mouth and smiled. It took all my will to not pull her into my arms and kiss her.

"Blue," I said, losing my thought and split between trying to recover or release it.

"My horse?"

I hesitated, staring into her eyes. "Nobody who ever called me JT made me feel the way you do."

"Who exactly's called you that?" she asked, squinting, feigning jealousy. She squeezed my hands again and stepped closer still, the front of her body just touching mine. She smiled bigger than before, perhaps seeing my skin change color as I felt a rush of blood.

"Nobody," I said. "I mean teachers, you know, schoolteachers."

Her eyes widened. "School teachers? Is that so?"

"Not that—no," I hurried to correct, unsure what I was

correcting exactly, but feeling awkward. "I'm—" I started to say.

"Well, I've thought of becoming a school teacher myself, one of these days. Are you saying a school teacher could never make you feel special?" Jesting, her eyes wrinkled at the corners, and those long eyelashes like brooms swept me deeper into her spirit.

"What subject are we talking about?" I asked.

"Now you're being silly. Before we get ahead of ourselves, we got some work to do. First thing's first. Like my grandma always said, you do the most important things in the morning. Don't put them off. So let's go get your sister."

I stared at her, amazed. "Let's do that," I said.

"You two hungry or what?" Carl yelled at us.

I dismantled Katie's shelter and brought Carl the rope for his other shoe. We sat beside him and the boys, silently gazing into the smoking fire, eating what remained of the cheese and meat, along with some bread Carl grabbed off the wagons after the massacre. Slowly, the sun broke over the horizon. I contemplated the violence we'd embark on that day, gazing in the direction of the trail, wondering if there were other trails, other ways to reach our goal that spared what remained of our innocence.

"We should go," I said, wiping my face. Everyone was packed and ready.

"Should we make a plan first?" Katie asked as she and Carl climbed on their horses.

"We need to see what we're dealing with," I answered. "Boys," I said to Harry and Arthur, uncertain of their ages.

Harry—draped in sewn fox skins but otherwise shirtless under his Stetson—looked at me with eyes that suggested my error. "Thank you for your willingness to help."

"Arthur and me," Harry said, "done no just work within the last moon. Carl said kidnapped kin of some folks being you, and saving a girl to save ourselves just work to stampede far away." I debated asking Carl for a translation but didn't, wondering how anyone could understand that. Didn't matter. I was grateful whatever their reasons were.

Our hearts pulsed the impending holocaust which occupied our thoughts as we snaked through the tight forest of barren trees back to the trail in the blue light of morning. White-hot embers spread throughout my chest, my stomach, my limbs, bursting from my fingertips. Stepping onto the trail, we lined up side by side, looking at each other, our muscles twitchy, our breath a thick fog tumbling out of sweat-beaded, rhapsodic faces.

Carthon's skinny legs wavered, shivering maybe, his knees discs on toothpicks. Blue raised and lowered his head while Katie petted his mane. Harry and Arthur's horses, both Appaloosas that looked like giant Dalmatian dogs, stood fixed and obedient, waiting for command. And Buck, maybe not the fastest horse—but he had to be the strongest—stood with tensing muscles, ridges rippling under his skin like a river current.

We all adjusted our seats, leaning over the shoulders of our horses, squeezing our reins, breathing deep, glancing one to the next. Katie's eyes glistened, and I knew she must be recalling her family. She swung her holster to her side, tightening the belt, then her ponytail. Her features were savage, reminding me of Pa's the night he ran up the hill in the dark with my whittling knife after that creep who touched Bethany.

Carl looked at me, his face a stone monument to retribution. I knew he pondered childhood under his Pa's merciless custody, transposing his experience onto that of every guiltless child, having told me that saving Bethany was saving himself. Our demons stood on the precipice to the world, awaiting the signal for release.

Carl's mouth was resolute, a slit of determination. He winked at me. I tightened my fists on the leather straps, then nodded and snapped my reins, driving my heels into Buck's flanks. A split second afterward, everyone followed suit. Carthon shot away impossibly fast, the rest of us struggling to see through the cloud of dust he laid down in our track. Our horses sprinted, sucking and spitting the quickening wind, dust sticking to our skin. Cacophony surged in from every direction, and it took a minute to realize that all of us— spontaneous, pure spirits in the moment—were screaming. Our inhibitions stripped, we were bolting through the thick forest of denuded trees, riding, our vision clearing as Carthon pulled even farther ahead of us.

Hazy shadows tightened into existence as the sun rose higher. The forest extended up and over low rolling hills, this part of the February trail empty of other travelers. We rode toward Council Grove over hard-packed dirt, past small trail cutoffs, detours to alternate destinations, the horses grinding earth underfoot. It wasn't long before they abated, the ground like rocks on their joints, so we slowed to a fast trot and let them catch their breath, then stopped by a stream.

"Everyone's okay?" I asked as the horses drank. Buck couldn't drink fast enough.

Harry hopped off his horse, checking on his and his brother Arthur's. "Your horses might maybe good riding fast like *whew*, but the horse here and there," he said, pointing at their horses and patting his horse's belly, "ain't no legs so much. Big boys likes water and walk. We walk yes no."

"We can't walk. Sorry," I told him, though I had compassion for their horses. They were beautiful animals, and I didn't know the circumstance of Harry and Arthur's condition or affiliation with Carl or how they managed to acquire horses of such showman quality. "How about Carthon? Blue? They doing okay?"

"You know Carthon," Carl answered. He watched Harry, who I could tell didn't like what I told him. "Might not be a bad idea if Harry and Arthur hang back, bring up a second raid on the white wagon if we're needing it."

Carl's idea had merit. We had no idea what we were in for whenever we caught up with the wagon. I presumed we'd face off against a lone kidnapper, but that was assumption through and through. "They capable?" I asked him.

"Are you?" Carl asked me in return.

Wow—I didn't expect that. In an instant, I was split between humility and resentment, trying to dial back my emotions, but knowing all my big talk was worthless until I willed it into the world. How many times did I consider the manners of justice I'd bring on Bethany's kidnapper, yet these were thoughts, stories, unchallenged in the safety of my mind. I'd never killed a man, and this would be my first. Story or not, something about that was scary. "Just saying, in case we're facing off against a small militia or something," I said.

"Small *militia*?" Katie asked. I couldn't tell if she was surprised at the possibility or thought I was insane for considering it. "Carl—what exactly are we looking at?"

"Like I told James," he answered Katie, "I saw a white wagon, real dirty, riding down the trail, and I could tell someone was inside. Never said it was his sister, but it stands to reason."

"So we don't even know if we're chasing your sister's kidnapper?" Katie asked, incredulous. She hopped off her horse and splashed water on her face. Her tone changed, and I could hear the anger. "So she could be halfway across Missouri, and you got us chasing *faith*? Are you serious?"

"I'm sure it's him," I said, confident. It had to be.

"You got no evidence," she said. I could tell she was dispirited, glancing back down the trail from where we rode. She paused, lost in thought. "You promise me, JT," she finally said, looking back at me while remounting her horse. "We make sure this white wagon's got your sister before we do anything that brings the judgment of God down on us. I'm all for justice, but not for mayhem."

"I promise you," I told her. I knew it was Bethany in that wagon—I just knew it. Don't know how or why, but my instinct wasn't nothing. It demanded to be listened to, like I was tapped into something much bigger at play, and no more explanation was possible. "I can't convince you," I said, "but it's her. I know it. Like the gears of destiny all turned so that this was the only path forward."

We rode another few miles over arid land, coated in a layer of fawn-colored powder. The forest thinned out, revealing below us an expansive plain carpeted with tall honeycomb hills, their convolutions high enough to hide within.

"Anyone see anything?" I asked, waving dust out of my face. The group shook their heads.

We descended into the lowland carefully, the dirt loose and rocky. "Look," said Harry, stopping before we reached the bottom and pointing ahead, off the trail to the north. A faint plume of smoke floated into the sky, seeming to come out of nowhere. "I know this land," he said. "Odd to be any such smoke—no, no, no. People *very* unusual way yonder out there."

I glanced at Carl. "Suspicious," I said, nodding. Together we led the group all the way down the hill, then off the trail into a steep ravine shrouded with shadows, which seemed to lead toward the smoke. Arthur's horse lost his footing along the bottom of the high crevasse and neighed loudly, to which I gave him a stern look. Should we be approaching the white wagon, our advantage relied on quiet. Arthur looked at Harry, who apparently didn't appreciate my silent reprimand, shooting me a stern look but keeping his mouth shut.

The sun wasn't yet high enough to penetrate the

labyrinth we traversed, crunching over sprouts of dead prairie grass and pockets of snow. We rounded the curves of this elaborately hewn piece of earth where storm and stone must have surely met each other's full force with adamant defiance. The network seemed to extend without end, occasionally opening into a small field here or there that abruptly ceased at the foot of even more steep hills. There was evidence of people, such as bits of trash thorned to sage bushes, but I figured that must have blown in since the wild terrain offered no comfort. With a cautious austerity, we advanced slowly through this strange environment, doing our best to follow the plume of smoke that quickly disappeared into the morning haze.

Further along, we approached the rising smoke, its source still hidden, until a familiar sound faded into earshot, just louder than the crunching brush under our horses' feet. I looked at Carl to see if he heard it too, but he shrugged his shoulders. Katie seemed frightened by our ominous and exotic surroundings, her wide eyes darting from the shadows and snow piles up to the hilltops. Carl and I looked at Harry, who most certainly did hear it. He held up his hand and moved it in a waving motion, like waves of water. That was it—it was the sound of a stream.

In silence, I led the group single file as we navigated toward the water through a tight, split between two hills, shadowed like night, our legs pulled up, the shoulders of our horses rubbing the ground by their sides, causing small tumbles of dirt and rock. They each slipped and regained their footing. The way gradually opened wider and spanned into a vast field to our right, a startling discovery in the middle of this bizarre landscape. We stepped past the boundary of the honeycomb hills and saw a land sunlit and covered in lush green grass. A few hundred yards off was a diagonal creek that zigzagged our direction through a narrow grove of young peachleaf willows, glittering sunlight filtering through.

The water was noisy, but not loud, and birds descended to its shore from tree branch perches, then back again, their silvery feathers reflecting the celestial fire which burned warm overhead, and somehow peaceful here. Near the birds and parked next to a campfire was a yellow and red gypsy wagon draped in strips of white silk along its roof. It was painted to resemble a mosaic of oriental rugs, gold filigree on maroon, each one aligned at right angles. It was as if the wagon itself was this serene, fleecy vestibule on whose entry fortunate souls would melt into the dreamy history of a thousand generations.

"Don't you see it, JT?" Katie asked me, whispering.

"See what?" I answered, hypnotized by the gypsy wagon.

"There," she said, pointing.

Beside the gypsy wagon was a white wagon, reflecting the sunlight. I squinted my eyes while they adjusted to keep from blinding. It was a box on wheels, sullied with spots of crud and mud splashes, with a bench seat built for one. The wagon itself was a cube and had holes drilled along the top — for air, I presumed. A miserable ride for anyone stuck inside.

"That it?" I asked Carl.

He nodded. "Yep."

We dismounted our horses quietly. I retrieved my guns and dug ammo from the pillowcase in the saddlebag. "Here," I said to Carl, handing him a pile of rounds and Pa's revolver. "You cover me." I gave Harry the .44 Henry rifle and a handful of ammo. "You know how to work a lever action?" I asked him.

Harry smiled, taking the rifle and quickly whipping the thing in a circle around his hand, yanking the lever open and closed as he twirled it under both arms and then up to a high-ready position, the stock tucked into his shoulder, prepared to draw down.

"What about you?" Katie asked me. She retrieved a small satchel with a shoulder strap from her saddlebag, inspecting its contents, then slung it over her head and tightened her ponytail.

"I'm good," I said, getting Pa's bowie knife from my saddlebag and unwrapping it from the flannel cloak. "I got a plan on what this looks like." Its sheen must have caught Carl's eye when I brandished it back and forth, feeling its weight, squeezing its soft wood handle.

"You trying to signal they got visitors?" he asked. "That part of your plan?"

I didn't answer but lowered the knife to my side, careful to keep it in the shade, then pulled the monocular from my saddlebag.

"So if that ain't it, what is it then? Your plan?" Carl asked.

We were concealed only by a bend in the hillside, and

there were no trees between our spot and the creek. If we were going to sneak up on them, we'd have to draw their attention elsewhere or pray to God they didn't see our advance across the field and through the tree grove. "How long you think it'd take to rush up on those wagons?" I asked.

"Horseback?" Katie asked. "Or on foot?"

"Good question," I said, thinking. If we were going to rush, might as well rush full-on and not half-ass it. "Horseback."

"You know Carthon could be there in a few seconds," Carl said. Smiling, he looked at the rest of our horses. "These other animals? I'd say a few minutes."

"Here's the plan then," I said. "Carl, you take Carthon and sprint to that hillside over there. If they see you, won't matter—you'll be faster than they can react. Tuck into that cleft there, looks like behind that pile of fallen rocks, and shoot off a few rounds over the wagons. While you're doing that, I'll ride up under the trees to the backside of their camp, hopefully unseen while they're trying to figure out whose firing on them. If you can draw them out, then I'll look around for Bethany and make sure she's there before we do anything else."

"What about us?" Katie asked.

"You guys hang back in case we need you to flank. If you hear me yelling, ride them horses of yours like they've never been ridden, and bring with you a hellfire vengeance for every injustice you've ever endured. Every injustice your kin ever endured." I looked at Harry and Arthur, still uncertain why they were willing to help me. They spoke a few words to each other in their native tongue, then nodded at me.

"Go on, Carl," I said, patting Carthon's head.

Carthon sprinted across that grass field faster than I'd seen him yet, kicking divots of sod from his hoofs far and long through the air. I raised the monocular to my eye and watched the wagons for any motion but saw none. If anyone was there, they must have been inside the gypsy wagon. Carl settled into his position, pushed Carthon deep behind the fallen rocks, then peeked his head out and looked at us. I signaled for him to fire.

Bullets rang out over the wagons, causing the birds to panic and fly off in a roaring murmuration, drawing attention to exactly where I aimed to ride. Carl looked over. "More," I said, signaling with my hands. The entrance at the back of the gypsy wagon was hidden from my view, but with the monocular I watched as a man—based on his boots and denim pants—hopped out and scampered for cover between it and the white wagon. Then a second pair of legs descended, covered in a long, layered gypsy dress. A woman I presumed. She stepped carefully to the ground, wearing anklets and sandals on her pudgy white feet. Both she and the man peered around the wagon to see who was shooting. By then, Carl had tucked himself back into the crack and was out of view. I watched the man reach up, his bandaged hand and grey-haired arm coming into view above the white wagon, knocking on the side of the gypsy wagon. A moment later, another pair of legs, those of a child, emerged from the back of the wagon wearing a pastel lavender day dress with a light petticoat underneath. I studied her shoes for purple stitching, wishing that damned magnifying device could bring me closer, but didn't see anything.

"What are you waiting for?" Katie asked me impatiently.

"That dress, it's Bethany's favorite color," I said, pointing.

"Well, are you going to ride or what!"

I threw the monocular back in the saddlebag and rode Buck as fast and quietly as possible—which wasn't that fast after all—while holding the bowie knife down at my side. I kept an eye on the folks between the wagons until we got to the trees. I crouched low under the branches while Buck trotted on the muddy creek bank, threading between the trees, ensuring we stayed behind the white wagon so they couldn't see us from the side. About twenty yards out, I hopped off Buck and tied his reins to a branch. Nearby were their three horses, each a different shade of grey, grazing. They eyeballed me as I walked through the cushiony grass until I was next to the white wagon, just feet away from these people. I stood with my back against the wagon, breathing deep and silent, clenching that heavy knife with all my strength and thinking of the creep that molested Bethany. Katie and the boys looked at me from the distance. I made an effort to gather myself, then nodded at them slowly, holding a finger up to tell them to wait.

Gotta make sure it's her, I told myself over and over, my nervousness growing out of control. I felt paralyzed and breathed deep, remembering the granary. A few breaths later I was able to push through the doubt and cement that fought to keep me motionless. *The fear was a conjuring.* Peeking through an air hole in the wagon, inside was much more comfortable than I expected. Beams of sunlight crisscrossed the interior, showing pillows and a few blankets—even a crate in the corner with bags of snacks and a jug of water. In my mind, I saw the face of that molester and knew whoever took Bethany was a different sort. Some greater level of sophistication, which I interpreted as a greater level of depravity.

While I scanned inside the wagon for a doll, a hair ribbon, any indication it was Bethany kept there, I heard the three folks on the other side whispering too low to make out the words. I strained to hear Bethany but couldn't. I couldn't see Carl from where I was either. I needed to tell Katie to tell him to fire more bullets—keep these people on edge. Waving both hands at her, I flung open my fisted fingers a few times and pointed toward Carl. She just stood there, perhaps unsure of what I was trying to tell her, so I held up my knife as if it were a gun and pretended to pull the trigger at the people here.

Harry said something to her, then to Arthur, and before I could stop him, he and Arthur sprinted their horses onto the field, running directly at the kidnappers. *What were they doing? I didn't tell them to charge!*

As he crossed the green grass, Harry pushed down his Stetson hat and untied his fox-skin cape which flew off behind him. He swung the rifle through the air from hand to hand like a baton and let out a tremendous screech, the same sound we'd heard during the massacre. I froze, realizing these Indian boys must be from the same group that killed Katie's family, and watched as her expression changed, her color running red. Still on horseback, Katie fell into a trance, fixed on Harry and Arthur. She walked Blue onto the grass, unconcerned with getting spotted by the kidnappers. I waved my arms to stop her, frantic, but she didn't see me. Like a woman possessed, her expression unbending, she pulled her gun and chased after them.

They all crossed the field, more gunshots ringing out. I heard the voices on the other side of the wagon speaking louder. A man was calling out directions, and the child stepped behind the white wagon along with the woman. I dropped to the ground to inspect their shoes, and there it was, Bethany's initials sewn into the cuff! It was Bethany!

More rounds came from Carl's direction, only moving closer, and I glanced under both wagons to see Carthon racing across the field toward the gypsy wagon. The gypsy woman gasped, and the man stepped behind the white wagon too, holding her and pulling Bethany to his side, all six of their legs clustered together, aquiver. Piercing the cacophony, the man pleaded for the assault to stop before gunshots split through the white wagon, splintering the wood, missing the group. They all crouched low to the ground, faces ashen with fear, strangers but for my sister. I looked into Bethany's terrified face from under the wagon, and she caught my gaze, her eyes growing large with surprise.

Shaking, and emboldened by determination, I got up, gripped that bowie knife, and sprinted to the back of the wagon. I came upon the old man, standing behind him—he didn't hear me in all the commotion. Trembling, I dropped the knife. In an instant, thoughts ran through my mind. I hesitated. This was a man before me, flesh and blood, and not a phantom. A man, once a boy, perhaps with his own Ma and Pa who tended his way through the early years. A man who—no doubt—lost that way and turned to lawlessness. Standing up slowly, he and the gypsy woman looked about, not noticing me there, with Bethany by their side. I could take her hand and be off, leaving these scoundrels once and for all. What more would killing bring to her safety at this point? But her safety was just part of this business. I recalled the promise I made to myself as Pa and I rode home from the lumbermill, the morning after Bethany was molested. Now was my opportunity to become the man I'd desired to be for so long.

I reached down and grabbed the knife. Throwing one arm around his throat, I plunged it deep between the old man's ribs. He gasped, his body convulsing, but I pulled harder on his throat with the bend of my arm, arching his back over my hip and shoving the knife to the hilt. Bethany screamed. I looked at her, so ashamed I didn't protect her before, pulled out the knife and sunk it again deep into his side, hot blood now pouring out over my hand. The man sucked for air and dropped to his knees while Carl rounded the gypsy wagon and jumped off his horse, shoving the woman to the ground and holding the revolver point blank to her forehead. Bethany's screams quieted until all that remained were the old man's gasps and the trickle of stream water in the distance.

For a moment, the chaos stopped. A brief moment of stillness set in, and I could swear I heard the flutter of birds' wings in the stream. Then two more gun shots shattered the stillness. Katie let out a scream that echoed in the valley. Setting the hilltops to quake, the gravely pitch of her voice separated into a searing symphony of anguish. Harry and Arthur's horses raced away, riderless.

Slowly, Blue trotted over, his hoofs audible in the grass as he carried Katie around the wagon beside Carl, her eyes wild and her hair a wind-whipped mess. I looked up at her, still holding the man in my arms. I gulped quietly while blood surged out through the slit between steel and skin, Bethany sobbing soundlessly behind me and pulling at my shirt.

"Got him," I said to Katie. She nodded, barely opening her mouth, then closing her lips again without saying anything.

"Where's Harry and Arthur?" I asked, but Katie just stared at me.

"James," Bethany cried, her body shuddering. "James, stop!" When I felt the man offer no more resistance, I released my grip and let him collapse to the ground, slumped onto his stomach and scarcely breathing.

"Bethany," I said, falling on my knees and pulling her into my arms, practically crying. Holding her felt like heaven. "You're safe now, Bethany," I said, shaking with excitement and barely able to speak. "You're safe." I smiled at Katie. She seemed to not notice but stared into the distance.

The woman Carl straddled on the ground was heavyset and dressed in fancy wear—colorful silks and garish gold-colored jewelry. Her many rings were massive, donning different colored gemstones, and her hair was tied back in a dark red scarf. She too was in shock, staring unblinkingly at the gun. "You gonna behave yourself, little lady?" he asked her.

She nodded, and Carl withdrew the weapon, uncocking the hammer and stepping back to keep an eye on her. Seeing the old man face down on the ground, she scrambled on hands and knees to his side, speaking to him softly.

"Anyone else with you?" Carl asked her. She didn't acknowledge him, so he shoved the end of the revolver against the back of her head. "Don't pretend you didn't hear me," he said. "Answer the question."

She shook her head frantically, her eyes filled with terror as she looked at him over her shoulder. "No, no—nobody else," she said in a cryptic accent that seemed both Russian and Italian. "Are you robbers? You want my things?"

"Unlike you and your partner here, we ain't thieves, woman," Carl said, seemingly offended by the suggestion.

Bethany cried into her hands. "You're okay, Bethany. Nothing bad is going to happen to you," I said. "Gonna take you home now."

"Where are Harry and Arthur?" I asked Katie again, but still, she didn't move.

Carl gave me a look to keep my eye on the gypsy

woman, and he walked around to the other side of the wagon, then walked slowly back. "She killed them," he said to me, indicating what Katie had done. His eyes were sad—understanding, but disappointed. "You killed them," he told her. "For no reason at all."

"Like hell I had no reason," Katie said, returning to life. "You heard that scream the other night, plain as I did. It was them that killed my family and all those people. You saying they didn't have it coming? You saying it wasn't them?"

Carl looked down, shaking his head. "No—ain't gonna say that. It was them the other night," he said.

Katie's eyes filled with fury, squinting at him. "You betrayed me. You betrayed me and JT, put us in danger, you son of a bitch." Her body twitched as I watched, antsy for some kind of catharsis, and she rested her hand on the handle of her holstered gun.

"Take it easy," I told Katie, helping Bethany to her feet. "We'll sort that out soon."

The woman wept, tending the old man. Bethany held the gypsy's shoulder gently. With eyes leaden by sorrow, my sister turned to me and moved her lips a couple times between quiet gasps of air before any sound came out. "*Wall*," she said, barely audible, then gradually louder. "*Wall. Wall.*"

"What's that, Bethany? What do you mean, *wall?*"

She took a deep breath and forced out the words, pointing at the dying old man. "Uncle Walter. That's Uncle Walter."

NINE

I grabbed the man by the arm and rolled him onto his back. The grass pillowed his head, and his skin was already pale from blood loss. "Is that you, Walter?" I asked. His eyes were clenched closed, and his wrinkled face was bearded in white hair that matched what hadn't yet fallen out of his balding head. He looked so different from the uncle I remembered—my tough uncle from New Hampshire—but it had been many years since seeing him. He opened his eyes, and there they were, penetrating and brown, with a glance that communicated strength and composure. Eyes that told bystanders this was a man of fierce integrity and unwavering goodwill.

"Why did you take Bethany?" I asked him, utterly confused and unsure if he heard my words.

"Did he hurt you?" I asked Bethany directly.

"No, James," she said, still crying. "Uncle Walter didn't

220

do anything bad. Why'd you hurt him?"

The gypsy woman rested Walter's head on her lap, combing his sparse hair away from his face with her fingers, a dozen thin gold bracelets jangling at her wrists. She looked up at me with contempt and disgust, her jaw clenched, and I could hear through those vicious eyes the curses she chastised me with in her mind.

"Why'd you do it, Walter?" I asked, desperate for him to answer. Kneeling by his head, I leaned close to his mouth, if only whispers remained. I felt dizzy and crushed inside. The rush of excitement that I'd brought justice into the world was torn apart by the love and respect I had for this great man. "Talk to me, Walter."

"Shh," the gypsy woman said to him, gently stroking his face, caressing his head. As she did, a cat walked up, rubbing its side on her back. It was Spooks, Bethany's missing cat. "He is a good man, you killed," she said. "A good man."

"Why did he kidnap Bethany?" I asked her, looking for Bethany. She was inside the white wagon, talking and holding her doll tightly, stifling her cries. "Why did he take her, and nobody knew? Why did you do that, Walter!"

"Relax," Carl said to me. His voice was calming. I looked at him as if the clarity he brought to every moment could be extracted and imposed down on this quandary. "Trust your instincts," he said.

Trust my instincts. As I looked down at him, my instincts told me Walter was a good man, and he was the same man he'd always been. I was desperate for understanding. "But why, Walter? Can't you answer me?"

"James," Carl said. His voice was muffled. *"James!"* He repeated himself over and over, louder each time until I heard him clearly, and understood he was trying to get my attention. I finally looked at him. "Can't you hear me? I'm right here yelling the whole time!"

"Yeah," I said, numb.

"Help me get your uncle up," Carl said. "Patch that wound."

We propped Walter up, Katie and the woman holding him while I lifted his shirt. He looked at me, his deep, compassionate eyes filled with tears, before coughing and spitting blood in the grass. He labored to speak but was unable. Again, he spit up blood. I was moved by emotion, and cried silently, anguish displacing my confusion. "Carl," I said. "Can you go inside the wagon for a rag? Anything to put over this wound?" He ran off and returned a moment later with a towel. I took it and pressed it to the cuts, but blood pushed its way around the borders and dripped down his back. "There," I said, pointing at the strips of silk along the top of the wagon. "Rip that down and hand it to me."

The silk ribbon was long, and I was able to wrap it tightly around Walter's body a few times, completely covering the towel, securing it in place with a knot. Inhaling slowly, his chest rose high, a faint gurgle from deep inside. The muscles of his neck jutted out profusely, surrounding his windpipe, each band of its anatomy visible. He could breathe. It was exceedingly strenuous for him, though I believed we could get him to Topeka where he could be saved before his energy ran out.

I watched him, waiting to make sure he didn't need anything before we'd mount up and ride. I sat by his side and listened to him, and also heard the breeze in the tree branches. Turning, I saw the birds dart back and forth from their perches to the creek and dip their beaks in the cool water. Overhead, wispy clouds glided slowly over the frost-colored sky. The scene surprised me by its tranquility. I turned to Walter. His skin remained pale, but he'd regained some strength.

While I tended Walter, Carl looked off toward Harry and Arthur, their bodies still and contorted on the field as they landed from their horses. Their repose was indistinguishable from those Rebellion soldiers of years past. Katie noticed his glance and seemed to turn inward, her expression becoming placid, her eyes distant. *What really separated any of us from each other?* I wondered, realizing with a visceral clarity how insane hatred was. Part of me lay dead with Harry and Arthur, and part of Katie, and Carl, and every living person—not physically, but spiritually, in that flow at humanity's back, now a little grimier, a little murkier.

"Will you help me bury them?" Carl asked Katie.

Her eyes sharpened. "Why should I bury them?" she said, her ire returning. "Let 'em rot out there. Let the birds get them. You saw what they did."

"Those two boys," Carl answered, "were more heroic than you'll ever know. It was them you heard that night, but they wasn't raiding. Harry and Arthur rode together between their kin, pleading for them to stop. Harry made that noise as a warning, so passersby would know to stay clear. One of his kin wasn't having it, so he swung his club but missed Harry, landing Arthur square in the throat, which is why he ain't said one peep since then. Their family chased them both off, exiling them, till I found them wandering in the forest." Carl looked down, then raised his head, his eyes red. "I been through some shit in my life. God help us all if there ain't no reparation in this world." He paused, and we all watched Katie take in his words, motionless. "You should bury them," he went on, "because they were helping us save Bethany as a way to make amends. Because they were trying to right a wrong, even if it wasn't their wrong to correct. Because those boys were full of life and goodness, and you snuffed it out for your own simple ignorance."

Katie looked at me, and I could see the struggle going on in her head, believing Carl but not wanting to, knowing he was right but unable to believe. She stood, antsy and shifting her weight, avoiding eye contact with him.

"If that's pride holding you back," I told her, "then know it's an illusion. You think it's real, but it's not. You should help Carl."

Carl walked off toward Harry and Arthur's bodies in silence. Reluctant at first, Katie looked at me, then followed him onto the field, her shoulders drooping. I continued to monitor Walter's gradual improvement, both of us watching Carl and Katie carry Harry, then Arthur's, body to the creek bank. The horses looked on as Katie fell to her knees and wept silently by their sides. Carl retrieved a small shovel from his gear and dug under the only white pine tree in the grove.

"We'll get you to town," I told Walter. "They'll help you there."

He reached out and touched my leg, nodding as if to tell me to slow down a little. Again, he coughed, this time bringing up less blood, and tried speaking. Words didn't come out, but his gaze fixed on me. He lifted his hand, resting it on my arm.

"What is it, Walter?" I asked. "What do you need?"

He looked at the gypsy woman, now standing next to me, and motioned for her to come close. She knelt down. Wheezing, he whispered, "Show him. Show him the papers."

"We don't have time, Walter," I demanded. The woman looked at me, confused. "Not now," I told her.

Walter coughed and spit in my direction, his expression insistent. Again he looked at the gypsy woman, signaling toward her wagon. He cleared his throat. "Please," he said to her. "Go."

Only because Walter looked stronger still, and blood had stopped trickling from the bandage, did I follow the woman to her wagon. "Do you know why he did this?" I asked her as we entered.

"Did what?" she asked, walking to the far corner. Inside, the wagon was embellished with shiny medallions. It was just as colorful and ornate as outside, except with soft linens and down, rather than wood, and it smelled like fresh roses in spite of the winter season. Light shined in through rectangular patches of weathered alabaster canvas along the walls just under the ceiling, setting all the colors on fire with an extraordinary vibrance. The woman stood at a medicine table, which was installed under an oval mirror and lantern sconce. An assortment of colored glass bottles were arranged in a wood lattice rack on its surface. From a shallow drawer, she pulled out a handful of letters, and squinted at me, slowly offering them. "Are you asking why he protected your sister?" she said, yanking the papers away before I could take them.

"Protect her from what?"

The woman shook her head. "He told me," she said. "He told me everything."

"I don't know what the hell you're talking about, woman," I said, frustrated.

"My name is Kezia, not woman. You show me respect," she demanded. "You pretend to not know, yet you lived with him every day of your life."

"Just give me the damned letters," I said, grabbing them out of her hand. There was no time for pointless bickering with this stranger.

There were at least a dozen letters, handwritten by my ma and all addressed to Walter in New Hampshire. They dated back over a year, and skimming a few I stopped at one in particular, reading it under my breath.

November, 1869

Dear Walter,

It is with a heavy heart that I again beg you to take up my request. I fear our situation is growing out of hand, and without your assistance I'll be forced to take matters into my own hands. I know you never approved of my romance with Sherriff Lock, and you probably think that miscarrying the baby he gave me was punishment for my sins. But you don't understand my plight. My desperate hope that life with Daryl should improve is nearing exhaustion. His beatings and violent rages have become more frequent. Thus, I write to inform you of my plan to leave him. Retain this letter, and refer to it as needed.

Upon hearing of your pledge to aid me, and with the help of Sheriff Lock, I will initiate our plan to frame Daryl for assault. We have a vagrant willing to scare Bethany to the extent of inflaming Daryl's passion for justice, but not exceeding the decency belonging to an irreproachable girl such as her. Worry not for this vagrant— the Sheriff assures me he will be safe. Take shelter from the cold in our barn, and I will bring you Bethany when Daryl is safely detained. I will entrust you with my daughter and ask you to make arrangements for her care. In a few months' time, and after Bethany's search and rescue efforts fail, I will convince Daryl she was killed. I will blame him for neglecting his duty as husband and father, and leave him—vindicated in the eyes of the courts and of men. I will rejoin Bethany, and together we will begin a new, valiant life.

Send word of your commitment as soon as you can, dear brother.

Sincerely,
Your devoted, loving sister, Cecelia

The information was shocking. I had my issues with Ma, but she remained my mother. I tried holding onto the image I had of her, but it crumbled in my grip. "These are lies," I told Kezia, shaking the papers at her. The whole situation here was ridiculous. Mute memories of Ma's recent peculiar behavior played in the back of my mind. Dumbfounded, I looked at Kezia as if she knew what I was reading. "They're all lies," I said again. But she looked at me with the same disdain from earlier. Thumbing through the letters, I found a more recent one dated January, 1870:

Dear Walter,

I've received confirmation of your arrangement to arrive next month, and am elated with your dedication to the welfare of your sister and niece. My heart is light with joy, and I am optimistic for the first time in many years. I must confess, in the absence of your commitment these past months, I'd fantasized about killing Daryl. It's a wonder that more women don't fantasize likewise, so many husbands abusive, especially under the wiles of drink the way Daryl is. He's poisoned our marriage and has poisoned James against me. The disrespect my son harbors for me is truly heartbreaking, and in spite of Benjamin's death, I dream James might return to me absent the pernicious influence of his father. A mother's capacity for love and forgiveness knows no bounds. And for this reason alone have I chosen to wait for your arrival, to enact our plan, and spare Daryl the vial of poison I've been hiding in my bedroom end table. If not for James's steadfast presence, I would certainly expedite my escape from this marriage.

Walter, accept my sincere gratitude. You are a genuine hero.

With love and appreciation,

Cecelia

"Did Walter show you these?" I asked Kezia, holding up the letters.

"I didn't read them," she said. She closed the drawer and rifled through the glass bottles, pushing the corks down before lifting them to read their labels. "He didn't show me."

"Did he ever talk about his sister? My ma?"

"Yes—he talked about her. He said she had trouble, but as long as you were there, she couldn't do anything." Finding what she was looking for, Kezia removed a pink bottle and tilted it up to the sunlight, inspecting its contents. "Has she killed him, then?"

"What are you talking about?" As I asked, she bristled past me with the bottle and returned outside. In the moment since reading this letter, it hadn't donned on me that I wasn't home and this might be the opportunity Ma'd been waiting for. *Holy shit... Would she really do it?* She'd been so different, so disconnected, I could honestly say it was a possibility. I stuffed all the letters in my trousers' pockets and followed Kezia out.

"Bethany," I said, leaning into the back of the white wagon. I noticed Kezia pulling away the wrap on Walter's back and pouring a viscous amber liquid over the wound from her jar. "We have to go."

Bethany stepped out and went to Walter's side. From the creek, Carl and Katie looked our way then walked over while I went into the white wagon and grabbed Bethany's doll and a blanket.

"What's going on?" Carl asked.

"I think my pa's in trouble," I said to them.

I handed the two letters I read in full to Carl, then held up the others for Katie to see. "Read that. My ma's been writing Walter for over a year, saying if me and Bethany weren't there, she had a mind to kill my pa. You coming?"

"You know I am, James," Carl answered.

"What about them?" Katie asked, nodding at Harry and Arthur.

"Let the dead bury their dead," Carl replied.

I ran and untied Buck, then brought him over. "Bethany, can you ride?"

"Yeah, I can ride."

"Good. Walter, do you think you can ride? Or would you rather wait here for help?" I figured he'd want to wait, his condition appearing much improved.

Though kindhearted, Walter was a tough son of a bitch. He took a deep breath, this time his face not scrunching in pain as much as before. "No, I'll be good," he whispered, his breathing now a deliberate task. "I can wait."

Without warning, Walter grabbed the side of his chest, rolling onto the grass. He clenched his eyes, gritting his teeth in sheer agony. Not breathing, his face turned red, the hue shifting to purple after a moment until he was able to force in a slight measure of air. Kezia and I dropped to his side, asking if there was anything we could do. But there was nothing. Bethany shook with fear. We all looked at each other, convinced Walter was going to die, though his ability to breathe steadily became easier and in a few minutes he returned to his prior condition.

"You're not staying," I told him. I looked around, knowing how difficult it would be to move him on horseback.

"Kezia," I said, pointing to a clearing to the west of our location, "is that the way you brought the wagons in?"

"Yes," she said. "But that's no good. If you ride to Topeka, that way is back-tracking. You will add an hour at least to the journey. His wagon is no good. The wheels. And my wagon is heavy. Slow."

Fuck, I thought. *How the hell am I going to move him on horseback?* If we had to ride horses, his best bet would be to ride with Carl, since Carthon was the fastest. But at the same time, he was also the least muscular, and Walter was a big man. Carl was skin and bones, and he'd have a time balancing Walter horseback while they rode. That left Buck, and while we wouldn't be the fastest to Topeka, he would surely have the strength to get us there.

"Carl," I said. "Help me get Walter onto Buck. Then you ride ahead to Topeka and get help. Bring a doctor and meet us on the trail where he can make sure Walter's okay for the remainder of the trek."

"Yep, let's do that," Carl agreed.

I got behind Walter. "Can you stand up? Carl, grab that arm." We slowly helped him to his feet, the pain causing him to breathe deep. "Just a little more," I said, pulling even harder. Walter just had to straighten his legs to be upright, but the pain was too much. He gasped, holding his breath, then let out a scream and fell to the ground. He rolled away from the stab wounds, arching his back and straining for the bandage, just out of reach.

Kezia and Katie went to his side, while Bethany stood back, staring in fear. "He can't do it," Katie said, looking at me. I wasn't sure he'd recover, his energy so spent. It took longer than last time, but he regained his breath, his color somewhat returning to his face.

"You go easy, Walt," Kezia said to him, stroking his hair again. She stared at me. "If this man dies, I swear to God and all His angels I will have vengeance. I'll enlist the devil himself to find you and make you pay." Having explained myself so much already, there was nothing else I could say to her. We had no time to spare.

I grabbed Buck and pulled him alongside Walter, then laid him down on the ground by his side. "Let's try one more time, Carl," I said. "All right, Walter, we're going to do all the work. You just have to bear the pain for a minute, and we'll be done." He held up a finger to me, asking for just a moment while he gathered himself, then nodded his head that it was okay for us to proceed.

"Same thing as last time, Carl," I said, "except we're not pulling him up—we're pulling him across Buck's back." As swiftly as we could, we dragged his body onto Buck. "Katie," I said. "We need your help." Together, we positioned Walter in the saddle, while he breathed heavy, gritting his teeth. "Almost done, Walter," I said, wrapping a rope around his waist and each leg.

"Up boy," I said to Buck, yanking on his bridle. Getting on his feet took that muscular animal no effort at all. Carl and Katie stood on either side of Walter, each holding a leg, balancing him as I tied the rope beneath Buck's belly. Unlike Buck, however, Walter had no strength left and wobbled unsteadily.

"He won't stay up there much longer," Katie said. "He's gonna fall off. You have to do something,"

I hopped onto Buck behind Walter, sitting bareback and grasping him in my arms. "I got you this time," I told him. Buck's spine was a biting chain of knots in my underside. This was not going to be an enjoyable ride. "I wish we could put you in a wagon," I said, imagining how comfortable he'd be in Kezia's plush accommodation. Looking again toward the flat clearing, I noticed puffs of dust and an escalating thunder rising from far off.

Three men on horseback, and a giant overweight woman in boots were coming through. The latter was in a bowler's hat and white nightgown with a rancher's coat overtop, carried in a small wagon drawn by two horses. They rode onto the grass, the sound of their chase quieting.

"You stop there!" the woman yelled at us, her booming voice carrying over the narrowing expanse between us. I saw the sunlight glint off a badge on one of the men's chests and assumed they must be lawmen. "You're under arrest for what you done to my Mel!"

"Let's go!" I yelled to the group. "Bethany, get on Walter's horse and follow close. Carl, Katie, let's go."

"You send word to me in Pecos, Texas that Walter is healthy," Kezia demanded of me. My capacity for her attitude quickly dwindled to nothing, and I had no interest in her words. "You make me wait too long and I'll find you myself." Her voice dripped with hatred. I looked at her, unsure if she was crazy or dead serious, while Bethany ran back to the wagon, reached in and pulled out a large purse.

"Spooks," she called out, throwing the bag strap over her shoulder. She looked frantically under both wagons and by the firepit.

"Leave him!" I yelled. Clarabelle and the lawmen were gaining on us rapidly. Our window for escape was closing. "We don't have time!"

"No," Bethany yelled back at me, starting to cry. Finally, Bethany spotted Spooks behind one of the wagon wheels and scooped him up into the bag. She hopped onto Walter's horse.

As fast as possible, we rode to the cut where we entered this prairie, my balancing Walter while commanding Buck requiring some struggle. I led us through the tight pass, advancing slowly. Though his breathing had improved, Walter was in significant pain. He tottered, perhaps not intentionally, and I strained with all my energy to hold him up. My underside cramped in agony, each step of Buck's like a knife stabbing me from beneath. I leaned into Walter to roll off my tailbone, feeling the wetness of his blood soaking into my shirt from his. Like before, our horses slipped on the loose dirt, navigating this steep cleft of earth, and regained their footing with difficulty. I held Walter's legs up with both arms, while pulling my own legs out of the way of the hillsides. Walter lost his balance through the rugged slot, falling sideways, but luckily braced from toppling off by the slope of dirt long enough for me to right his bearing. Buck breathed heavy, whimpering, his massive muscles twitching—I assumed from exhaustion—but we finally made it through, though we weren't to the trail yet. I studied the ground to see if I'd recognize our path.

"Follow me," Carl said, taking the lead. He navigated us

with deftness through the maze of small mountains back onto the trail. We stopped and looked back, not hearing the lawmen. "Ha-yah!" he yelled, snapping his reins, and we climbed the long hill that led out of the basement of this labyrinth as fast as we could.

As he ascended, Bethany's horse slid on the loose dirt and fell on his front knees with all his weight, throwing Bethany from his back, and dislocating his shoulders. The disfigured horse floundered onto his back and wailed in ear-piercing agony, his forelimbs splayed out like bat's wings. He skidded to the bottom of the hill, screaming, while Bethany watched in terror.

"Don't look at him, Bethany," I yelled to her. "Don't look at the horse, just look at me." I turned to Carl. "Can you make sure Walter doesn't fall off?"

As Carl rode over, I hopped off of Buck and handed him the reins. "I got him," Carl said. He negotiated Carthon alongside of Buck so that Walter was right by his side. Reaching over, he wrapped his arm around the older man's shoulder. "I got you Walter, don't worry."

"See if you can't get him up this hill," I said to Carl before running down the hill to Bethany's aid. Katie brought Blue to Buck's other side, and together she and Carl led Buck and Walter to the top without incident.

Bethany's horse cried so loud. He tossed his head left and right, slamming it in the ground, desperate to be rid of the suffering. "Come on," I said, facing my sister and making sure she was okay. "Can you get up this hill?" She was strong, and fighting the urge to glance at the horse, stared at me with stoicism. "Go on. Get up there," I said, pointing toward the others. As soon as she walked away, I slit the throat of Walter's horse with my whittling knife, careful to avoid the deluge of steaming hot blood, then caught up with her, holding her hand the rest of the way.

"I'll take her," Katie said from atop her horse, reaching her hand out to Bethany. She stepped up on Blue's stirrup and swung onto his back.

I climbed onto Buck, taking the reins from Carl and noticing Walter's color running white, his eyes heavy. From a distance, concealed by the hills, the lawmen yelled for us to stop, then yelled at each other trying to figure their way out of the maze.

"Let's move," I said. "I don't think we've got much time. Carl, bring help. Whatever you have to do, just bring it."

"I'll see you soon," Carl said. Snapping his reins, he disappeared down the trail for Topeka.

"Thirsty," Walter said in a whisper. It was clear our horses could use a drink as well.

"There's a stream a few miles up," I said. "Let's get there first. You gonna be okay, Walter?" He nodded, turning his head to the side slightly as if trying to look at me. His breathing seemed steady, though his deliberate movements and determined countenance told me he was still in pain. "Carthon's the fastest horse I've ever seen. Carl will be back soon with help. Maybe even meet up with us at the stream." I knew that wouldn't happen, since there were many miles between the stream and Topeka, but I wanted Walter to stay positive. "You're going to be okay. Trust me. You just have to stay strong."

We made it to the stream without any indication the lawmen were approaching. As the horses drank, I looked back for them, nervous, then up the trail to the forest where Katie and I found Carl and the Indian boys. "I don't think you should come down, Walter," I said. "If you do, I'm not sure Katie and I can get you back up." He didn't answer, holding his body as still as he could.

I hopped off Buck and walked to fill my canteen, my ass screaming in agony with every step. I handed the water to Walter, but he was unable to take it from me. After leading Buck to a rock, I stood on top of it and held the water to Walter's mouth. His eyes were closed, not necessarily squeezed shut from pain, but resting as if exhausted. He tilted his head back taking small sips, his white beard aglow in the sunlight, and I noticed his lips a shade of plum.

"You all right?" I asked him. Again, he didn't say anything. I lifted his shirt to check the wound and saw runny blood staining his skin. It was more watery than normal blood and ran into the back of his pants. "Looks like this is giving you problems," I said. I pulled the silk ribbon and towel away from the cuts to inspect, and all around the injury his skin was purple. Parts of the cuts opened and closed like little mouths as he shifted in the saddle. "Katie," I said. "Check this out."

She came over and looked, no more experienced with such injuries than I was. "Maybe it's just cleaning itself out," she said. "See that clear liquid? That's better than blood, right?"

"Walter," I said. "You sure you can't talk?" He looked at me and nodded, holding his lips shut. Through the pain he had a peace about him. "All right then," I said. "Let's make for that forest and wait for those lawmen to pass us by."

We rode for a half-hour or more to the forest edge, then trotted into the dense wood until finding a clearing. The ground was soft. The felled tree trunks and blackened campfire rocks reminded me of where we'd camped the night before. "Let's stop here. Just until those guys pass. Then we've got to get back on the trail so Carl doesn't miss us. Walter, I hope it's okay, but I want to leave you up there still. Hopefully Carl returns with a doctor and a wagon soon, so you won't be on horseback much longer."

I hopped off of Buck while Katie brought Blue alongside my horse and steadied Walter from falling. Bethany, sitting in front of Katie, reached her hand out and put it on Walter's knee. "Keep an eye on him for me, will you Bethany?" I said.

During the war, Ma and Pa kept her sheltered from the carnage. She was only two then, too little to really understand what was happening, but such sights would have been devastating just the same. Ever since Pa and I got back from Westport, I sometimes thought I smelled faint hints of the putrid, rotting stench of death on evening breezes and wondered if I was the only one. I'd ask Bethany, "You smell that?" and she'd always look at me funny, like I farted or something. But I was happy my mind played tricks on me. Even from the slightest offense, Bethany remained undefiled. So much had changed these past few days...

"Keep quiet if you can," I said, trying to smile at her.

I walked back to the trail, hiding in the trees, waiting for the lawmen. After maybe twenty minutes, the three of them rode directly past our location and kept on riding. They were an ornery-looking bunch, ugly with greasy hair that flowed from under greasy hats, and even their horses were unbrushed. I watched another ten minutes to make sure they didn't return and decided it was safe to keep riding.

"*James,*" Bethany yelled as I turned to walk back. She stood just outside the clearing, her bag with Spooks still over her shoulder. "James, hurry!" I rushed to her.

Walter's limp body hung from Buck's side, one leg tangled in the rope and bound up next to Buck's saddle while his head and upper body lay on top of the dirt, bent at the waist, right where I stabbed him. Katie yanked on the rope, trying to free him. I pulled the whittling knife from my belt and cut the rope away. Walter's body flopped onto the ground, motionless. His hair was dirty with dry leaves, and his face scraped by the rough earth. I raised his shirt, seeing nothing escaping the wound this time. His lips were more purple than before, his skin a shade whiter, and I suspected his heart was stopping.

"What do we do?" Katie asked, frantic, but nowhere to put her energy.

Bethany stood behind me as I knelt by Walter's side, his breath now little gasps. I knew there was nothing I could do—nothing, in all likelihood, a doctor could do either. This was it. "I'm sorry, Uncle Walter," I said, placing my hand on top of his hand. I lowered my head, barely able to look at him. "I'm so sorry."

He gazed up at me, his eyes growing distant, perhaps watching the clouds in the sky. Something about those brown eyes of his caught my full attention. He moved his mouth, the sound of his breath barely audible. He mustered his strength, straining to speak, staring directly into my eyes. "James," he said, his voice a slight rustle. "It's okay. I forgive you."

As I looked at him, all I could think of was the ride he took me on as a child, through the New Hampshire birch trees—a prelude I realized to the mysterious experiences I'd had on the Santa Fe. I recollected a crystal sense of transcendence, a oneness with nature, and in this instant as I leaned over Walter, looking into his eyes, I recognized as plain as day how *all* our so-called knowledge was a feeble construct of an imperfect imagination. Fear truly wasn't the only conjuring. His eyes widening, fixing in the heavens as though charting the trajectory of his spirit, Walter gasped a final time. Then he rested. The earth pulled to reclaim its vessel as the color of his skin washed down, his jaw dropped, and all the joints of his body sunk into the duff, releasing their tension.

I felt myself hovering weightless, my stomach nauseated. In a bright flash, I launched out of myself, the world around me fading, tumbling into pieces as I flew faster and faster. I saw my knowledge as a far-off monument, resilient in a blinding hot sun. Flying closer, I recognized that monument was built from sand, which crumbled before me. I didn't just lose Walter—I lost *everything*.

Katie touched my shoulder. I looked up at her red, sorrowful eyes as she stood over me in silence—the blue sky past the outline of her radiance, a halo. Her loving smile snapped me back to her presence. The world, like those grains of pollen, seemed to assemble all around me at the moment I gazed on it. Constantly refreshed, I sensed a transfigured reality, one in perpetual flux and utterly dependent on our involvement.

I reflected on wanting so badly to be like the men I always admired, judging their worthiness in terms of ferocity rather than sensibleness. I was angry at myself for wanting so badly to earn redemption in my mother's eyes and respect in my pa's, rather than cutting the umbilical cord once and for all and damning the opinions of others—no matter who they were. A small hatred for my parents kindled in my chest, but I knew it was misplaced and that my horror belonged toward me, for my own faintheartedness to chart an independent path through life. Ma was right about my being a coward—more than I could ever imagine. Manhood wasn't meeting and exceeding the virtues of other men but detaching from all those stories and being exactly who I was created to be—exactly who I decided to be.

"Should we bury him?" Katie asked softly. I looked at her, tears running down my face, then looked over at Bethany who stood next to Buck. My heart ached for what she was surely feeling. I walked to her, not thinking to answer Katie.

"Hey," I said. I reached down and petted Spooks, still in her bag. "I'm sorry, Bethany. Nobody knew what happened to you. We all thought you were kidnapped. Another trail creep." She looked at me, understanding, and I knew she loved me still. "You know how things are at home. I hoped if I rescued you, things'd be different."

"Uncle Walter said everything was planned," she said quietly. "When Ma took me to him that night, he gave me a big hug and said I was going to stay with a close friend of his until Ma came and got me."

"I know," I said. "That was in the letters. She was going leave Pa for good and get you once he thought you were dead."

Bethany looked at me with huge eyes. "But what about you, James?"

"I don't know … I guess live with Pa." We both cried, realizing Ma planned to split our family, keeping me and Pa in the dark while she ran away with Bethany and Sheriff Lock, presumably. "I guess Ma wanted me to think you were dead too."

We all stood over Walter's body for a moment in silence. "He deserves a proper burial," I said. Though I pondered a thousand reasons to leave him where he lay, there was no room in my decision for argument. With Katie and Bethany's help, we used the rope to pull him onto Buck, then wrapped his body with it, around the saddle horn, and cinched it tightly against the swell so he wouldn't bounce off. We mounted our horses, Bethany again with Katie, and walked toward the trail. I held Buck's reins with one hand, and placed my other hand on Walter's back, holding this holy man as yet every moment I could. Back on the Santa Fe, we brought the horses to a run, making our way through the forest.

After some time, Carl raced directly toward us, Carthon keeping pace with another man riding in a buckboard wagon drawn by two horses. We all stopped when we caught up to each other.

"Suppose you won't be needing me after all," the man in the wagon said. He gazed at Walter's body, and perhaps noticed the reverence with which I tended it. Looking further up and into my eyes, I could see his were wet and welling with tears. He tipped his hat at me, holding the brim with his thumb and first finger.

"I'm sorry, James," Carl said, sadness in his eyes. He nodded, whispering silently to himself, then turned to the man in the wagon. "Thank you anyway," he said. "I'm sorry I don't have anything to offer for your kindness."

"Wouldn't be kindness if I expected payment," the man said. He made the sign of the cross. "Godspeed."

Our mood was somber as we rode the trail back toward Topeka, and Leavenworth after that. There was little cause for optimism. Taking Ma's word for it, Pa was in serious danger. Even if she didn't use the poison on him, Sheriff Lock might try and expedite his trial and sentencing—a sentence of death, he'd promised. We needed to get back to show the evidence—Ma's handwritten letters—that Pa was framed and this whole scheme cooked up by the crooked sheriff and a wicked woman.

We passed Topeka and made it to the Kansas river by sundown. On shore, another man sat in the chair where the big man was seated a couple days prior. The big man's dead body was no longer in the water. Carl fired the revolver in the sky to get this man's attention, and we called out, waving our arms in the air to bring the ferry over so we could cross. He got up from his chair and moped onto the float, pulling the overhead rope to draw himself across.

The ferry approached, and I saw it was no man piloting the craft, but a scraggly, parsnip-headed boy wearing the same wool suit of his predecessor. Without waiting for him to lower the ramp, the three of us rode our horses onto the ferry. From nowhere, the lawmen came into view, gaining quickly on us.

"Where did they come from!" Katie said.

"I have no idea," I said. "Hey boy, we gotta get across. *Now*."

He held his hand out, the sleeve of his coat draping low off his arm and looked at me through half-shut eyes. "Fifteen cents," he said.

"Come on," Katie said, "they're catching up."

"Each," the boy said. He slowly turned his body, counting us on his fingers. "One ... two," he said, adding another finger to his count. He looked at me again. "Three."

"We ain't got time for this shit, boy," Carl said. He maneuvered Carthon around so that his backside faced the boy, grabbed both of Carthon's ears, and gave them a sharp yank. Carthon reared up on his front legs and kicked with his back legs, launching the boy off the ferry and into the turbulent water. We watched for a second while the boy's triangular head bobbed above the water like a cork, catching his breath, his arms flailing but his indolent facial expression unchanged, looking at us through dull, disinterested eyes.

Carl winked at Katie and me. "He gets a kick out of it," he said, laughing into his fist.

The lawmen were yards away now, but we managed to pull far enough offshore that their horses couldn't jump onto the craft. They yanked their sidearms from their holsters, brandishing them and telling us to stop, to bring the ferry back to shore. One by one, they walked their horses into the water, holding the overhead rope for support, and slowly crossed the river behind us.

"If they get across, they're likely to find us eventually," Katie said as we all heaved on the overhead rope, slowly gliding across the river.

"Well, we ain't shooting them, if that's what you mean," I said.

"I didn't say that, but we gotta get rid of them."

She was right. We had to lose them. "Grab hold tight," I said to her and Carl. "I'm going to cut the rope. They'll be forced to go back or get swept down the river." I waited until they were far enough in that the water flowed hard, then sliced through the thick fibers from the back of the ferry. Instantly, the rope went slack, and the ferry swung downstream, traversing the remainder of the way across the river in the process. In a tug-of-war, we all fought hand over blistering hand to keep the ferry from plunging downstream, while the lawmen were powerless against the current, them and their horses getting washed away.

"Keep holding!" Carl yelled. Bethany stood behind him doing her best to yank on the rope. But the water was too strong, and with so much weight on the craft, there was no way we had the strength to pull ourselves across.

"What about them?" Katie asked, muscles bulging from her graceful arms.

"They're … fine," I said between breaths, glancing at the lawmen long enough to see them and their horses scrambling for the riverbank. I gathered the slack of rope from behind Bethany and tied it to the side of the ferry before our grips exhausted, and we all let go. The ferry jolted as the rope ran out, and the horses pranced in place to keep their balance.

"This isn't going to hold," I said, seeing the ferry pull apart. Not far away was a fallen cottonwood tree, its thick branches in arm's reach. I stretched out and grabbed hold, bushwhacking as hard as I could. Carl, Katie, and Bethany grabbed branches too. I jumped into the water thinking I'd have more leverage to hold the ferry, freezing cold up to my waist, but that raft was too heavy, the current too strong. While the others held their branches, I grabbed Buck's reins and pulled him into the water. He splashed in next to me, then jumped onto the shore, followed by Carthon and Blue. "Come on!" I yelled at the others, the raft snapping and cracking apart.

Katie hopped in and reached her hand out for Bethany, the massive timber where the rope was tied now separating from the rest of the boat. We leaned sideways; our feet driven into the silt to keep from getting swept away. "Hurry!" Katie said to her, but Bethany was petrified. Strands of rope popped like wire strings under the strain. Carl picked her up and handed her to us as the rope broke free. He jumped onto the cottonwood branches, navigating through the web of wood to dry land just before the river consumed the raft, turning it into chum which leaped to the surface, a lunging flotilla of wreckage. Together, Katie and I helped Bethany to shore, the horses just watching.

Dripping wet, the three of us lay on dry land catching our breath, staring up at the sunset sky. Behind us, Carl whispered to the horses, patting them down. "Everyone good?" I asked.

"Horses are good," he answered. "Likely cold due to being wet, but I wouldn't know anything about that," he finished, unable to contain his laughter.

"Katie," I said. "Will you help me throw Carl into the river? *Please*?"

She looked at me and rolled her eyes, then craned her neck to see him. "You're damn right I'll help you, JT!"

I had no energy to get up. "Well," I said, "we got a full day of riding before making it home."

"Look around, JT. We ain't got a full day," Katie said.

Bethany sat up and looked at me. "I'm hungry, James."

Not only were we hungry and exhausted, but our journey back to Leavenworth would take us through wooded ground and made us vulnerable to wolf attack—or worse. I was desperate to get home for Pa but calmed by the same sense that told me Bethany would be okay. Again, there were no words, no logic, but a feeling that said we should get our rest and tomorrow wouldn't be too late. Throughout childhood I struggled to understand what people meant by having faith. I always assumed faith was a decision, an intention of the mind rather than an opening and a receiving by the heart. And to be fair, maybe this wasn't faith at all. Maybe it was some sort of psychic listening. But words were clumsy, and however I described it would never really capture the sense. I hadn't chosen my mysterious experiences on the trail, and I wasn't choosing to believe Pa would be fine for one more day, but both were undeniable.

I helped Bethany to her feet. "Let's camp, then," I said. We walked our horses toward the trail, then hopped on and rode up to where I'd seen encampments before. I found a clearing with an intact ring of rocks not far from the river where we built a fire, lighting buffalo dung with a kindling of dry weeds, and took turns taking our horses to the river for a drink.

"Sorry I forgot your blanket, Bethany," I said. "You can have my jacket though." I untied my boots, then took my pants off and draped them over a rock next to the fire. I stood near the flames to dry, Katie eyeballing my sun-starved legs.

"What?" I asked her. "Never seen legs before?"

"I've seen legs," she said with sass. She tilted her head to the side, raising one eyebrow. "Just never ones that skinny. How do you get around on those delicate little things?"

"Barely," Bethany said. "He can't even run!"

"I can too, Bethany—quit lying!"

"Ask him to race, Katie. You'll win no problem. Even our pa can beat him, and he's old."

"Be quiet, Bethany," I said.

But she stared at me, squinting, her smile devious. I hesitated to look at Katie, hoping she wasn't starting think of me different. "Did I tell you James's nickname?" Bethany asked her. I turned toward Bethany, curious what she'd say. "You've heard of the boogie man, right?"

"That's enough!" I said. I must have been beet red, my face was burning so hot. "Look, here comes Carl. Hey, he's got something."

Carl walked over with a dead rattlesnake draped over his shoulders, its head crushed. He looked at my legs, laughing into his fist. "Man," he said, pointing. "And you think Carthon's legs are scrawny. You're one to talk!" He handed me the snake and proceeded to take his pants off too, draping them over a tree branch.

I glanced at Katie. "Don't even think about it," she said, securing the buttons of her dress.

"What?" I asked, feigning innocence. Bethany looked at me with naive curiosity. "I'm just going to clean this," I said to the girls, holding up the snake and retrieving my whittling knife.

"You do that," Katie said.

We cooked the meat over the open fire, sitting close to it for warmth. The evening was peaceful, and a low and calming murmur of night insects seemed to aid all of our moods. Firelight flickered off our faces as we huddled together, the horses resting, standing behind us.

Katie picked pieces of snake meat off her stick and popped them in her mouth. "Never had snake before," she said. "It's actually not bad."

"You ever think how scared people are of snakes?" Carl asked. "Pioneers cross this country surrounded by food, yet how many of them practically starve their way across? I'm telling you, it doesn't take much to survive out here. Once you get aligned with nature, you'd be surprised what you see."

Katie glanced at him with narrowed eyes and a distant gaze, her expression uncertain. I believe like me, she too was deep in thought—the first chance we'd had to slow down and regather ourselves. Our first opportunity to contemplate what we'd been through. For Bethany and me both, Walter's death was crushing weight.

"Well," I said, "I'll be happy with a steak once we're home."

"Given your cooking," Carl said, smiling and holding up his stick of snake meat. "Me too." After a chuckle, we noticed Bethany crying quietly, hiding her face and holding Spooks close. "Has your brother always been this bad at cooking?" Carl joked, trying to cheer her up.

Katie moved close to her and wrapped her arm over her shoulder. "I know how much your uncle Walter meant to you." She paused, thinking of her own ordeal, I'm sure. "Those moments go so fast," she said, almost speaking to herself.

I looked at Bethany, knowing I killed Walter to keep her from being harmed, not knowing at the time she couldn't have been any safer. I ended a good man's life for choosing to believe my worst fear was true. There seemed an obvious split between truth and opinion, though inside I knew that the logic which separated them was bullshit. It was *all* a conjuring: our grief, and even Walter's death. Though hardly salve for the misery I felt, my Gnosticism was insanity to those who didn't know, so I vowed to keep these thoughts to myself.

"It feels like this might be a dream," Katie said, looking at her hands in her lap. "Like none of this is real. How do we know this isn't a nightmare, and we won't wake up at home in bed?" She cried quietly. "I miss my family so bad. I don't have anywhere to go."

"Neither do I," Carl said to her, his crossed eyes and face scar glimmering in the orange light.

"We're a family now," I said. "I'm not sure what life looks like back in Leavenworth with everything going on, but we'll forge our own path if we need to. I promise you both, until I die, you'll have me by your side, come what may."

TEN

Dead and dormant shrubs hissed as a cold easterly breeze pushed us back. Riding the entire day as quickly as our tired horses would allow, we made it home. Bethany was home. I guess I expected to feel different, like a big shot having seized my treasure. But I didn't. We were all exhausted. I smiled at the others, their shoulders stooped, their hands gripping the reins loosely, and their tanned faces lined with dried white sweat.

The aftermath of rescuing Bethany and killing Walter was a kaleidoscope of emotions, thoughts, memories, and desires that made me dizzy and nauseous. What I did to Walter was a tragedy I'd live with forever, his face joining the others that had long faded from my dreams—those Rebellion soldiers, now resurrected in my sleep. I was grateful Bethany's countenance wasn't among them but still worried for my pa, thinking Ma might have done something to him.

"Here we go," I told Katie and Carl, speaking over the wind and pointing at the pecan trees. "Our house is in the valley, just past this grove."

Nobody said anything, but we resisted the tempest and made our way forward, stopping in the cold shade of a pecan tree and staring down the hill at the panorama. Rising out of turbulent, golden prairie grass, picturesque in the setting orange sunlight, was our house, white smoke twisting chaotically from the chimney. Past that stood the barn and paddock where Fred and Clyde walked in place, shoulder to shoulder, next to the sliding barn door, waiting for it to open. Except for the whistling branches, the scene was silent.

"You live there?" Katie asked.

I nodded.

"It's nice," she said quietly, smiling at Bethany.

"Think your folks are home?" Carl asked.

"My ma, probably." My imagination put my father's face in the company of the Rebellion soldiers. "Hopefully my pa's home. Or locked up in jail at least."

We rode down to the paddock as the sun fell behind the westward hillscape, shade sliding over our property. Fred and Clyde hurried to the fence, excited, and Bethany could hardly help herself, jumping the long way off Blue and running to see her horses.

She pulled the top of her coat closed as the wind blew faster. "I didn't know if I'd see them again," Bethany said. Her expression grew distant, like she was deep in thought, perhaps wondering what exactly would have happened if I didn't take her away. "You think we're going to be in

253

trouble?" she asked, petting Clyde's nose.

She didn't know about the letters Ma wrote until I told her. Our whole way home today, Bethany cried, trying to understand why Ma would do that. So much of what she wrote was a lie. None of it made sense. We talked, questioned, argued, and eventually just accepted Ma was who she was, and that she'd been like that for a long time — always wanting more than Leavenworth had to offer. Walter had promised Bethany a bright and joyful future, saying over and over how much Ma loved her. As much as we hated it — her stunt having caused harm and death — we understood this was Ma's way to try and get the life she always dreamed of.

With Carl's help, we laid Walter's body on a fresh bed of straw in Buck's stall and covered him with a wool Navajo blanket, stitched with the image of a thunderbird. I closed the sliding barn door and secured the horses outside in the paddock. We stood by the fence looking at the house. It was quiet, a lantern flickering in the window by the door, and apart from the chimney smoke, there was no other evidence they were home. "I don't think they know we're here," I said. "If they'd seen us, I'm sure they'd have come outside."

Uncertain of what we were getting into, we all walked across the yard and stood outside the veranda. "You thinking about hurting Ma?" Bethany asked me.

The images of death stood salient and demanding in my imagination, despite my desperate desire to the contrary. I saw Ma's face in the soil of Westport, her vacant, lifeless eyes looking up at me, and my reaction as I returned her gaze, ambivalent. To be honest, I *had* thought of hurting her but was done with violence for now. "No," I said. "Are you?"

"Don't be an idiot," she said, but I could tell she had more on her mind.

"You know Uncle Walter was an accident," I said. "You know that."

"Just don't hurt her, James," she said.

"Let's go find Pa, then."

The navy sky turned charcoal as the sun dropped further behind the horizon, an already bright moon high overhead. I gazed around the property, recalling so many memories. The nostalgia was a heavy sadness for what was and never would be again. I hadn't realized my excursion into the dark prairie would mean I couldn't come home. I looked up at my bedroom windowsill for that stubborn black bird, but he wasn't there. Perhaps that meant he found a new life, a willingness to forage his own pine nuts.

The veranda creaked as we walked over it, and I peeked through the crack in the window curtains, but only saw a plate of chocolate chip cookies on the dining table. I pushed the door open.

"Pa," I said, walking into the house and nearly tripping over Buster. I picked him up and carried him to his blanket by the fireplace. He started to raise his head when I put him down, his eyeball straining backward to see me, but gave up and closed his eyes. Katie, Carl, and Bethany walked into the front room behind me. "You here, Pa?"

"Pa?" Ma asked, calling out from the bedroom. Her voice was callous, maybe disappointed even. "No love for your mama?" After a moment, she walked into the front room wearing a tousled skirt and wrinkled blouse, collar turned up on one side, wiping her hands on a towel. Spotting Bethany, she threw it to the ground, ran over, and scooped her up.

"Bethany! You're home!" she said, stroking her hair away from her face and kissing her cheek. It all seemed so fake to me—perhaps it wouldn't have if I didn't know the truth. I felt foolish, wondering how many times I never questioned her sincerity. "You don't know how bad I missed you," Ma said. I believed she genuinely cared for Bethany. She looked me square in the eye, then averted her gaze, standing Bethany back up on the ground. "I'm so happy your back." Stepping away, she looked Bethany up and down. "Let's get you cleaned up, some fresh clothes. You must be hungry," she said. Grabbing the towel from the ground, she draped it over the plate of cookies. "Don't eat those," she said.

Bethany started to reply, but I interrupted, "Where's Pa?"

At that moment, Sheriff Lock walked out of the bedroom and into the front room, tightening a strap on his leg brace and checking the buttons of his shirt. "You're back," he said, looking at me. "I have a mind to lock you up as well ... but I guess I won't. Not today, at least."

"Brought some trail rabble with him," Ma said, rolling her eyes at Katie and Carl.

"Where's Pa!" I asked again, demanding an answer.

"Listen to that ugly mouth, Cecelia," the sheriff said,

holding onto a dining chair. "That's one lucky boy. I'd string him up if he spoke to me like that. Disrespectful bastard."

"He's in jail still," Ma said. "He's a murderer."

"He's not a murderer," I said. "You know that."

"Don't be naïve," Ma replied. She grew impatient while we stared at each other a moment, all of us quiet. "What are you waiting for? You expecting something from me?"

"No. Nothing, woman," I said. "But you know Pa protected us. For some fool reason, he loved you. Not for long, I'd guess though, once he finds out."

Her eyes opened wide, then settled on Bethany who looked at her with surprise and disgust. "Don't you look at me like that," Ma said to her. "I'll slap that face off if you don't get it right." She looked at Hank, tugging on her skirt again, then back at Bethany. "Where did you go? You had us all so worried. Were you hiding somewhere?"

"As if you didn't know," I said. Ma's face reddened while she studied all of us in turn. I let her stew in whatever awkwardness she was obviously feeling. After a long moment, I went on, "I know all about it. Were you really planning to poison him?"

Hank's eyes narrowed as he looked at Ma. "He doesn't know anything," she whispered to him.

He turned to me. "Don't be preposterous, boy."

Such a condescending dick. "Why are you here, anyway? This ain't your house. You get on! Get the hell out of here, Hanky!" I said, running my finger under my nose.

His face turned bright red with anger, the veins popping from his neck. "Like father, like son," he said, grunting. "I'm gonna tear you into pieces, you little son of a bitch."

Ma watched, wearing a sly smile as Hank hurried past her, hobbling on his bum leg, shoving dining chairs out of his way. What a buffoon—so easily provoked. Quickly, I stepped outside on the veranda and behind the wall, and when Hank ran out, I tripped him. He fell flat on his face, clutching his leg in agony. Ma ran out to tend him.

I ran back inside and yelled at Katie, "Lock the door!" She secured it while I went to Ma's bedroom and rummaged her end table. By then, the sheriff and Ma were banging on the door, demanding to be let in. Stockings, brassieres, and undergarments filled her drawers, along with a copy of Mary Shelley's *Frankenstein*, but nothing else. Not finding the poison, I pulled the drawers all the way out and dumped them on the bed, throwing everything on the floor piece by piece to make sure I wasn't missing anything. In the meantime, their banging on the door got harder. The book was the only thing that seemed out of place. It didn't belong in an underwear drawer, so I flipped through it, thinking the pages might be cut out to make room for a small vial—but nothing still. Maybe it was all lies, more of her fantasy life intruding into the real world. I scrambled elsewhere around the room, looking through Ma and Pa's large dresser, which I emptied. Again, nothing.

Katie yelped from the front room as Hank threw a porch chair through the window and climbed in, yanking the curtains to the ground, then shoving Katie out of his way to unlock the door.

"You fucking animals!" Hank yelled. "You're awful!

Plain awful humans!" Bethany stood there fixed on him while he grabbed her shoulders and shook her violently, screaming in her face. "You're horrendous, just like your pa!"

Nobody touches Bethany, especially you, I thought, my mind a steel beam of determination. Pa's bowie knife was wrapped in Buck's saddlebag, but I always carried my whittling knife on my belt. *Just like my pa. That's right, and you're going to find out what that means.* Enough violence wasn't enough, after all. I unsheathed the knife and came at Sheriff Lock with unflinching purpose.

"Stop!" Katie cried. "Don't do this again! For God's sake, *just stop!"*

I looked at her, her expression crinkled in distress. Hank turned and saw me with the knife, coming directly for him. He went to Ma's rocking chair where his belt and holster were hanging and grabbed his revolver. As he raised his arm to aim it at me, Carl appeared and swooped up the kerosene lantern, swinging it against the back of the sheriff's head. Kerosene splashed all over the sheriff, which ignited instantly, setting his shirt and hair on fire. Carl stomped out the fire in the house while Hank stumbled outside to the oak tree, lighting up the night, dragging his leg and patting his body frantically while he hollered in pain like some hysterical goblin. Ma ran after him with a blanket, wrapping him in it as he fell to the ground.

"You did this," I yelled at her. "All of this! You did everything! Couldn't be happy with a normal life, so you made up some lies about how Pa treated you, convinced your brother to steal away with Bethany, even paid that fucking

259

creep to molest her! With that lousy son of a bitch Hank ...
the two of you are going to pay for what you did."

Perhaps not hearing me, Ma tended to Hank in the
moonlight outside, trembling and anxious. "Look what you
did to him—he's burned!" She turned to me. "You've been
rotten for years. Just a boy. A reflection in your no-good pa's
eyes—never a man. I've dreamed for so long about getting
rid of you. If only you knew," she screamed. "If only you
knew!"

"If only I knew what, woman?" I asked her.

"You never remembered what you did to me," she said.
"What you did to Benjamin. If you did, you'd have the
decency to hate yourself as much as I do. But I didn't forget.
I'll never forget the day you touched me with your evil little
fingers and caused our baby to break free of this world,
splashing out in blood and water—dead. I wished so hard it
was you in my womb, instead of him. Everything would be
different."

My God—that was it. Not until she said that did I
remember when she was pregnant. I was little and worried
because she'd been in bed with tremendous pain for so many
days. The doctor had said she was sick, and when I laid my
hand on her stomach, the baby slid out. That was why she
blamed me for his death.

"What do you know, anyway?" she went on. "I didn't
pay anyone to take your sister. And mind your mouth saying
I wanted to hurt her! You tell me where you got her—who
you got her from."

"You know already, woman. Quit your games," I said.

As she knelt by Hank, she looked uncertainly at me, surely knowing I knew more than she had presumed. Her voice turned low, demonic even. She stood up and got face to face with me. "Where's my brother?" she asked, her eyes bloodshot, spitting as she talked.

I didn't answer. She stared at me, this complete stranger to us all, with the eyes of a snake, her whole body almost slithering in the moonlight as smoke rose off Hank's smoldering clothes behind her. It disgusted me to remember that I actually thought rescuing Bethany would bring healing to our relationship. She waited for me to speak, and waited, but I owed this woman nothing now.

Beside me, Bethany watched, shocked, her face white, apparently unable to understand everything that was happening. "Look at your daughter," I said to Cecelia. "Look what you've done. Or is that too much?"

As if becoming a different person, Cecelia returned to Hank's side, gentle and earnest. "Honey," she said, whispering, "think of the life we'll have! Now that I'm free— free to live the life of adventure Daryl was impotent to deliver." She stroked his face with the back of her fingers. Hank moaned while she fussed about. "Quit you're sniveling, Henry," she went on. "Those burns aren't serious. Come on," she pulled on his arm. "Let's get you cleaned up so we can leave already. Maybe take the train to New York City, or San Francisco."

"How does he know?" Hank asked in a quiet voice, perhaps supposing I couldn't hear. He brushed her off and staggered to his feet. "Damn, woman. Give me some space!"

Katie, standing behind me just outside the front door, put her arm around my waist. "It's okay, JT," she said. "Leave it be. That's the past. Let it stay there. Come on, let's go check on your pa. Show him Bethany's home safe." The four of us walked to the paddock to fetch our horses.

"Let me help you, darling," Cecelia said to Hank as we left. "Don't talk to the mother of your child like that."

"I got no child with you," he said. "That one died in your womb. I don't owe you nothing."

Cecelia's voice softened as she spoke. "You don't owe me," she said. "Just let me help you. Come on now, let's go inside where we can get you undressed, and I can get you washed up. You like that, don't you?"

Apparently done with the fussing, he demanded again from her, "How does he know? How does James know what happened?"

While Katie helped Bethany climb onto Clyde, and Carl hopped onto Carthon, Fred was eager to get back into his stall. He followed me inside the barn, where I got a bridle and buckled it over his head, then clipped a rope to the curb strap under his jaw. Watching me in silence, Katie leaned on the sliding door, a black silhouette in the evening light, the edges of her delicate features glowing.

"You okay?" she asked me. What power did this earth possess that was able to manifest such perfection, such a sublime creature as her?

"Yeah," I said. I looked at my hands which were still shaking from the confrontation. "I'll be good."

She walked to my side, moonlight illuminating her

features. She tilted her head slightly, her moist eyes sparkling as she ran her hand down my arm, catching my index finger with her pinky. She brought my hand to her waist. "Good," she said. Forgetting to breathe, I stared into her blue eyes, which shined in the white reflection of the moon, my mind vacant in her presence. Recalling the glory I felt at the top of the pecan grove before Bethany's attack, Katie was proof that angels were real.

It took some tugging on Fred, but that lazy horse finally moved. Hand in hand, Katie and I exited the barn to where Carl and Bethany were mounted on their horses. "You ready, Bethany?" I asked, closing the sliding barn door. I put a bridle over Clyde and handed her the reins. She was crying, but nodded yes. "We'll take Fred for Pa." I patted my trousers' pocket. "Hopefully these will get him out." I climbed onto Buck and flicked his reins. We all rode toward the oak tree where Cecelia and Hank were still arguing. "I read the letters!" I said. "That's how I know."

We rounded the backside of the house and got on the main road toward town. The sweet lemon smell of winter honeysuckle calmed my nerves as memories of childhood sprang to mind, a time when ignorance was innocence. But as we rode, everything felt different. I felt like a visitor in a foreign territory, the years of memories stacked atop one another like cabinet cards someone had handed me. I could just as easily put the photos away and go on with my life in some other place. A sense of déjà vu crept over me as I watched our group ride through the cold, windy, moonlit evening, each of us sober, determined. We had been initiated into a transfigured innocence in spite of our vulgarity, no longer ignorant, and carried inextinguishable sparks, outside of space and time.

I used to believe we were a typical family, before Cecelia's attitude toward me had calloused my emotions for her. Before, she was just Ma, and our family made its way through the years as every other family in Leavenworth did. There was no other deciphering her behavior apart from a mental illness that, perhaps similar to myself, found a commonality between the real and the imaginary. Where I found purpose and unity with all creation, she must have found absurdity and loneliness. My disdain for this woman diminished, seeing she must be suffering, accepting who she was on her own terms. We all made our own ways through life, defined by our own choices, not anybody else's. A shameful spirit left me as I contemplated that Cecelia's choices didn't define me. They didn't make me a bad person.

Every one of us made choices that defined our futures. This moment—an intersection of our four lives—was simply the culmination of a thousand past choices, inevitable, and exactly the way it was supposed to be. I understood, seeing it clearly for the first time: perfection had nothing to do with our judgment of things, but with their order. Perfection itself was a precise and inviolable organization, indifferent to our opinions. The surface of each moment exactly coordinated to every other moment without gap or corruption. This was the geometry of justice. And the plans of men—irrelevant. My soul drowned in regret for what I did to Walter, and I knew in time justice would find its way to me one way or another.

"Can you make it?" I asked Bethany, seeing her nodding off to sleep as she rode on Clyde. Her crying had stopped, though mine had begun. "Do you want me to hold you?"

"I'm just tired," she said. A smile emerged on her face. "I don't want you touching me, you nasty boy," she said softly.

I led the group as we crossed the bridge into town and down the street to the sheriff's station. Most of the shops along the road were dark, but a few windows glowed with lamplight. A rose-hued bubble-glassed lantern lit the display at *Cordelia's*, the candies, comfits, and sweetmeats all snug in their jars. Like a child's dream, those treats shined at me, tempting me to retreat into a past version of myself, though the enchantment was now gone.

At our destination, we strapped our horses to the hitching post alongside a number of other horses. I recognized deputy Charlie's, Nathan's, and the diminutive mayor's pintsized Shetland pony. On the veranda outside, we stood listening to townsfolk within, clearly protesting Pa's jailing. Their voices were angry, and the windows bounced as people stomped, yelled, and demanded his release. Over the noise, I heard deputies Charlie and Nathan trying to quell the excitement.

We walked into the back of the room, a couple dozen flinchy and irritable people there, including Peggy, Boris, Dominic, and many others clamoring to be heard. "It's a fact he killed a man," deputy Nathan said, holding his hands up as if to halt a horse-drawn wagon.

"He explained to you," said a neighbor named Jacob—

whose real name was Quingee. "The man attacked his daughter! What do you expect?"

"Not only is the supposed *mo-les-tation* hearsay," Nathan said, drawing out the word sarcastically, "it sure is convenient how the victim who could best affirm the accusation isn't here. In her absence, what do I expect? I expect due process."

"From you incompetent bastards!" someone said. "You want us to believe that?"

Nathan looked around, trying to figure out who'd spoken, his face red and pissed. "There was no molestation," he said, his voice loud and demanding. "It's a sham. Daryl's a liar, trying to get off."

"You know damned well he's no liar," another person said, their voice indistinct among the commotion. "You're a snaky son of a bitch, aren't you?"

"Fact remains, unless there's evidence to the contrary, he's guilty!"

"What happened to due process?" asked Peggy.

"Help me out, Charlie," Nathan said, but Charlie leaned back against the sheriff's desk and crossed his arms. "Anyway," Nathan went on, "no man's above the law."

"That's bullshit!" yelled Samuel Burton. "I get harassed constantly for how I dress. Ignorant folks have no appreciation for ancient Celtic wear!"

"Who, Sam? Tell me," Nathan said, aloof.

"Well, the school kids, that's who."

"They're kids, Sam," said Mr. Furrough, the farmer, looking him up and down. "And no one's buying that

266

Scottish ancestry fiction. I don't imagine the Scots wore chintz and fancy boots. We all know you. You're a good man. Just be yourself."

The mayor wasn't as compassionate. "Grow up, Samuel," he said. "And for God's sake, put on shirt and pants once in a while."

"I'm just saying," Samuel said, his face growing red with embarrassment. "Are kids not accountable?"

"What makes a kid?" the mayor interjected haughtily, practically screaming to be heard as his ridiculously high top hat bobbed on his head. "Age? *Sensibility*? Anyway, this is all beside the point. We're here about Daryl, and unless anyone is under the illusion he's a child, we must reckon with the fact that he killed an innocent man in cold blood, whose only crime was destitution. A white man, no less. That carries penalties."

"What difference does color make?" asked Mrs. Roush. She and Jacob looked at each other in disbelief. "This is Kansas. The war's over—or don't that mean anything?"

"Regardless," the mayor yelled. "Cold blood! Don't you hear me? *Cold blood!*"

I pushed my way to the front of the room. "It wasn't in cold blood," I said.

"Give him some space," Charlie said to everyone, seeing me struggle to get through.

Pa looked at me as I emerged, his eyes wide with surprise. Nathan and the mayor were likewise surprised, but not more so than when I pulled Bethany forward and into their view. Their jaws dropped, knowing we had her testimony about what happened that night. Seeing Pa, Bethany ran to his jail cell, thrusting her arms through the bars.

"Pa," she said, squeezing him tight. "You're *safe*."

"My sweetheart," he replied, holding her with his good arm. "*You're* safe. I love you, sweetheart." Tears ran down his face. "*My sweetheart…*"

"This ain't how justice works," the mayor insisted. "We're in charge—not you all—and I'm telling you it was in cold blood."

The crowd grew angry and someone yelled back at him, "This is a travesty! Daryl is an honorable man. He's no butcher!"

Someone else chimed in, "Yeah, I've known him for years as a God-fearing man who goes out of his way to defend the innocent—even the Indians!"

"Ask Bethany. She's right there!" someone said.

"Daryl's fierce but principled," another yelled. "He's never deviated from righteousness."

They shrieked and hooted to release him. "This is still America."

"What if that was your daughter?"

"Such assaults on family justify a harsh requital!"

"We have rules," the mayor said, growing focused in his anger. The little man appeared so desperate for control, unprepared in the company of the self-reliant, and said what comes naturally to a bully. "We're the government, and you do what we say or face the consequence. Whether you know it or not, there's a social contract. Your duty is to obey!"

"You're crooks!" one person said.

Others joined in. "And liars!"

"Cheats!"

"*Bastards!*"

"Who voted for stubby anyway? Did anybody here?"

"Times are changing," said deputy Nathan, visibly frustrated, "whether you like it or not. Mark my words, one of these days when your kids or your kid's kids are fat and cozy, you'll do what we say and won't have a second thought about it. We'll threaten you openly, take away your rights even, and you'll be too cross-eyed to realize it. You'll even defend us locking up anyone who endangers your fat and cozy status—authority-deniers like Daryl here."

"Listen to this skinny tyrant!" Boris said. "Who does he think he is?" The crowd quieted, scandalized over what they heard.

Squinting, Nathan snorted and spit on the floor of the sheriff's station. "I'm deputy and my name is Nathaniel Harris, your plantation overseer," he answered. "That's who. You've had your say, now get out."

The crowd grew raucous, angry and defiant, and was getting out of hand, turning destructive. "Look," I said, "the mayor's in charge, not Nathan. And I'm telling you, his account is wrong. I've got proof right here."

I reached into my trousers' pocket for Ma's letters and pulled out a handful of pulp. *The river! Dammit!* I hurried to the desk and tried to flatten them out, piecing together fragments that pulled apart. "Pa," I said, frantic, "these were letters from Ma. I swear. They proved you were setup!"

269

"Son," the mayor said, "what do you take us for?" His voice was condescending. "You know better than to try a foolish trick like that. *Please*. I can't even read what's written there!"

Katie and Carl stepped to the front of the crowd. I looked at them and sighed, shaking my head. *How could I be so stupid?* Carl donned a shrewd smile and winked at me, then retrieved the two letters I'd had him read back in the honeycomb hills. He handed them to me. Thank God for Carl!

"Here," I said to the mayor, unfolding the letters. "I'm no liar. This here's the evidence."

The mayor took a moment to read both letters, and the more he read the more he squirmed, shuffling his feet and clearing his throat. He glanced up at me, then lowered his head to continue reading, his ears turning red. When he finished, he took Bethany aside and spoke with her, too low to hear. I watched as Bethany nodded to his questions, then grew teary-eyed, embarrassed, looking down and touching the hem of her dress. I guessed she was telling him about the molestation—an admission anyone would prefer to keep private. The mayor walked over to Charlie. "Unlock the cell," he told him. "Let him go."

"What are you talking about, mayor?" Nathan asked. "This man's a criminal."

"It's true," the mayor said. "Daryl was setup, no doubt about it. I dare say, if Bethany was my daughter and this happened to her, I'd have done exactly what Daryl did." Nathan stood in front of Pa, blocking his exit from the jail cell. "Move yourself, Nathan," the mayor said. "That's an order."

"You ain't got the authority," he replied. "We'll wait for the sheriff's return."

The mayor's patience ran thin. "Your duty is to *me*, boy, not the sheriff. I'm in charge. You understand?"

Charlie smiled at Pa as he walked out of the cell. "Good for you, Daryl," he said. Pa nodded, placing his hand on Charlie's shoulder, then scooped Bethany up and walked out of the building. In hindsight, I might have been more discrete in what I said next, but I couldn't help myself. Cecelia was my mother, but no longer my ma, and the truth needed to come out.

"Listen everyone. You haven't read these," I said, holding up the letters, "but they prove that Cecelia and Sheriff Lock paid a vagrant to camp out on the trail until seeing Bethany, at which time he was to molest her. *They arranged for her molestation.* Then they wanted to trick all of us into thinking that she was kidnapped, even though she was safe with my uncle. She wanted to leave my pa, accusing him of hitting her. Have any of you seen him raise a hand to anyone in our town in all these years? Or even seen a bruise on my mother? She sacrificed her daughter, and she and the sheriff both lied to us all so they could continue their affair."

Hearing the news of Hank's corruption—standing in his house—so enraged the crowd that they took to breaking furniture and kicking holes in the walls. I have to admit I was shocked at their response, never thinking these otherwise docile folks had it in them to do this. Like Pa said, push any man far enough, and you'll discover what's inside.

"You probably helped him, the sheriff, didn't you?" someone asked the mayor.

"I didn't know!" the mayor yelled, trying to quiet the group. "I swear, I didn't know anything! I understand you're angry, but stop what you're doing. I'm dropping all charges—Daryl will face no prosecution for what happened. Now please, stop your destruction!" His action came too late, and the group moved on to smashing windows and breaking lanterns on the floors. Soon the drapes caught on fire and overtook the station.

Orange flames raged, flickering, licking high into the black air, illuminating the section of moonlit road and nearby buildings. Safely away from the heat and embers, Katie, Carl, and I sat next to Pa, who was holding Bethany—all of us on horseback. The townsfolk were blinking in the yellow light of the fire, nobody speaking, just watching with awestruck expressions. I couldn't help but wonder if they felt they'd gone too far, but as I looked at them, there was a peace in their eyes. Reflecting on my own contribution, I was at peace too, satisfied with this result and believing the town's corruption was beyond redemption. We needed to start over. And while not perfect, we were a solid people made up of good folks who strived to do the right thing. There was cause for hope for the future of Leavenworth.

We watched while the mayor, furious now, yelled at deputy Nathan to do something, to arrest this mob. Nathan ignored the mayor, quiet and smirking, a glint in his face suggesting he enjoyed the mischief and destruction. Charlie eyeballed the mayor, then took the star from his shirt and threw it into the pyre.

"That explains her regard for that son of a bitch," Pa said. He hadn't read the letters. I was tempted to tell him that Cecelia was plotting his murder, and that Benjamin was not his child, but resisted.

The fire quelled, running out of wood to burn, and Charlie trotted over to us on horseback. "Why don't you all come back with me, to Papa's house," he said, glancing at me with a look that said he knew Hank had moved in with Cecelia at our house, though he was unsure if I knew that.

"Just the same," Pa said, "I'd rather head home."

I looked at Charlie, nodding, then at Pa. "Charlie's right, Pa. Why don't we head to Mr. Elton's? It's been a long day, and he'll be happy to see you're out."

"I'd love to see William, but I have a house and a bed and I'm anxious to lay down in it," Pa said, his voice rigid.

I explained to him what we found when we arrived home, that Hank was living with Cecelia, sleeping in his bed, while he was in jail.

"I built that house," Pa said angrily. "Like hell that snake will stay under my roof. He'll leave, and she'll join him."

Once home, we found only Cecelia there, crying in her chair, a blanket pulled under her chin, clutching one of her novels to her chest. Apparently, Hank left her, opting to walk to the nearest neighbor for a lift to his own place.

"You'll leave this house, Cecelia," Pa said. "That means now."

She slouched in her chair, squeezing her crossed arms against her body. "I'm alone now," she said. "You ruined my life! You promised a good life when we got married, a life of excitement and happiness. But you gave me nothing I wanted. Only this dreadful town in this dreadful state. It consumes everything, and offers nothing. My great regret, Daryl—that's my great regret. Moving to this dreadful state."

The woman was blind to what was in front of her—a family who loved her at one point in time but now just felt sorry for her and wanted her gone. She was sick, it was plain to see, but that didn't mean we owed her an obligation to allow her into our lives, to drag us down in her misery. I sympathized with Cecelia, as much as any stranger in similar straights, but felt thoroughly detached from her. She was on her own, and at least for now, there was no redemption for her. In silence, we all watched from the veranda as she rode off into the night, riding Fred toward town, hoping to find someone kind enough to take her in.

"I'll be fetching him later, mind you," Pa shouted at her. "Don't think you get to keep Fred."

It was a long day, but after she left, none of us were tired anymore. I thought of telling Pa about Uncle Walter in the barn, but didn't. We rode to Mr. Elton's after all, Pa holding Bethany the whole time as they rode on Clyde. Back on the Santa Fe Trail, the wind had quieted, the starlit night becoming silent but for the clop of horse hooves. A half-mile away we got to his property north of the ridge, which was vast and sat in a valley. It glowed in the radiance of the pearly moonlight under a crystal-clear onyx sky, adjacent to the hundreds of acres of farmland he owned.

"You go ahead, Pa," I said, and he rode down to the house while Katie, Carl, and I stopped our horses and watched the quiescent evening setting.

"That his place?" Katie asked.

Mr. Elton lived in a massive A-frame farmhouse that could have been lifted from the pages of a fantasy storybook. Its sod roof was covered in dormant grass and the sides of the house were overlaid in parchment-colored sandstone and had ample windows, each with muslin curtains drawn shut, some with lantern light glowing yellow from inside. "It's something, isn't it?" I asked.

"It is that," Carl said. "Ain't never seen anything like it. There must be a lot of rooms. You think he'll let us stay there?"

I could hear the emotion in his voice, having no idea about his youth apart from the scant shards he shared, and that the extent of what he endured had pushed him to choose hungry and homeless as the better option. I felt compassion for my brother. More than that—responsibility. The stirring of my conscience, something I ignored for so much of my life in favor of duty or others' expectations, was that invisible trickle from the other side of the veil into this. Duty was fine, but only so far as it was grounded in integrity, moved by the current at the back of all humanity, pushing us toward breath, not suffocation.

"My brother," I said to Carl, "we'll live good lives and follow where our conscience points. Let's see what room we end up in."

We rode down the hill, stopping beside Clyde and Charlie's horse. Carl jumped off Carthon and wrapped his arm under his horse's head. He was petting the side of his face and gazing around in awe as Mr. Elton came to the door, happy to see me.

Mr. Elton grabbed a lantern by the window and stepped outside. "James!" he said, his wife Maria standing by his side. "It's great to see you. Daryl and Bethany are inside. Come on, all of you, come inside."

"Honey," he said to Maria, "can you get some food on the table? Have Daryl and Bethany join us in the dining room." He kissed Maria on the cheek in a display I'd never seen from him, overjoyed with our return. "We'll send wire to Independence and Franklin and tell Bingo and Tommy that Bethany's returned safe."

Maria stepped outside and gave me a big hug. "You did good, *mijo*," she said, squeezing tight. "Very good. You got what you needed." She couldn't have known what I prayed for all those years prior at Blessed Porres church, but perhaps she knew all prayers eventually traced their descent back to an elementary yearning, a desire not actually for wholeness with the cosmos—since that was an unalterable aspect of reality—but rather an *awareness* of that wholeness which most people were ignorant of, and the personal transfiguration that comes as a result.

Everyone except for Bethany sat down for a meal. She slept in the Elton's *Jasmine Room*, one of the sanctuary guest rooms he built for travelers passing through. We ate and drank, grateful how things turned out—all things considered—though still in shock of it all.

"I thought she was going to shoot us," I said, telling Pa and Mr. Elton how Carl and I met Katie as we all finished our meal. "She was the most beautiful thing I'd ever laid eyes on, about to kill us dead."

"Oh, you're exaggerating, JT," she said.

"*JT?!*" Pa said, leaning forward in his chair. "You hate that name! She must be something if you let her call you that!" I didn't know what to say, but could feel my face turning red. "Well," he went on, "it's nice. Regardless, I'm glad you found each other."

"I'll miss my family," Katie said. "I miss them now. My pa was helping all these other families make their way across the country. People he picked up along the way. In the weeks we had together, we became a community. Sometimes you don't know what you've got until it's gone."

Pa nodded, agreeing, while Mr. Elton looked at Maria and smiled. "And sometimes you know exactly what you've got while you've got it," he said. She returned his smile with so much love, I instantly grew longing of their relationship, glancing at Katie.

"Would anyone like dessert?" Maria asked, standing from the table. "I'll bring a plate and coffee. You decide."

"That's kind, Maria," Pa said. "Maybe a little more wine."

"*Mijo?*" she asked Charlie.

"Thanks, Mama," he said. "I'm fine."

"These have been eventful days for you all, that's for sure," Mr. Elton said. "Maybe one day you'll write a book about it. Immortalize it." He looked at Katie. "Immortalize your family. They were good folks, I know it, and it's a terrible loss." Turning to Carl, he went on. "You haven't said much about your family."

"Not much to say, I guess," Carl replied. "Left home with Carthon, my horse, a few years back, when I'd had enough of my father's beatings. I know what abuse looks like," he said, looking at Pa. "It's a serious accusation, cheapened when people lie about it." Carl's hand drifted to the scar on his face, and his eyes grew wet. "If it's all the same, I'd rather plan for a better tomorrow than reminisce on a hurtful past. Your son is a good man, Daryl. He showed me kindness when a thousand other people pretended I didn't exist. As I told him before, I'd aimed to rescue someone like myself, someone oppressed and neglected, treated like an animal. We didn't know Bethany was in good hands until it was too late, so my purpose remains. My better tomorrow will be helping others make good, free lives for themselves."

"There's something I didn't tell you, Pa," I said. "I killed Uncle Walter, not knowing who he was. I assumed it was a trail creep, like that molester, one of those migrants we've been hearing more about lately. All I wanted to do was rescue her. I brought him back with us for a proper burial. He's safe, in Buck's stall. "

I loved Walter without exception, and separate from my unyielding grief, a small part of me was numb over what happened. In a sense, he was just another face in the battlefield of the fallen. I didn't know how to integrate the awful part of myself that killed him with the rest of me. *Was*

278

either part even true, or were they both a conjuring as well? I made peace with my action by knowing one day my own face would join the anonymous assemblage of barren visages, our features disappearing in the sands of time.

"I was wrong for not making sure," I said. "I should have done more."

"What more could you do, James?" Mr. Elton asked. "How could you know?"

Pa looked at me, his eyes growing distant, and sat quietly, contemplating, turning his glass of wine like a dial on the table. Settling his gaze on the glass, he sighed. "That man was everything to me," he said. "When Roger died, he looked after me the way a big brother does. Before I went off to war, he gave me that bowie knife I keep in my night stand. Said to open the heavens with it, allow justice a way into this God-forsaken world. I've dreamt about the men I killed in war," he continued, somber. He wiped his mouth with a napkin. "I told you before I never contemplated those men's families—and I didn't lie." He swirled his wine and took a sip. "But those men have haunted me. Choices have consequences. Wish I had known earlier to choose my scars carefully. Justice," he said, now looking at me, "is the most fundamental yearning of our souls. But it's an inferno that consumes your humanity if you let it. We'll bury him proper, don't worry, son."

Maria returned with coffee and dessert and sat next to Mr. Elton. Pa asked me to see the letters, so I showed him. He read them slowly, taking everything in. I watched as he read about Cecelia's desire to kill him and about Benjamin's real father. "She never was able to detach herself from her fantasies," Pa said. "To extract herself from those delusions of adventure and glory that filled her books." He pushed the letters away and leaned back in his chair. "Cess was never happy, even before we married, but I hoped I could change that. When she wasn't stuck in her head, she was so full of life and emotion. She made living rich, spirited." He paused, thoughtful. "Perhaps I should have done more too," he said to me. "I'm sorry, son."

"Can we resist the current of history?" Mr. Elton asked. "What can we really change?"

"Do you think *people* can change?" I asked him, thinking about Cecelia.

"Well," he said, "people do change." He took Maria's hand, smiling at her. In his younger days, Mr. Elton was a different man, motivated by blind hatred. But he changed. His love for his wife was genuine, regardless of race.

"You keep the letters, Pa," I said. "Just in case you need them for anything."

Pa looked at Katie and Carl. "You two are more than welcome to stay with us. Our home isn't big, but you're family now, and we'll figure things out."

"I think we might be on our way, Pa," I said. In the silent plains of my soul, I knew this was right. Looking at Katie and Carl, they nodded agreement.

"Thank you, though," Carl said.

"I've lectured you plenty on duty," Pa said to me. "It's the boy who is duty-bound to the orders of other men. But it's the man who binds himself to his conscience. As I look at my son sitting before me, and consider the boy who ventured into uncertainty, overcoming himself to do so, I see he's returned a man."

I slid my arm over the table and squeezed Katie's hand in mine. "As we rode home, state law was after us. Not sure they've given up." I paused, thinking. "There were others besides Walter. Casualties. Topeka law made a run for us, but we got away. Wouldn't be surprised if they kept on."

"What do you have in mind, then?" Pa asked.

I thought before answering. "Can't trust the worst in people that causes them to seek positions of authority. You might not have gotten out tonight if it wasn't for that crowd there."

"In the hierarchy of law and order," Charlie said, "law takes a firm second place."

"Justice shouldn't need persuasion," I said. "Perhaps it never will be uncorrupted, but until it is, what law or order calls justice can't be trusted. There is a higher justice, though—I've felt it. A justice that exists outside of time, and there's no escaping it."

"You do what you think is right," Pa said. "I will always support that." He and Mr. Elton looked at me with knowing expressions.

"We'll follow our own path," I said. "We'll make do, and make honorable lives for ourselves. You'll hear from me. I'll write from time to time. I admire you more than you know, Pa, and I always hoped to make you proud. It's time to venture on."

Exhausted, we picked at the desserts until our eyes

started closing on us. Mrs. Elton showed us to our rooms. The house was a mansion, bigger inside than out by all appearances, carrying a faint scent of wildflowers and cotton. It's funny I never went inside all those times I hung out with Guts. We walked down a long hallway past rooms on both sides, candelabras on all the walls, through sitting areas and another kitchen, then to the travelers' bedrooms and where we'd sleep.

"Each room has its own bath with linens and towels," Mrs. Elton told us. "You should have everything you need."

We thanked her for everything, then walked through the rooms she showed us to, amazed at the extravagance. "These rooms have chandeliers!" Carl said, flabbergasted. He pulled Katie with him, pointing at all the adornments. "I've never seen a chandelier!"

I turned to join them, but Mrs. Elton took my arm. "We will all miss you here, *mijo*, and you are always welcome back," she said to me. Her smile and kindness were everything I hoped for from my own mother. I wasn't a jealous sort but recognized how incredibly fortunate her sons were to have her as their ma. "It seems you learned so much on your adventure. Remember those lessons in your heart. Use them as you grow older, to guide your choices." She paused, nodding and looking knowingly into my eyes.

I waited for her to say more, curious what she was thinking, just as Carl and Katie ran back down the hall toward us. Carl's excitement replaced the tone of our conversation, so Maria wished us all a good night and left.

"Who are these people?" Carl asked.

"Old friends of my pa," I told him, knowing he served with Mr. Elton in the army but not knowing anything more about his earlier life.

"Honestly, guys," Katie said, "I can't keep my eyes open. I'm going to bed."

Carl walked back up and down the hall again, taking in their collection of oil paintings hanging over ornate wallpaper, admiring the oriental rugs on the floor and the decorative molding at every corner. At the far end of the hall where we hadn't walked, by itself in the shadows, was a door that seemed to lead outside. "I'm going to check that out," he said, then hurried off.

I turned to Katie and took her hands once more. We stood in front of the room she would stay in. "I guess that's it, then."

"What's it?" she asked.

"Well, the end of our adventure. Right?"

"I wouldn't say that," she said, glancing to see Carl heading away.

"It's been a long day," I said, my eyes growing heavy. I looked at the door to the room next to Katie's, where I would sleep. We hadn't talked about what she did to Harry and Arthur, and it weighed on me, but not because I judged her— God knows I had no basis to do that. It was something else, an uncertainty, an unpredictability about her that excited and terrified me. She must have seen it in my eyes, reading my mind.

"Are you thinking about the boys?" she asked. "I wouldn't blame you if you were. I can't stop thinking of it. To be honest, I don't know what came over me. When I heard him screech like that, something took over. I barely remember it. I wouldn't blame you if you hated me as much as I hate myself."

"How could I hate you? If it wasn't for you," I said, "I'm not sure what I would have done when we found Bethany. I'm not even sure I would have found Bethany, but for your company. We make mistakes—some of them massive—but we learn by them. Don't hate yourself, but carry what you did with you, and make different choices in the future. That's all any of us can do." I could tell my words touched her, as her eyes grew glossy. I released one of her hands and took the other in both of mine, holding it tight. "You've been a comfort and a confidence. I never thought of myself as a romantic before, but you made me one."

She wiped her eyes then pulled her ponytail out and shook her hair, long strands flowing over her shoulders. "I made you a romantic?" she asked. Carl was at the end of the hall pulling the door open to sheer blackness, another room inside the house, maybe, since the moon was bright outside.

I stared at Katie. "It feels like I've known you my whole life. It's the weirdest thing. Like we're meant to be together, and we always were."

Katie blushed, smiling. "I'm actually not that tired anymore," she whispered.

I looked over her shoulder into her room, seeing a giant four-poster bed with a plush purple comforter. "What'd you have in mind?" I asked, my exhilaration causing my body to shake.

"We could come up with something, but first," she said, undoing the top button of her dress, "I've got to get out of these dirty clothes and get cleaned up. No way can I sleep with this layer of dirt on me."

Stuttering, I could barely speak. "I don't blame you. You should do that, definitely."

She stopped, thinking. "What's next for us, JT?"

"As in the next few minutes?" I was confused, curious she asked that.

"No, you silly, when we leave here?"

"Oh. I don't know. Maybe we jump on the train west and get off where it seems right. We could go all the way to San Diego, then down to into Mexico if we wanted to."

"That'd be nice," she said, unfastening the next button. "Maybe one step at a time. Right?"

I was enchanted beyond all rationale, breathing fast and unable to think. "Yeah," I said, watching her fingers. I'd agree to anything she said. "One step at a time."

She leaned in and kissed me—a passionate union I'll remember forever, our lips pressed into each other's, hers as supple and silky as I imagined. I held my breath, and held her, embracing her with the palms of my hands, squeezing her close, my soul yanked from my body, elevated in an unspeakable bliss. Though sweaty and covered in dirt, I inhaled her riveting scent, freezing that moment in my mind, wishing I had the power to stop time. "In that case," she said, stepping into her room. "I'll see you in the morning." And she closed the door.

Before heading out, we planned a small burial for Walter next to Benjamin under the magnolia tree. Word spread that Walter—a dear friend of Pa's—was an honorable and upright man of integrity who did his best to do what was right, though not perfect. Unknown to nearly everyone in town, he quickly became a symbol of our striving and humanity. In droves, folks turned out to pay respect, if not to the man, then to what he represented, or for who he was to our family. Clad in black, the crowd extended past the paddock and the oak tree—even Bingo and the widow Finny were there. It surprised me that Cecelia made no effort to come for her own brother, but after a moment of thought, that surprise left me.

It was a clear and brilliant morning, the sun's rays bouncing high in the atmosphere, tinging the heavens with shimmers of rainbow colors. With hats in hand, we all stood, solemn, listening to Father Breen from Blessed Porres offer prayers and scripture:

"From the Gospel of John," Father Breen said, "we take comfort, reading these words: '*And I have given them the glory you gave me, so that they may be one, as we are one, I in them and you in me, that they may be brought to perfection as one, that the world may know that you sent me, and that you loved them even as you loved me.*'"

At the conclusion of the ceremony and before filling the grave, Bethany walked over with her doll in hand, stood by its edge, and looked down at Uncle Walter wrapped in a satin shroud. Circling near her feet, Spooks watched as she dropped in her favorite toy, crying. "No matter what, Uncle Walter," she said, "I'll always be with you."

Any horse not hitched to a wagon was secured in the paddock, and they too watched quietly. Following the service, I went to them, petting Buck who seemed to actually understand what was happening. Clyde and Fred shouldered each other for a position near my hand, until something caught Fred's eye. He stared away, into the sky, so I followed his gaze and spotted a single white magnolia flower growing near the top of the tree. A moment later, Katie and Carl joined me, followed by Mr. and Mrs. Elton.

"I understand your pa's giving Buck to you," Mr. Elton said to me. He glanced at the three of us. "I know you've all got big plans, so to get you started, Maria and I bought you rail passes. They'll take you *and* your horses anywhere you want to go," Mr. Elton said, handing them to me.

"Thank you, Mr. Elton," I said. Taking the tickets, I noticed he also included some cash. My gratitude for them and this community was overwhelming. I was sad to leave, but excited for the next chapter. "I'm hoping you'll change your mind about politics and take over as Mayor here. We need good folks running our towns." He smiled, and we all exchanged our farewells. Genuinely good folks never sought authority over others, and if he was to take office, I knew it could only happen by write-in.

Late that summer, I wrote to Pa. The notes I'd sent to him up to that point were postcards, brief to avoid raising suspicion it was me, should any law be monitoring. This time I was more verbose in my letter, telling him Katie and I finally got married—she wore her mother's wedding ring— and that Carl helped officiate the service. We'd settled into a

Nevada desert town called Winnemucca. It was a quaint, dry place where locals were living peacefully with the Natives, a Paiute tribe. The area was infused with enough money and excitement from the railroad and seasonal cattle herders to keep life interesting. It was a small town, though, and safe— well insulated from the news of the outside. Katie'd taken a job with a feisty, tough old woman, a half-Paiute named Nahimana, or Mana for short. She ran a room and boarding house on Main Street, and also schooled some of the local Native kids who wanted to attend regular school but weren't allowed. I wasn't surprised to hear Katie was a natural with the children. Carl'd taken up card games as a way to earn a living while understudying with the local preacher, a white-haired ex-convict named Boo. When they weren't serving the local community, they'd ride to nearby districts in search of runaways or abused kids and try and offer help. I've never seen Carl so happy, able to make good on his promise to himself time and time again. And as for me, I'd picked up work at the railyard with a man named Frank, who ran the operation with his brother Teddy. In my spare time, I'd been chronicling our adventure on the trail, to maybe turn it into a book one day, like Mr. Elton suggested. Beyond that, we hoped to make it back to Leavenworth soon for a visit, seeming enough time might have passed that the law would have forgotten about us.

Pa wrote back, saying in fact, the law hadn't given up on their search for us, the *Santa Fe Gang*, who they said owed a debt to society if the balance of justice was to remain intact. He also said it wasn't local law anymore, but state law was involved, encouraged by politicians, after blaming us for the death of a ferry boatman and suspicion of slaughtering an entire wagon train along the Santa Fe Trail. Their reasoning was familiar, such a rigid and fundamental concept of righteousness. A relic of my own myopic childhood when I was incapable of seeing past the conventional wisdom. Such were politicians, ever the infants—and such were lawmen, ever the lackeys. He wrote that the horses were doing well, healthy, and the house was in good repair. Bethany'd added to the family, taking on the responsibility of a couple guinea pigs as pets, named Quizzy and Ziggy. Other than that, it was quiet on the home front, Buster constantly sleeping— which would come as no surprise. Pa and Bethany had become quite the pair since our departure, him teaching her about survival and the wilderness, and her a quick and eager learner. They both looked forward to seeing us again but warned caution on all fronts.

Without going into depth, he mentioned that a scandal had broken. The governor, a shareholder in the transcontinental railroad, sent his suits up and down the Trail to sow fear of the migrants—especially foreigners who couldn't speak English—and exaggerate tales of violence and wrongdoing to stimulate train ticket sales. Closer to home, Sheriff Lock wanted nothing to do with Cecelia after it got out what they had planned. The mayor pulled some strings, and nobody was held accountable for conspiracy to hurt Bethany or false testimony to law enforcement about her kidnapping. Since Pa's release from jail, Cecelia had become an outcast, living alone in the old cave-like sheriff's station, windows broken and covered in vines and cobwebs, with only her fantasies to keep her company. He suspected Mrs. Elton and the church were providing her needs, including library books, since by all accounts the only time she left the building was to the outhouse.

After signing farewell, he included one final note at the bottom of the page—a note for which I've carried his letter in my pocket every day since. He wrote that he loved me, and he was proud that I was his son.

John grew up in the chaparral-covered suburbs of northern Los Angeles, spending most of his youth outdoors in that hot, dry environment. He studied biology at the University of Redlands, then joined the Army and served in the Chemical Corps while studying philosophy in his free time. After this, he spent many years working in the biotechnology and life sciences engineering sectors, primarily as a project manager. His lifelong passion is writing, and he earned an MFA in Creative Writing from Mount Saint Mary's University in Los Angeles, California.

CPSIA information can be obtained
at www.ICGtesting.com
Printed in the USA
BVHW030847220323
660915BV00017B/710